SAMUEL

THE COOPER BROTHERS

NIKKI ASHTON

Cover design – JC Clarke from The Graphics Shed

Formatting by—JC Clarke from The Graphics Shed

Proofed by – Brooke Bowen Hebert

To those of you who learned to love and trust again

Samuel

"I am hers, she is mine and he is who we created"

CONTENTS

Prologue	1
Chapter 1	9
Chapter 2	19
Chapter 3	25
Chapter 4	31
Chapter 5	37
Chapter 6	43
Chapter 7	49
Chapter 8	55
Chapter 9	67
Chapter 10	75
Chapter 11	79
Chapter 12	85
Chapter 13	95
Chapter 14	105
Chapter 15	109
Chapter 16	115
Chapter 17	121
Chapter 18	125
Chapter 19	131
Chapter 20	139
Chapter 21	149
Chapter 22	157
Chapter 23	165
Chapter 24	175
Chapter 25	181
Chapter 26	187
Chapter 27	195
Chapter 28	201
Chapter 29	209
Chapter 30	215

Chapter 31   223
Chapter 32   229
Chapter 33   237
Chapter 34   247
Chapter 35   255
Chapter 36   263
Chapter 37   275
Chapter 38   279
Chapter 39   287
Chapter 40   293
Chapter 41   299
Chapter 42   307
Epilogue   315

Playlist   321
Acknowledgments   323
Nikki's Links   325
Book Links   327

PROLOGUE

SAMUEL

the past

Out of breath, I pushed on the buzzer for the maternity ward, desperate for them to answer.

"Come on," I muttered to myself, putting the small, pink bear under my arm pit, I squeezed anti-bac liquid into my hand from the pump next to the door.

"Hello," a voice echoed as I was just about to press the call button again.

"I'm here to see Alison Carmichael," I replied, one hand on the door ready to push it open.

There was a pause for a few seconds. "Okay, come on in."

I heaved a sigh of relief as it buzzed to indicate it was open. I pushed through and ran down the short corridor to the main part of the ward.

"End bay," the nurse on the desk said, giving me a huge smile.

With a tight hold of the teddy bear, I rushed off with a quick 'thanks', desperate to see Ali and the baby. I couldn't believe I'd missed the birth. She'd promised to call me as soon as she went into labour, but for reasons only she knew, she'd not texted me until half an hour ago insisting I get there as soon as I could. Admittedly, I'd been in college all afternoon and she'd have known

1

I'd have gone to the pool afterwards, but she'd promised, so I was pretty hurt that she hadn't called. I knew we were keeping everything quiet, shit I hadn't even told my parents I was going to be a dad, but I still should have been the first person she called. I knew I couldn't go into the delivery room with her, her mum was doing that, but I could have been on the ward waiting.

Excitement swilled in my gut as I approached the bay the nurse had directed me to. I was going to see my baby – mine and Alison's baby.

When I rounded the corner, Alison was the first person I saw amongst all the other women propped up in bed or sitting in chairs feeding their babies and she looked beautiful, considering the amount of pain she must have gone through.

Her blonde hair was piled on her head and her cheeks were pink as she lay back against a mound of pillows, her eyes directed at the Perspex cot next to her.

Picking up my step, I moved to stand at the end of the bed and reached down to touch her foot under the cover.

"Hey," I said quietly, not sure if the baby was asleep.

Alison's head shot around to look at me and her eyes widened. "Sam," she gasped. "Where have you been, I texted you ages ago?"

"Sorry." I held up the pink teddy bear. "I wanted to get this."

I grinned and moved to the side of the bed without the cot and bent to kiss her cheek. I was desperate to see my daughter, but I wasn't so much of a dick to ignore the mother of my child.

"God, you look beautiful," I said, cupping her face. "How was it?"

She shifted on the bed and winced a little. "Okay, as I expected; painful."

My eyes darted to the cot and I took a step, but Ali caught hold of my hand, her eyes looking over toward the door.

"No, Sam. I need to talk to you."

She flattened her lips against each other and I saw tears in her eyes as she squeezed my hand.

"Why?" I asked. "What's wrong? Is there something wrong with her?" I glanced over at the cot, but could only see a tiny, pink woollen hat peeking out from the top of a white blanket.

"No," Ali replied, swallowing hard. "Nothing like that."

"What then?" I dragged the chair that was behind me closer to the bed and flopped down onto it. "Alison, what's wrong, tell me?"

She took a deep breath and glanced at the baby and then back to me. "I'm sorry, Sam, but she's not yours."

I felt as though someone had punched me in the stomach as it lurched, and my heart stopped. A shiver ran over me as I followed Ali's gaze to the baby. I pulled my hand from Ali's and slammed it against my chest.

"Nope. No way," I hissed, shaking my head. "She's mine. She has to be."

My voice broke as I said the words that I was desperate to be true. She had to be mine. I loved Alison and she loved me. She'd been my coach since I was fourteen, but things had changed when I reached sixteen, our relationship had become sexual and had been that way for over two years. The last eleven months had been the best of those two years because things between us had become more intense - she'd left her husband and we'd begun making plans for the future.

"But-."

Alison shook her head and silently cried. "She isn't, Sam. I'm sorry."

"I don't understand. You told me she was mine. You let me pick her name, we're going to call her Sadie. You said, Ali."

My words and eyes implored her, needing her to tell me she'd got it wrong or that it was all a sick joke, but she simply swiped at the tears on her cheeks.

"Who's the fuck is she then?" I hissed, trying to regulate my breathing. "Tell me."

I pushed up from the chair, almost sending it toppling and rushed around to the cot, needing to see for myself whether she had my olive complexion and dark hair. As I pulled back the blanket, Ali and I both gasped at the same time.

A perfect, pale brown face peeked out at me and I felt the ground fall from beneath my feet. Every hope and dream I'd had of starting a family with the woman I loved flashed before my eyes and disappeared in a puff of air.

"She's Roger's," I gasped, thinking of her Jamaican husband whom she left a year ago.

Alison let out a quiet sob and nodded. "I'm sorry."

"So you keep fucking saying," I growled, not caring how loud I was. "But you haven't explained how she's his baby, when you've been separated for eleven fucking months. You said you left him. You told me you couldn't stop the feelings you had for me, so you left him a month before we got together."

The woman in the next bed gasped, but went back to reading her magazine when my hard gaze landed on her.

"I-." Alison stopped abruptly as her eyes widened in horror at something behind me.

I swung around to see Roger, her fucking husband, strolling in. He had a huge bouquet of flowers in one hand and a teddy bear in the other. I looked down at the small pink bear that I still had clutched in my hand and felt bile rise in my throat.

I wanted to puke. I wanted to run. I wanted to stay and tell him everything. I wanted this gorgeous little girl to be mine.

"You're back?" Ali said, her voice rising in pitch as Roger looked over at me.

"Couldn't keep away. Hey, Sam," Roger cried, giving me a huge grin. "Great to see you man. You just come from practice?"

I heard Alison whimper behind me as her hand moved to rest on top of the sleeping baby. "Sam just came to give Abigail a teddy bear, and tell me about practice. He almost did a personal best, didn't you Sam?" she asked, her voice high pitched and anxious.

My throat prickled and my chest tightened as the baby's name registered. She wasn't mine, she hadn't got the name that I'd picked.

"Well, that's really nice of you, Sam. Not many swim coaches get that sort of treatment baby, do they? And almost a personal best, great going man. That guy you've got standing in for Ali must be cracking the whip."

Laughing, Roger moved to the other side of the bed and leaned down to kiss Ali, just as I'd done only minutes before. It was the simple act of a man kissing the mother of his child, yet it felt like a knife to the fucking heart. When he pulled away, Ali stiffened and stared at me as she worried her lip.

"Hasn't she done well, hey?" Roger asked, nodding towards the baby. "I told her the day she did the pregnancy test it was going to be the most beautiful baby in the world, didn't I babe?"

She'd been with him when she took the pregnancy test.

The same pregnancy test I'd found when her bag fell off the seat one night at the pool, when we'd been the only ones there, practicing late into the night as we'd always done. The same fucking pregnancy test she'd shown me with tears of joy and a huge smile on her face and said 'surprise'.

Looking down at the baby, I thought back to that night. I'd just reached eighteen and Alison was my thirty-three year old coach, but I'd hugged and kissed her and told her how happy I was that she was having my baby. We'd had sex in the changing room and then gone back to her house that she *used* to share with Roger. That was the one and only time I'd stayed the whole night, but after that Alison had said we needed to be careful in case the neighbours saw and put two and two together once she started to show. She'd said, if anyone found out about us she could have her coaching license taken away and I'd end up with some shit community coach who had no idea what my potential was.

"She's perfect," Alison said, painfully dragging me back to the present.

I looked at her and felt my jaw tighten as her eyes silently begged me not to blow up her life, like she'd made mine implode with her lies.

"She's gorgeous, Roger," I replied before clearing my throat to rid the thick emotion from my tone. "Looks just like you."

Alison drew in a jagged breath but Roger's deep laugh drowned out the noise of her discomfort.

"Nah," he said, shaking his head with a huge grin. "She's all her mummy. My eyes maybe, but the rest of her beauty all comes from Ali."

"H-how did practice go?" Alison asked.

I raised my brows, wondering how she could ask such a mundane fucking question after ripping my damn heart out.

"Fine," I bit out.

"Not the same without coach, I bet," Roger said, laughing. "God knows I missed her like mad those four months I was in Jamaica."

"You were in Jamaica?" I asked, realising why she'd risked taking me to her home just the once and why since that time we only ever had sex with the smell of chlorine around us.

"Yeah man. My dad was ill and then died, so I had to sort things out. I went the week before Ali found out she was pregnant. That was one hell of a Skype session, when you told me and showed me the test, wasn't it baby?"

Roger grabbed Ali's hand and leaned in to kiss her forehead, his eyes closing as he did, and I knew at that moment I couldn't break his fucking heart, it wasn't his fault. As much as I wanted to and have him feel as shitty as I did, it wasn't fair to him or the baby. She'd played us both.

"I'd better go," I said, taking in a long breath. "I just wanted to say congratulations."

"Hey thanks man, appreciate it," Roger said, sitting in the chair I'd vacated earlier. "Come again, any time."

I nodded but didn't say anything. I knew I wouldn't be going back. I wouldn't be seeing Alison, Roger, or their baby ever again.

"We need to talk about your training," Ali said tentatively.

I narrowed my eyes and curled my lip as though I'd just smelled shit in the air. There was so much I wanted to say, so much I could say, but the man sitting holding tightly to his wife's hand didn't deserve it, so I just nodded and left.

As I moved down the corridor to the exit, I couldn't stop the tears from flowing. I'd loved her, as much as an eighteen year old heart could. I'd been willing to be a father and a partner at a young age because she was the woman I loved. She'd helped me be great at the sport that I loved, she'd taught me how to be a generous lover and had given me dreams of a future full of her and our baby, and now it was all gone, ripped to shreds.

Reaching the exit door, I realised I was still holding onto the teddy bear. I didn't want it. I didn't want any reminder of the day my heart had been crushed. I looked around and seeing a waste bin, threw it in. I then went to my car and seeing my swim gear on the passenger seat, threw it into the back, knowing I'd never visit the pool again. I was going to start living my life like every other teenager and I'd make sure I'd never fall in love ever again.

1

SAMUEL

the present

I let out a long breath and gave my sister-in-law a look that most definitely said 'I fucking hate you at this minute'. Amy, the cocky little shit, just grinned at me.

"You're going to love it," she said, bouncing on her feet like a demented toddler.

"No I'm not," I ground out. "How the hell did I let you talk me into it?"

"You love me, but most of all you love Bella and you hate to see her upset and she'd be really upset if she had to give up her swimming lessons."

I stuck out my tongue at my niece in Amy's arms, making her giggle. "She's two fucking years of age Amy, she's hardly being trained for the Olympics."

Amy's face fell as she kissed Bella's soft dark curls. "Don't say that, she's really good."

"She splashes around doing the doggie paddle, so unless they've decided to include it as one of the strokes in the four by two hundred meter medley, I think she's got a way to go."

"She might have inherited your genes," Amy grumbled. "Hopefully, the only ones of yours she has, but she still might end

9

up being really good, and if you don't do this and she isn't able to come to Water Babies, we may never find out."

I rolled my eyes and looked over Amy's shoulder at the pool which was filled with kids playing with floats until their swimming lessons started – lessons that fucking Amy had talked me into taking when the regular teacher broke his leg.

I'd been a good swimmer in my youth, actually better than good, I was a county champion and according to Alison, my coach, I was on the edge of being picked for Team GB. In hindsight though, I didn't think so. If I'd been that good one of their top coaches would have picked me up, or at least wanted to know why I gave it all up at eighteen. The thought of why I hadn't carried on caused a shiver to run over my body and a little bit of bitterness to seep through my veins. The consequences of having an affair with your coach were harsh, because aside from ripping my heart out and shredding it, Alison Carmichael had taken away my desire to carry on in a sport that I loved. It didn't matter whether she'd over exaggerated my chances of being a top swimmer or not, that's what coaches often did to get the best out of you, but I'd been sixteen years of age when she took my virginity and the thought of it made me feel sick. She'd taken advantage of me and my stupid teenage crush and rush of hormones, so the thought of stepping inside a pool again was abhorrent to me. My need to swim was soon replaced with a desire for girls and booze, which definitely did end any chances I might have had.

"I actually don't understand how me teaching the intermediate class impacts the Water Babies," I groaned. "*Their* teacher hasn't gone missing with a broken bone."

Amy sighed in exasperation and shifted Bella on her hip. "I told you this before. If you don't do the intermediate class, Victoria will have to, which means there's no one to teach Water Babies."

I glanced at the pool again, my fingers twitching at my side as water splashed against my leg. The clear water was calling me and I suddenly realised how much I'd missed it; cutting through the water with a feeling of weightlessness, the warm ache in my muscles and the smell of chlorine on my body.

"How many in the class?" I asked.

"Seven, all new starters tonight." Amy smoothed a hand over her daughter's head and pouted. "It would be a shame to waste the DBS check that you passed with flying colours. I mean, why go to all that trouble, Sam, if you're not going to do it?"

"How my damn brother lives with you I'll never know. You're a pain in the fucking arse."

Amy grinned. "I know, and stop cursing in front of my baby. She said balls yesterday."

"And?"

"Eli was naked at the time and she was definitely pointing at the goods when she said it."

Laughing, I shook my head and leaned in to kiss Bella's head. "Okay, but if I hate it I'm not doing it again next week. They'll have to find someone else."

Amy grinned and padded off toward the baby pool while I strolled over to the small group of kids now all waiting on the side of the pool. They were various heights and weights, all chatting excitably. All except for one poor kid who was squeezed into a pair of swim trunks, looking about as happy to be there as I was. I was betting his parents had been told he needed to lose weight and this was the nightmare resolution they'd come up with. I made a mental note to keep a special eye on him and more importantly, make sure he didn't sink to the bottom of pool. All the kids I was teaching were supposedly already able to swim, but I had a feeling this kid hadn't swum for a good while.

As my gaze ran over the rest of the kids, my heart stopped and despite the cool air blowing around the pool, a sticky heat broke out all over my body. My mouth went dry and I felt as though I was going to be sick as my gaze reached the last one standing alone, pinging the elastic of his goggles and looking over at the older kids doing life-saving drills in the deep end.

He was tall for his age, which was eight, had broad shoulders for his age and dark hair that was styled to perfection in a high fade with a side parting. This kid was bright, did well at school but had a cocky mouth on him at times. How did I know these things about this kid?

I knew because he was *my* kid. My eight year old son, Frankie West, who I'd never spoken to in my life.

As each kid did a width of the pool using front crawl, my gaze kept being drawn to Frankie. I'd avoided eye contact with him for the whole hour, nervous that he might realise who I was, nervous about actually looking at him and feeling something. I didn't think for one minute he'd figure out I was his dad; his mum had made it quite clear that I wasn't ever going to be part of his life – not that I'd cared, it was for the best. Watching him now though, I couldn't help noticing the aching feeling of guilt and regret that enveloped me. It wasn't a totally alien feeling, over the last few years I'd found myself thinking about him and his mum a lot, especially around the time Elijah and Amy were doing the dance of second chances. All the shit they went through had made me wonder what my life might be like, if I was given another go at happiness.

Once I got over the shock of him being there, I'd watched Frankie carefully, looking for anything that he might have inherited from me. As soon as he entered the water, I knew what it was. He was damn good, and most definitely had my swimming genes. His body position was perfectly horizontal and his head central

12

and still, just as it should have been. His kick wasn't coming from the hip, but even at just eight years of age, he almost had a text-book form.

As Frankie gave a final kick and reached the edge of the pool first, my gaze went back to the other six kids. As I thought, Timothy, the chubby boy, was struggling and lagging behind the rest. Props to him though, he wasn't giving up. Finally, he finished and I looked up at the huge clock on the wall seeing that it was time to finish.

"Well done guys," I called as they all held on to the edge or started to tread water. "You've worked hard today. Now for next week, I want you to practice in the mirror."

"The mirror," a slight boy, who I think was called Toby, scoffed.

"Yes, a mirror," I replied, crossing my arms over my chest. "I want you to practice your arms and head movement and check the positioning in the mirror."

"Are we doing the crawl again next week?" Frankie asked.

My heart thudded like a damn nervous teenager and I was glad my hands were tucked under my folded arms to stop them from shaking. I turned to Frankie and cleared my throat, it suddenly felt full and tickly.

"Yes, probably."

I breathed in through my nose, anxious as he studied me. I wondered what he was thinking, and hoped it wasn't that I was a dick. I wanted him to like me for the six weeks that I'd be teaching him to swim. The six weeks that I'd finally be in his life.

"What?" I asked, as he tilted his head still watching me carefully.

"You didn't even think you'd be back next week did you?"

My eyes widened as I took a half-step back. "Um, I don't think I ever said that."

"No, but you thought it," he sighed, pulling himself out of the pool. "Otherwise you wouldn't have looked so nervous when you came over and you'd have had a plan and you don't."

"I might have one," I argued.

The look he gave me was pretty fucking withering and I instantly saw myself in his attitude. I'd heard from my source that he was a smart mouthed kid and now I was seeing it first-hand. Quite rightly he didn't believe me.

"See you next week," he sighed and ran off toward the changing rooms.

"Hey, no running," I shouted, anxious that he might fall.

Frankie stopped and then started to do the tiniest steps, with an exaggerated tiptoe walk. I bit my lip trying not to laugh – the little shit.

"Okay, kids," I said turning back to the rest of the group. "I'll see you all next week."

They all pulled themselves out, except Timothy who swam for the ladders, and left the pool with a chorus of goodbyes and that they'd see me the following week. As Timothy stomped past me, I called after him.

"Hey Timothy."

He stopped and sighed, probably expecting me to tell him he wasn't very good, no doubt.

"Yeah."

"Well done today, dude. You did really well."

His face broke into a grin as he crossed his arms over his chubby belly. "Really?"

"Yeah really," I replied, nodding vigorously and giving him a smile. "I know you didn't find it as easy as some of the others, but you never gave up and you finished every drill we did."

"Thanks, Sam." He looked towards the coffee lounge that

overlooked the pool and then back to me. "Bye, see you next week."

I couldn't help the huge smile on my face as he started to run and then suddenly pulled up and started to walk, making me laugh quietly.

As I started to walk to the changing rooms, I heard a knocking on the coffee lounge window that overlooked the pool. I turned to see Amy holding Bella, both of them now fully clothed. She gave me a thumbs up and mouthed 'well done'. I gave her a thumbs up back and mouthed 'fuck off', with a huge, false grin on my face. Amy laughed and waved Bella's hand at me to say goodbye.

———

When I left the leisure centre half an hour later, after being cornered by Timothy's exuberant mother, a light drizzle had started and I couldn't wait to get back home and get a warm shower. I might have only stood on the side of the pool shouting instructions to a group of eight to ten year olds, but I was knackered.

Throwing my gym bag over my shoulder, I pulled up the collar of my jacket and started to walk toward my car.

"Sam."

The voice was one I would never forget, although not as sweet as I once remembered. It had a hint of steel to it and when I looked up, there was fiery anger in her eyes too.

"Well if it isn't Maisie West," I sighed, unable to stop the grin creeping on my face.

"What the hell are you doing?" she snapped, holding her hands out in front of her. "I told you, you'd never have anything to do with him, ever."

"Hang on a minute," I hissed. "I didn't know he was in the group, not until I walked into the pool."

"You can't be around him, Sam. You just can't. You have to tell them to get someone else."

She wrapped one arm over the front of her padded black coat, while her other hand shakily covered her mouth.

"I'm not a fucking monster, Maisie, and it's not as though I said 'oh hey Frankie, I'm your dad, nice to meet you'."

"This is not funny," she continued. "If my partner finds out you're teaching Frankie, he'll go ballistic."

I huffed at the mention of her partner. I knew all about him from my source – okay, it was my friend Hannah who lived two doors down from them and had a little girl in Frankie's class. Apparently, Maisie had been living with some guy called Josh for four years and he worked in insurance and drove a fucking Audi prick wagon.

"I could give two shits what your partner thinks," I replied. "Now, I'm sorry this happened, but I didn't damn plan it. I have no intention of telling Frankie who I am, so chill your fucking boots, Maisie."

She glanced behind her and when I followed her gaze, I noticed a red hatchback with a small dark head bobbing around inside.

"What's he doing?" I asked.

"What?" Maisie swung around and then snapped impatiently. "Listening to music, he likes Northern Soul."

My eyes widened and Maisie tutted.

"I didn't encourage it, he just heard it and liked it."

"Playing our tunes were you Maisie?"

"Oh fuck off," she snapped, "and make sure Frankie doesn't find out. Believe me, if there were any other decent swimming lessons close by he'd be there in a flash."

"Whatever you say, Maisie, whatever you say."

Without another word, I pushed past her to go to my car and wondered whether I should ask the leisure centre to find someone else.

"Ah, fuck her," I snarled to myself as I started the engine and drove away, not thinking about why I was feeling just a little bit excited.

2

Maisie

the past

As Sam changed the vinyl record on what he told me had been his parents' stereo, I watched him carefully, loving the sight of his hard, tight, naked bum and strong, wide shoulders and muscled arms, one of which had an amazing tattoo of an old fashioned fob watch and it was surrounded by thorns from a rose that was dropping its petals. Everything about Sam was gorgeous and for some reason he seemed to like me – a lot. At least I thought he did, I hoped he did. I wasn't normally the sort of girl who slept with someone straight away, but when Sam had walked me home a week ago after seeing him in Ziggy's, the local nightclub, he'd been sweet and romantic. He'd given me his jacket to wear and when I complained that my feet were aching, he dropped to his haunches and insisted I'd got onto his back. He carried me the rest of the way home and then kissed me at the garden gate, like some clichéd, cheesy chick film but I didn't care, it had been perfect.

When I'd seen him at Alex Drake's party tonight, I knew he was watching me, his dark eyes were on me every time I glanced at him, but he didn't seem to be bothered to speak, spending a lot of his time in the kitchen with his sister-in-law, Amy. Finally though, he came over to me and we'd chatted for a couple of hours. We'd

19

kissed too and when he'd asked if he could walk me home I'd been more daring than I'd ever been and said no, but he could walk me to his home. As his mum and dad were on holiday, he'd brought me up to his old room rather than go back to the apartment he shared with his brother and his sister-in-law and within minutes of walking through the door, we'd fallen into bed and given each other an orgasm pretty quickly.

"What's this?" I asked, instantly liking the song that was playing.

"This," he said, slipping back under the duvet and snuggling closer to me, "is called 'Do I Love You' by Frank Wilson and is one of my favourite Northern Soul songs."

I shook my shoulders in time to the bouncing beat and smiled. "I like it."

"Yeah, well I like how your tits bounce when you do that," Sam groaned, reaching down to take my nipple in his mouth.

"Sam," I gasped, loving the sting as he sucked hard.

"You're so fucking perfect," he rasped, kissing his way up my chest with his hand in my hair.

"No I'm not."

"Yeah you are."

His teeth nipped at the soft flesh below my ear and I groaned, feeling him getting hard against my leg. I dropped my head back onto the pillow, giving him better access to my neck, and was rewarded with his lips and tongue on them, making me moan with the pleasure of it.

"Sam," I whispered. "I think I need you to fuck me."

Sam laughed softly and looked up at me, resting a hand on my stomach.

"You are so not what I thought," he said, drawing lazy circles around my belly button.

"In what way?" I breathed out, desperately thrusting my hips up, hoping that he'd move his fingers lower.

"You need me to fuck you? Just never expected such a little potty mouth who was so demanding."

I gave a lazy smile, my eyes half-lidded as his lips found my nipple again. "The quiet ones are always the worst, apparently."

"Or maybe the best," he groaned, lowering his hand to where I wanted it and inserting two fingers inside me.

I gasped as he crooked them and started to rub against my sweet spot. Then when he moved down the bed and his mouth started to suck on my clit, I wanted to scream with the feelings that were passing through me like an electric current.

After a few seconds I growled out an irritated sigh. "Sam," I pleaded.

His mouth left me as he lifted his head and grinned up at me through my parted legs.

"So fucking impatient."

With a chuckle he removed his fingers and manoeuvred himself between my thighs, he reached for a condom and rolled it on, before hitching one of my legs up onto his hip. His mouth slammed onto mine and without any further hesitation, he pushed into me.

I gasped and quickly matched his rhythm with my hips, my fingers digging into the hard muscles of his back. My cry of ecstasy seemed to urge Sam on as his thrusting went faster and deeper and his fingers pinched into my thighs as I clung onto him. The song he'd been playing on his stereo started again and its quick beat became Sam's metronome as my heavy breaths duelled with his groans of pleasure in the silence of the room.

Everything about Sam was hard and powerful and it wasn't long before I could feel my orgasm building. As my skin heated as the first waves of my climax started to roll through me, Sam's phone began to shrill out from on top of his chest of drawers. He didn't stop or hesitate as he continued to pump into me, his lips helping to bring me to my pinnacle with heated kisses along my jaw and down my neck.

As the phone stopped ringing, my orgasm hit and I cried out as the pleasure engulfed me.

"Oh shit."

Sam continued moving in and out of me, hard and fast, and as my body started to relax into the overwhelming euphoria, he came hard, cursing and gripping the pillow next to my head.

As we both gasped for breath, Sam's mobile started ringing again.

"Who the fuck is that?" he groaned, pulling out of me and moving onto his back, his chest heaving heavily.

"Answer it," I said breathily.

"Later." Sam turned his head to me and grinned. "Well that was pretty fucking awesome."

I gave him a shy smile, not sure why, seeing as he'd pretty much seen every part of me, naked.

"You hungry?" he asked, leaning up on one elbow just as his mobile stopped ringing again.

"Yes," I replied. "And you know what I could eat?"

"What?" He reached up and pushed some hair from my face, letting his hand linger of my cheek.

"Cornflakes."

Laughing as he got out of bed, Sam removed the condom and wrapped it in a tissue before throwing it into the small waste bin by the door. "Really, not toast or pizza, but cornflakes?"

I nodded and turned onto my side, giving me a better view of his gorgeous face and dark brown eyes...and naked body.

"Okay let me-."

As his mobile started again, Sam stopped talking and looked at it over his shoulder.

"Fuck it, whoever it is must be desperate to talk to me."

I glanced at the old fashioned alarm clock ticking away and saw that it was almost one in the morning, and suddenly my heart started to beat faster. No one called at this time, unless it was an emergency. Sam padded across to the stereo, turned it down, and then snatched up his mobile, as I watched him warily and waited, holding my breath as he answered.

"Eli, this better be fucking important."

I guessed that Eli was already speaking, because almost immediately Sam dropped his head back and let out a sigh.

"I've no fucking idea," he cried, looking agitated. "Last time I saw her she was talking to that tall girl with the tattoos, Bernadette or something, the one who looks like Pink...no, who told you that?" Sam scratched his head and looked around the room. When his eyes landed on his jeans he moved over to them and snatched them up from the floor and put them on, his mobile wedged between his shoulder and his ear, still listening.

"Okay, calm down," he said as his zipped up his jeans. "Give me half an hour and I'll be there...no, just stay at the fucking apartment and keep calling her mobile...I have to get a fucking taxi Elijah, so shut the fuck up...I'll be there."

He stabbed a finger at his phone, ending the call and threw it onto the bed.

"I'm so sorry, Maisie," he sighed, shaking his head. "Elijah got home and Amy isn't there. He said some of her stuff is gone and a couple of people at the party said they'd seen her run out in floods of tears but he has no idea why or what the problem was."

"Oh my God," I cried, scrambling out from under the duvet. "Do you think she's okay?"

Sam shrugged as he picked up his t-shirt and turned it outside-in, before pulling it on. I picked up my underwear and clothes and while Sam put on his socks and shoes, got myself dressed.

Finally we were both ready and when Sam turned off the stereo, we turned out the light and left his room with the lingering smell of sex in the air.

3

the present

I ran a hand down my face and waited for Elijah and Amy to say something. I'd finally told them about Frankie and I wasn't sure it had gone down too well.

"You've known you had a son for eight years and never once told any of us," Elijah ground out from between gritted teeth.

"Pretty much."

"Don't you dare be so fucking flippant about it," he snapped. "This is a child we're talking about. How the hell could you leave her on her own with a kid? I thought you were a better man than that?"

Eli's eyes were blazing with anger and were so concentrated on me, he didn't even register that Amy had taken his hand in hers. I'd only ever seen him this mad during his years without Amy, particularly when she first left, but never expected this level of anger to be aimed at me.

For some ridiculous reason, I'd decided to tell them both about Frankie and Maisie and the fact that Frankie was in my swimming group. I'd thought he'd be supportive and understand why I'd not been in my son's life, but he clearly wasn't. I got it, I really did, especially as he and Amy had suffered the loss of a child years ago,

25

when Amy had a miscarriage. Children were a sensitive subject for him for a long time, but now that they had Bella, I thought he might be a little less judgemental; obviously not.

"It was Maisie who wanted to do it on her own," I protested.

"Really, like I believe that," he scoffed. "And if she did, why the fuck?"

I leaned forward, resting my forearms on my knees and weighed up what I was going to say. It was true, it had been Maisie's wish that she did it alone and I had nothing to do with the baby, but I hadn't exactly argued or given her an alternative. I'd been a prick.

"Okay, truth?"

Elijah's eyes went wide. "It'd be a fucking start."

"We'd had sex a couple of times and then it ended. She knew it wasn't what I wanted."

"But you really liked her," Amy added. "You told me you did."

My gaze went to my sister-in-law who was now slowly rubbing Elijah's back, trying to calm him down.

"I did, but I didn't want a baby and she did. Maisie said she'd rather do it alone than have me giving a half-arsed, uncommitted attempt at being a dad."

"So you just said okay and let her go and have your child without a care from you?" Elijah asked, throwing his arms out in front of him. "You didn't give a shit about him for almost nine years. You're a fucking twat, Sam, and I can't believe you're my brother."

"I couldn't do it," I hissed. "I couldn't fucking do it, not ag-."

I stopped myself from saying any more. I had never told him about Alison Carmichael and the baby that was never mine. I'd never told anyone. Was that because I still cared about her or felt loyalty to her? Was it? Fuck! I hated her and what she'd done to me. There were two reasons I hadn't told a soul about how she'd ripped my heart out and broken me – her husband and her daughter. They didn't deserve to have their lives turned upside down, and if I was being truthful, I felt fucking ashamed of what had happened, what I'd allowed to happen.

I knew that these days what she did may well have been seen as grooming, but I wanted it just as much as she did when it started, for fuck's sake. I'd wanted her as soon as I realised that my dick wasn't just for peeing out of and if truth be told, I'd done everything I could to make her notice me as more than a protégé. Maybe it was a teenage crush and if she'd not made a move on me I'd have grown out of it, but she did and I let my teenage dick rule my sensibility. Did I think she'd do it to some other teenage boy with raging hormones? Who the fuck knew, but even the thought that she might do it again wasn't enough for me to let the world know that I'd been a stupid idiot and let myself be manipulated. Over the years while the pain and embarrassment hadn't gone away, it had lessened and I'd learned to deal. It didn't mean it hadn't taught me a lesson, it fucking had, hence why I'd been quite clear to Maisie that a baby was of no interest to me.

Once bitten, twice shy.

A burned man dreads the fire.

Fool me once, shame on you, fool me twice, shame on me.

Whichever phrase you chose to use, it applied to me. I'd vowed I'd never fall in love again, or let another woman make an idiot of me, and the situation with Maisie had felt a little too familiar.

"Oh well," Elijah said with a heavy hint of sarcasm. "If you couldn't do it, I totally understand why you'd let her bring up your son alone. It explains it all."

"Eli," Amy whispered softly. "Calm down, you'll wake Bella."

"Oh yeah," he replied. "Because that's what you do when you've got kids, you take care to make sure they're happy, safe, and sleeping soundly, unless of course you're Samuel fucking Cooper, who just 'can't do it'."

He pushed up from his seat and stormed out of the room. As Amy and I sat in silence, I heard him stomp up the stairs, probably going to check on Bella if I knew him.

"He'll calm down," Amy sighed. "I don't think it's just about you not helping to raise Frankie, I think he's hurt too."

"Hurt? What the fuck about?"

"You didn't tell him, Sam. He's your brother and you didn't tell him. All this time you had a son and you didn't tell the one person you're closest to."

I went cold at the thought of him finding out about Alison. His reaction emphasised the fact that it was too late, he could never know after all this time, otherwise he might never speak to me again.

I shrugged. "Maybe I was ashamed."

They were words I'd never voiced before, but there was a ring of truth in them. I *was* a little ashamed about it all – that I couldn't be a father to Frankie, didn't *want* to be a father. The circumstances of why I felt like that didn't matter. I was a fucking twat, just like Elijah said.

"Are you going to tell your mum and dad?" Amy asked.

"Fuck no," I groaned. "No way. They'd insist on meeting him and Maisie's made it very clear Frankie is not to know I'm his dad."

"So why tell us?"

"Because..." I sighed and considered what my answer was, because I had to be honest, it suddenly felt like a stupid damn idea. "It's unsettled me. Seeing him, talking to Maisie, knowing that he likes Northern Soul and that he could be an amazing swimmer, has made me feel strange. Complete even."

Amy's eyes were soft as she watched me from her chair by the open fire. It had taken me a while to trust her again after she and

Elijah had gotten back together, but once I got my head from up my arse and realised she wasn't to blame for what happened, and I finally heard the truth from Lauren Proctor after Eli and Amy were back together, we got our old friendship back – me taking the piss out of her and her thinking she could boss me around.

"There's parts of him that are so obviously me, Ames, and I'm kind of proud of that and I think I just wanted to share it. I needed to tell someone, 'you see that kid, the one that's a great swimmer and likes cool music, well he's mine'."

"You know to deserve those parts, you need to do the shit parts too."

I nodded, knowing I was being totally selfish.

"Do you want a relationship with him?" Amy asked.

I flinched back, my eyes widening at her words. "No. Not at all. Yeah, it's weird and kind of cool that a part of me is running around, you must get that, every time you look at Bella, but I'm not ready to be his dad. I won't ever be."

Amy nodded. "I do understand why you feel pride, but I also want everyone to know she's mine and Elijah's. I love being her mummy and can't imagine watching her from the side lines. It would kill me and I know Elijah would feel the same."

I knew what she said to be true, because Eli had pretty much said the same thing to me when Bella had only been a few month's old. He'd said he'd die before he'd let anyone else bring her up. The difference was, Elijah was born to be a father and had the love of his life alongside him. Yes they'd suffered along the way, but I think everyone knew deep down they'd always end up back together – it took them some convincing, but they got there in the end.

"How was it talking to Maisie?" Amy asked, smirking.

"Well we didn't swap numbers or holiday snaps if that's what you're asking."

29

"You really liked her all those years ago."

"Yeah, but we had sex twice in one night and like I said, it fizzled out."

"How come?" Her brow furrowed.

"Well that would be because I was trying to hold my brother together after his wife left him."

As soon as I saw the hurt mask Amy's face, I knew it had been a shitty thing to say.

"I'm sorry," I said on a sigh. "But you'd gone and he was falling apart and so I didn't have much time for Maisie."

Amy nodded and shifted in her seat, pulling her feet underneath her. She was makeup free and her deep auburn hair was in some sort of plait, hanging over one shoulder and I couldn't image anyone more perfect for my brother. She was beautiful and sweet and she was just who he deserved. Like I always said, he was the good brother.

"So what now?" she asked.

I shrugged. "Nothing, I suppose. I spend an hour with him once a week for the next six weeks and treat him like the rest of the kids in the group. I go on as normal, as a single man without kids, with a business to run."

"And you think you can do that, carry on as normal?"

Trust Amy to ask the sixty-four-million dollar question. She never did let me have an easy ride.

"Yep, of course I can. Nothing has changed. I already knew he existed, I just never met him before."

Amy looked at me sceptically and nodded. "Well, if you say so, Sam."

I did say so and I had to do so too. Nothing had changed really. And if I kept telling myself that, I may actually believe it.

4

MAISIE

the present

I watched Frankie closely as he ate his dinner and sighed. He looked a lot like me. He even had the same pattern of freckles across his nose but with Sam's dark hair and brown eyes, and the way he held himself and his cocky little attitude, he was all his father and it worried me. How long before people started to realise and talk, and maybe let it slip to Frankie?

It had been easy to keep it all a big secret when Frankie was small, but now that he was growing, he was becoming more and more like bloody Samuel Cooper every day. No one had ever suspected before, because we'd only had one night together, after Alex Drake's party, and even though he'd promise he'd call me, he never did. I got one apologetic text telling me he was sorry but he was too caught up in helping his brother get through his wife leaving him to be able to have a relationship. The next time I'd seen him had been when I'd told him about Frankie, to say he looked horrified was an understatement. I knew straight away that a child was not what Sam wanted, so I gave him the easy way out and told him I'd do it on my own. He did say he'd support me at appointments and with money, but I knew for my own sanity that unless I wanted my own heart smashed to smithereens, he'd have

31

to be all in and no way was that going to happen, something that became blatantly obvious on the day Frankie was born. That was the day I told him to go and never come near us again.

For the first four years of Frankie's life, I regularly received money from him, but after about a year of being with Josh he said we didn't want or need Sam's money, so my solicitor wrote to Sam and told him. Personally, I'd have taken it and put it in an account for Frankie, but Josh was adamant and proud. That ended up being the next time I saw him, when he asked to meet me and discuss the money. Can't say it wasn't weird being next to him again, looking at the larger version of my son, but we meant nothing to each other, so while he argued about the money, that was all it had been – a quick twenty minute meeting in his car arguing about money.

I couldn't believe I'd been lucky enough to avoid Sam in over eight years. Apart from that onetime, I'd seen him at a distance from time to time, but never as close as we'd been earlier at the leisure centre. Our town was fairly big and I rarely went out at night to pubs or clubs, and if I went shopping it wasn't locally. I knew it had been a subconscious avoidance tactic, but to be honest, it hadn't been that difficult. The first few months of Frankie's life I dreaded bumping into Sam or any of his family, but once life got busy and I moved out of mum and dad's house into my own place, I kind of forgot about him. Yes, I'd liked him and we'd had two rounds of great sex, but he hadn't been the love of my life, but he had given me Frankie and I'd be eternally grateful to Sam for that.

When I heard Josh's car on the drive, my stomach clenched. He wasn't a local, so he didn't know Sam personally, but had a hatred for him that was almost to the point of being poisonous. Sam wasn't the only person Josh hated and it had to be said it would be easier to say who he didn't hate, and there were some days I wasn't sure whether I was even on that list.

"Hey," I said as Josh breezed in through the kitchen door.

"Hi. How come he's only just eating his dinner?" he asked, nodding at Frankie.

"Swimming lessons," I replied around a swallow and glanced warily at Frankie. Thankfully, he was listening to music and too interested in his spaghetti hoops to feel the need to comment on his new swimming teacher. If Josh found out Sam was running the lessons, he'd be sure to put a stop to them. I'd told him a couple of years ago Sam had been a talented swimmer, so when Frankie started to show an interest and appeared to have the same ability, Josh hated it, always stating it was a waste of money. Frankie loved it though, so I put my foot down and insisted that he continue going. If Frankie mentioned the name Sam, it wouldn't take Josh much to put two and two together and I was sure my hiding it from him even for a few hours would create another row and I just didn't have the energy – I also didn't want my son to have to give up the thing he loved.

Josh let out a sigh. "Huh, you know what I think of that." He then reached across the table to rip Frankie's earphones out. "What have I told you about listening to music at the table?"

Frankie looked up at him from beneath his long dark lashes and blinked a couple of times.

"Not to do it during dinner as it's family time, but I'm the only one eating so I thought it would be okay."

"Frankie," I warned in a low tone.

"But that's what Josh said."

"Don't split hairs," Josh snapped. "It's probably crap anyway."

Frankie picked up his iPod and turned it off and without looking up at Josh said. "Out on the Floor is one of the best Northern Soul songs ever."

I was sure I heard Josh mutter 'weird bloody kid', but before I could say anything, he disappeared out of the kitchen into the hall.

I had no idea what was wrong with him these days, when we first met, he had so much more time for Frankie. He'd spend long periods playing with him, even building a wooden garage for Frankie's toy cars, but after about a year he started to be too busy and had better things to do, and then in the last year or so Josh had made no secret of the fact that he found Frankie irritating.

"Frankie," I sighed. "Why can't you just think about what you say to him?"

He looked up at me and while there was some defiance behind his eyes, I could still see he was simply a little boy who didn't understand why he couldn't say what he thought. It had been just the two of us for just over four years and I'd believed in letting him speak his mind and talk things through with him if what he'd said wasn't appropriate – my own parents had brought me and my sister up that way, and I thought we'd turned out okay. To be fair, Frankie had always been a good boy, well behaved and polite but with a strong personality, and it made me feel awful that Josh was starting to chip away at my son's confidence, trying to turn him into some meek and mild child who never spoke. I'd tried to make Josh see what a lovely nature Frankie had, but when I said anything he wouldn't listen, insisting that I let Frankie get away with too much. It caused lots of rows and I was pretty sure that was why Frankie listened to his music so much, so he couldn't hear us arguing. I knew in my heart that it was only going to get worse, because the older Frankie got the more he looked like Sam and from what I remembered of him from all those years ago, his son had the same damn cocky attitude at times too.

"I'm supposed to tell the truth," Frankie said with a pout. "And that's the truth. No one else was at the table, so why can't I listen to my music?"

"It's not good manners," I explained, kind of seeing it from his point of view. "Just like Josh or I don't bring our phones to the table, we don't want you listening to music."

"But you talk about grown up stuff."

"Hey," I warned as Frankie rolled his eyes. "I've warned you before about rolling your eyes at me. Don't do it."

"Sorry Mummy."

He looked at me sheepishly, before going back to scoop up a forkful of spaghetti hoops.

As I washed the pan that I'd warmed Frankie's dinner in, I heard Josh moving around upstairs. He'd be having a shower and changing out of his suit into track suit bottoms, a t-shirt, and his slippers as he did every night. Josh was nothing if not predictable, it had to be said.

"Mum."

Frankie's voice drew me away from the sink, to turn around and face him.

"Hmm."

"What were you talking to Sam about?"

It was a good job I wasn't washing a glass, because I was sure I'd have crushed it as my hand fisted so tightly.

"Your swimming," I said, trying to sound unaffected by his question.

"But you were shouting at him."

I took a deep breath and looked over my shoulder. "I wasn't," I lied.

"Yeah Mummy, you were." Frankie wasn't looking at me, but scrolling through the music on his player. "You had your shouty face."

"I was asking him not to push you too hard, that's all."

"What do you mean?"

I moved over to sit with him and rested my forearms on the table in front of me.

"It means," I started. "That I don't want him trying to make you do things in the pool that you're not ready to do. I think you should stick to becoming a stronger swimmer, not learning a whole load of new strokes."

It wasn't a total lie, I wanted Frankie to enjoy swimming club, not think of it as an extension of school.

"But I'm good, Mum," he said, his brow furrowed as he stared at me. He didn't understand why I'd hold him back, but he was also daring me to contradict his conclusion that he was a very gifted swimmer.

I couldn't help but laugh, eliciting a sigh from Frankie.

"I am," he stated.

"I know," I replied, nodding my head and grinning at him.

God, he had enough confidence to sink a battle ship and he definitely didn't get that from me.

"So why can't Sam show me extra things to try?"

"Well, he can, but I don't want him to make you try too many things, I want you to have fun as well."

"I do. Today was much better than when Danny teaches us, last year he just got us to swim up and down. Sam played games with us that taught us the strokes."

His little face was full of consternation and I knew he had already had a fascination with the man who was his father. I knew then that I had to find a different swimming club for him, because I couldn't stand the thought of his heart being broken if he found out who his father was and that he wasn't interested in him.

5

SAMUEL

the past

I looked over at Elijah and groaned, he looked grey and as though he was about to puke – again. He'd been on a permanent bender since Amy, his wife, had fucked off and left him almost three weeks earlier. According to *her,* she caught him in bed with Lauren Proctor at Alex's party. Elijah couldn't remember anything, except at one point seeing some hazy figure that he couldn't focus on, writhing on top of him and wondering if it was Amy before passing out again. It was only when Luke, his mate, threw cold water on him and told him that Amy had apparently rushed out of the house in tears, and that Eli needed to get up, that he realised something was wrong. He'd finally got hold of Rachel, Amy's friend, who chewed his balls off over what he'd supposedly done.

Eli had rushed to Rachel's house, but Amy wouldn't see him and Rachel had slammed the door in his face. When I got to Eli at one in the morning, after a frantic call from him, he was huddled in Rachel's doorway, even though I'd told him to stay at our apartment, and was insisting he was staying there until Amy came out. I managed to persuade him to go home, but he was back there at six the next morning waiting it out. Amy however, still refused to go to

37

the door. After four hours of Elijah constantly banging on the door or calling her and Rachel's mobiles, Amy finally spoke to him, but no matter what he said, she didn't believe that he hadn't realised it wasn't her on top of him. Eli had gotten angry and so had she, both of them screaming at each other, until finally she'd shut the door on him. I'd tried to get Amy to see reason, we all had, as she'd known how paralytic he'd been. He could barely stand up, but she wouldn't listen. Now she'd left town and no one was telling Elijah where she'd gone. It was all a big fuck up, because they were obviously too damn immature to be married in the first place.

"They have to fucking tell me," he slurred, pointing at me with the neck of a beer bottle. "She's my fucking wife. I have a right to know."

Without waiting for me to answer, he pulled his phone out of his pocket and started to text what I guessed was probably the fiftieth text that day to her.

"She has to come back. And why the fuck wouldn't she believe me."

I shook my head and sighed. "I have no idea, bro. Now how about you get upstairs and sleep some of the alcohol off. You need to go to work tomorrow, otherwise you're gonna get the push."

Elijah shrugged. "Don't fucking care."

At that moment, Mum came into the kitchen asking me silently with her eyes whether I'd been able to talk any sense into him. I gave her a short shake of my head and felt my heart constrict when I saw tears welling in her eyes.

"Eli, sweetheart," she soothed, moving over to wrap an arm around his shoulder. "Why don't you let me make you something to eat? I think I've got a homemade chicken pie in the freezer, it wouldn't take long to heat it up."

"I don't want your fucking pie," he growled, shaking off her touch.

"Right," I snapped, snatching the beer from his hands. "You don't get to speak to Mum like that and be a total wanker to her at the same time."

I emptied the contents into the sink and slammed the bottle onto the draining board before turning back to my brother.

"Can't tell me what to do," he said, glaring at me. "Neither can she and why isn't she on one of her fucking crusades?"

Mum whimpered beside me and I reached for her hand and gave it a quick squeeze.

"Because she's looking after your sorry arse." I grabbed him with my hand around his bicep and pulled him toward the door into the hallway. "You're getting some sleep then you're going to get a shower and eat something, because if you want her back, you're going the wrong way about it. As if she'd want to come back to you in this state?"

Elijah tried to pull away from me as he swung a hand in my direction, but I dodged it and he stumbled.

"Oh god," Mum whispered.

"It's okay," I told her over my shoulder. "You get the pie out and when he's had a couple of hours of sleep, he'll be ready for it."

She flattened her lips together and nodded, leaving me to deal with my broken brother.

Dad came back into the lounge with a grim look on his face, rubbing a hand over his thick thatch of dark hair. For a man of fifty-seven, he was still in good shape and looked a lot younger than his years, but the past few weeks had aged both my parents.

"Nope," he said. "They won't tell me. All Lee said was that she'd moved away for a while and Elijah would be hearing from her solicitor. I tried to tell him that Elijah had no idea what happened until he spoke to Rachel later that night, but he says Amy is adamant what she saw."

"Alcohol," Mum snapped. "Bloody alcohol, it's damned evil at times. I know my son and I know how much he loves that girl, he would never do that to her if he was sober."

"He says he didn't do it at all, Mum. When he woke up all that was missing was his t-shirt, he even had his boots on. Luke has vouched for that, but she won't listen."

"Well if he hadn't been in that state, that stupid Lauren girl couldn't have taken advantage of him, and what the hell is Amy thinking, just running away like that. Twenty whole minutes she gave him to talk, after being together for six years."

"Hey, Yvetta, come on," Dad said, rubbing a hand up and down her back. "She saw what she saw and she's in an emotional state of mind. She's still grieving love, we have to remember that. I agree she should try and think more logically about it all and listen to Elijah, but we have no idea what her mental state is like at the moment."

I thought back to my conversation with Amy in the kitchen at the party, and she was definitely still struggling with losing their baby, especially as it was coming up to her due date.

"This is why I don't do damn girlfriends," I muttered, as my phone call to let Maisie down ran through my head.

During our night together, I could imagine myself falling for her, wanting to make it something more than a hook-up that was for sure, but Elijah's current fucking shit storm had soon put an end to that. I needed to be there for him, he was struggling, and even though Luke and Alex tried to help at times, they were about as much use as a one-legged man in an arse kicking competition. They had no idea what to do with him, except help him get plastered. It had also shown me that even the best of relationships could turn fucking toxic and I did not want to go there. I'd had my heart ripped out once, and it was once too often. No, Maisie West was best finding some nice bloke who took her out three nights a week, rang her every lunchtime, told her he loved her after a month, and then proposed after six, only to marry her a year later. She was pretty, funny, and sweet and she did not need me and my black heart fucking her life up because I couldn't commit.

"Oh," Mum said, gasping and putting a hand to her cheek. "I totally forgot, a pretty blonde girl called here for you earlier. Said she needed to speak to you, but has lost your number and didn't have the address of your flat."

My heart gave an extra beat. "Did she give her name?" I asked, wondering if by huge coincidence it was Maisie. Although there'd been a few pretty blondes in my life, Maisie was the only one I'd ever brought to Mum and Dad's house.

"She didn't say, but she left you a note. I'm so sorry love, it went clear out of my head with Elijah coming home in that state."

"It's fine Mum."

That was another thing worrying me – when was my brother actually going to go back to the flat and continue to live his life. He couldn't stay at Mum and Dad's forever, and call me a fucking shithead, but I couldn't afford it on my own, especially as I was saving like mad to have enough to offer to my boss to buy the recruitment agency I worked for.

Mum's hand came into my view as she handed me a piece of paper. I unfolded it and read the neat handwriting.

Sam, I'm really sorry that Elijah is having a bad time and I know you explained why you can't see me anymore, but I need to talk to you. Do you think you could give me a call on my new number 07783 098451. Thanks, Maisie.

· · ·

I swallowed, my mouth suddenly feeling dry, as my lungs began to work extra hard. There were a couple of reasons why a girl wrote you a note like that, and seeing as I'd worn a condom that night, both those reasons didn't seem possible – so why was my fucking heart hammering at one hundred miles an hour?

6

the present

It was official, my brother hated me. He hadn't spoken to me for three days, and it didn't look like he was going to any time soon. Amy had told me to be patient, but that was something I definitely wasn't, so I'd made her tell me where he was and I was going to meet him.

Walking along the path to the kid's park, I could hear Bella's chuckles of enjoyment as Elijah pushed her on the swing. Her little legs kicked excitedly as she clung on to the chains, her dark curls blowing behind her.

"She loves that, doesn't she?" I said, coming up alongside him.

"What are you doing here?"

"Well it's not to go on the slide, Elijah," I retorted sarcastically. "Hey Bella."

I waved at my niece and blew her a kiss.

"Unca Yam," she cried before bursting into giggles again.

"Hi beautiful."

I couldn't help but break out the biggest smile in my arsenal for the light of my life. I bloody adored her and couldn't ever contemplate her not being around now. She filled all our lives up with joy.

43

"See, Bella loves me," I muttered to Elijah's back as he continued pushing his daughter.

"She's two, she doesn't know any better."

"'Gain Dada."

We both grinned like love sick idiots as Bella held her hands in the air.

"I'm not sure what you want me to say," Elijah eventually said, glancing at me.

"I don't want you to say anything. I just want you to try and understand."

His gaze landed on me and lingered there for a few seconds before he exhaled and turned back to Bella.

"I can't, Sam. I can't understand how you can have a son and not want to spend every fucking waking hour with him. How you can just dismiss him from your life. How the fuck do you do that?"

I could do it because I was screwed over once before, because I fell in love with a child growing inside the woman I loved, only to be told it was all a big fucking lie – was what I wanted to say, but knew if I told Elijah that he'd hate me even more for keeping that from him too. Truth was, I was also ashamed, ashamed that I'd let myself be tricked by someone who I trusted and loved. Someone who stepped so far over the line she was in danger of falling off a cliff edge.

"It's just not me," I replied with a shrug. "The whole couple and family thing. I'm too busy with work and too fucking selfish to give anyone else any time. I was even more selfish then; when Maisie got pregnant. I was working towards buying the business and it was my only focus. I'd have been a shit dad to him and that wouldn't have been fair."

"Yeah," Elijah said, grabbing hold of Bella's swing. "But he'd have had a dad and I think you're kidding yourself. I see you with Bella, you're great with her. Do you think Amy would have let her stay overnight with anyone else when we went away for our anniversary, aside from our parents?"

"I dunno."

"No, you know she wouldn't. You asked us, instead of Bella going to one of the grandparents, could she stay with you and Amy said yes straight away, because she trusts you and knows how good you are with her, so don't give me the 'I'd have been a bad dad' shit.

He moved to pull Bella from the swing and blew a raspberry on her cheek when she started to complain about it. I watched carefully as he strapped her into her buggy and gave her a cup of juice, wondering whether to follow him or just walk home and let him work himself out of his shitty mood.

"Another thing," he snapped, turning to me. "Why the hell didn't you tell me? I'm your fucking brother, we tell each other everything."

I inhaled deeply, wondering how I could tell him without sounding like I was using him as an excuse.

"It was a difficult time, bro," I sighed. "You were going through your shit-."

"You could have told me," he hissed, glancing down at Bella who was snuggling down in her buggy. "I know I was in a bad place, but you're my fucking brother; I'd have been there for you."

I placed a hand on his shoulder. "It wasn't just losing Amy, you'd lost a child. How the fuck did I tell you that I wasn't going to have anything to do with mine without you hating my damn guts."

Elijah's eyes softened as he swallowed. "I could never hate you," he said in a quiet voice before turning back to the buggy.

As he started to walk toward the gate to the little park, he glanced over his shoulder at me.

"We're calling to see Matty and Carla, Bella is going to play with Jacob if you want to walk with us part of the way."

45

I nodded and walked over to him, edging him out of the way so I could be the one to push the buggy.

"So, you telling Mum and Dad?" Elijah asked.

"No." My response was short and sharp. No way were they to find out, it would only lead to a load of arguments and problems.

"Do you not think they have a right to know?"

"The point is, Eli," I said, carefully manoeuvring the buggy over a cracked paving stone, "I have no rights, which is fine. I don't deserve any, don't want any and we both know they'd go ape and insist on meeting Frankie, and that's not what Maisie wants. Not what I want."

We stopped at the edge of the pavement and turned to each other.

"You have no desire whatsoever, to be in his life?" Elijah was evidently stunned as his eyes grew big and stared at me. "Seriously?"

I didn't answer immediately as we crossed the road, double checking no cars were coming, but when we reached the other side I pulled to a stop.

"I admit, it felt weird seeing him at the pool, spending time with him. Yeah, there was part of me that enjoyed it, I felt proud that he was good and probably got that from me, but being a dad, a family man, that's you Eli, it's not me. The kid is happy, or seems it, and me suddenly announcing who I was, could only mess with his head. Even if I wanted to, it wouldn't be fair on Frankie."

Elijah looked down at Bella and ran a hand over her sleeping head, before bringing his gaze back to mine.

"I don't get it, Sam. I really don't understand how you can feel like that, but it's your decision so I'll respect that."

"Not just mine," I added. "It's Maisie's too."

Elijah nodded and took the buggy from me as we were at the junction where we needed to go in different directions.

"You told me once not to live a life of regret because, and I think your words were, it's a dark shit hole of a place, which means you know what regret feels like. If this is it," he said, placing a hand on my shoulder. "If this is your regret, then do something about it. Talk to Maisie and see if you can get to know your son."

I shook my head and opened my mouth, but Elijah wouldn't let me speak.

"No, just hear me out. If you want to have a relationship with him, speak to Maisie. Whatever you decided before he was born may not be what's best for any of you now. Things change, people change, so don't think you've got to keep to those choices. I know what it's like to live half a life, to think you're living the one you want when it's far from it and you're right it is a shit hole of a place. I hate that I hurt Mia, but I honestly thought I loved her, it just took Amy coming back for me to realise it wasn't enough. Don't make that mistake, Sam. Don't leave it until someone gets hurt before you admit the truth to yourself."

My brother pulled me in for a hug and then with a squeeze of my shoulder strode off in the direction of his brother-in-law's house, leaving me wishing I'd kept my secret to myself, because if nothing else, my damn brother spoke sense from time to time.

7

Samuel

the past

I approached the table where Maisie was sitting in the coffee shop and could see straight away that she was totally fucking stressed about something.

She was chewing on a thumbnail and her eyes were firmly fixed on her mobile on the table – probably waiting for me to text her that I wasn't coming. Despite the frown lines on her forehead though, I had to admit she looked beautiful. Her long blonde hair was cascading over her shoulders, curtaining her perky tits in a tight green V-neck jumper, evoking all sorts of thoughts. Memories of our night together flooded back and a small voice in the depths of my brain told me I should ask her for another chance – take her out and stop using Elijah as an excuse for being a cowardly shit.

When I'd almost reached the table, she looked up, her pretty brown eyes spotting me. Instantly she stiffened and I saw her draw in a breath before giving me a wary smile.

"Hey," Maisie said, pulling out a chair for me. "Thanks for coming."

When her gaze darted around the room, as I took a seat, dread filled my stomach. This was about what I had dismissed so easily, because like a knob head, I'd thought we'd be safe and it couldn't possibly happen to me.

"Fuck," I muttered, rubbing a hand down my face.

Maisie's head whipped around and startled eyes stared at me.

"What?" she asked around rapid breaths.

I looked at her for a long moment, trying to search for something in her face that told me I was wrong, that this meeting was all about her wanting us to try and be a couple. Unfortunately, no matter how carefully my eyes scrutinised her, I could see nothing but fear, anxiety, and stress. It could have meant anything, but it was the sparkle in her wary eyes and the pinkness of her cheeks that proved to me I was right – I'd seen the signs before.

"You're pregnant, aren't you?" I groaned.

Maisie's mouth dropped open as she nodded slowly.

"Fuck." A cold sweat ran over me as I watched Maisie's face crumple and tears spring to her eyes.

"I have no idea how it happened," she whispered.

I reached across the table for her hand, not sure whether it was to comfort her or myself, I just knew I needed to do it. This couldn't be happening to me. I was always so damn careful. It didn't matter if the girl was on contraception, I never ever went without a condom.

"It's fine," I said and then closed my eyes as I shook my head. "Obviously it's not fucking fine, I mean it's not your fault. We were both there. Fuck."

My head dropped to the table and Maisie moved her hand from mine, laying her tiny cool palm on top of my huge one.

"I just don't know how it happened," she said close to my ear. "I'm on the pill and we used a condom. It's impossible."

My head lifted slowly and I looked up at her.

"My sperm is obviously as good a swimmer as I am," I deadpanned, not really finding anything funny about the situation.

Seemingly, neither did Maisie because her face was impassive. "You've not forgotten to take it?"

Maisie shook her head. "No, the only thing I can think of is I had some antibiotics for a chest infection a few weeks ago, but otherwise..." She shrugged and made a little whimpering sound.

"But we used a condom," I stressed again, still unable to fathom what had happened.

"Have you had them a while? *Is* there an expiry date on condoms?"

I had no idea, but Maisie had made a good point, I'd left the packet of condoms in my old room when I left home to share with Amy and Elijah and I wasn't sure how long I'd had them before that because I just didn't take girls back to Mum and Dad's house.

"Whatever the reason, it happened," I replied, sitting up straight. "So, what next?"

I held my breath, not sure what I wanted to hear coming from Maisie's mouth, because I couldn't deny that a very small bit of that same excitement I'd felt when Ali had told me she was pregnant was there, but as images and memories of the day when Ali gave birth pushed to the forefront of my brain, dread quickly washed it away.

"It is -."

"Yes," Maisie snapped, pushing back in her seat. "I told you, I hadn't been with anyone for ages."

I let out a breath and rubbed a hand down my face. "Yeah, I know, I'm sorry. I'm just trying to get my head around it."

"Yes, well that makes two of us," she hissed. "And don't think I want anything from you, I don't. I just thought you should know."

I nodded and while a silence fell over us, I once again let my mind wander back into that black day that hardened me against beautiful, sweet women like Maisie.

I knew she wasn't like Alison, but who would blame me for

wondering and wanting to be sure. I'd been prepared to face anything for that woman, to give up my dreams of swimming for my country and get myself a decent job to support her and our baby. I'd even been prepared to cut my family out of my life if they wouldn't accept her, but all those sacrifices were immaterial because she'd lied to me and made me believe in a fucking fairy tale.

"I'm not getting rid of it." Maisie's voice was small and timid, evidently she was scared that I was going to argue with her, but I would never force her to do anything.

"I don't expect you to, if it's not what you want," I replied, leaning forward to emphasise my point. "I'm not cruel Maisie, it's-."

"It's just that this isn't what you want."

Taking a second before answering, I took in a deep breath and then let it out slowly.

"No, it isn't, but I'll support you and the baby financially. I'm not sure I can offer you much else."

"Okay." She swallowed and looked up at the ceiling.

"I'm sorry."

Maisie's gaze came back to my face and she gave me a small smile. "I didn't expect you to get down on one knee and propose, Sam. I also didn't expect you to jump around with excitement. I knew that this would probably be the outcome, I hoped though that you might want some involvement in your child's life."

"I can't Maisie. It's not me and I know that makes me look like the biggest shit on the planet, but you'll be glad I'm not around to let him or her down, honestly you will."

She looked unsure, but smiled anyway.

"You're probably right. As for supporting the baby, you don't need to, we'll be fine."

I shook my head. "Nope, no way. I'm doing it, even if you

choose to put the money away for their university, or their wedding, or whatever, I'm going to contribute." So, it would take me longer to save the money to buy the business from Hazel, but I was sure she'd be okay to hang on a little while longer. "I guess we should consult a solicitor."

"You think so? Can't we do it between ourselves?" Maisie chewed at her lip and I almost reached up a hand to stop her. Her lips were perfectly shaped- a deep pink and far too pretty to be chewed.

Instead, I pulled my hands away from the table and stuffed them into the pockets of my jeans.

"I'd rather we get something official written up," I replied. "I want you to feel secure financially."

I heaved out a breath as Maisie watched me. Her brown eyes warily searching my face and I wished I wasn't so closed off to having a relationship with her, but I couldn't allow myself to be distracted from my aspirations again. I couldn't put myself in a position where I might end up feeling torn apart again. I wanted to buy the business and nothing was going to stop me.

"Because?" she asked.

"Because, that's all I can give you. I'm sorry. I have things I want to do; I want to buy my boss out. Nothing can distract me from that and I don't want to be a dad."

Pressing her lips together, Maisie nodded and then reached down for her bag with one hand, while the other felt behind for her jacket on the back of the seat.

"Okay," she said, pushing to the edge of her chair. "If you want to get something organised, I'll do whatever needs doing – I don't know, sign papers, organise my own solicitor – just let me know."

"Will do," I replied, my voice flat.

"You've got my number, from the note?"

I nodded. "Did you save mine from my text?"

Maisie looked at her phone and nodded before she dropped her phone into her bag and stood up.

"I'll be in touch," she said as she pulled on her jacket. "Unless...well unless you don't want to know, or..."

"Yes, that's fine," I interjected seeing she felt uncomfortable. "Keep me updated and I'll let you know about the solicitor thing."

She nodded, gave me a small smile and was gone, leaving me to wonder why I hadn't stormed out or called her a liar like I'd always thought I would if ever a girl gave me that news again. I felt surprisingly calm, despite what I'd just found out. There was definitely a sense of fear within me for what this might mean for my future, but knowing that Maisie was being sensible and cool about everything helped. All I had to do was decide whether to tell my parents and my brother who was in his own pit of hell.

8

the present

As soon as I let myself into my parents' house, Frankie shot past me and down the hallway into the lounge.

"Grandad," he yelled at the top of his voice. "I'm going to be in the school play."

Mum popped her head out from Dad's little study and grinned. "Was that whirlwind my grandson?"

"He's a little excited," I replied, taking off my coat and hanging it on the coat rack. "He got a part in the school production of Charlie and The Chocolate Factory."

"Wow." Mum came into the hall and gave me a hug. "That's ambitious."

"I know, but they're not doing a Christmas play this year so they can put all their efforts into it."

"Your dad will be disappointed, he always enjoys the Christmas play."

"He's got three months to get used to it."

I followed Mum to the kitchen, shouting a hello to Dad as we passed the lounge. Immediately I went over to the sink and picked up a potato and a knife. "How many do you want me to peel?" I asked.

"Ooh about six, I'd say. Libby and I are off the carbs," Mum announced.

"Again?" I asked, wondering how long it would last this time. My mum and my sister had tried every diet known to man and it was a different one each week. No carbs though had been done at least twice before.

"Hmm," she replied, examining a bag of carrots. "That woman off the telly is doing it and she's lost ten pounds."

"Which woman?"

"You know the big lady, the one with beautiful, long red hair."

I had no idea who she was talking about, but gave a murmur of recognition anyway.

"What is it for tea, anyway?" I asked, thinking it was probably best not to get into the whys and wherefores of Mum and Libby's latest fad.

"Homemade steak pie."

I opened my mouth to say something, but changed my mind. I was too het up about the fact that Frankie had another lesson with Sam the following day and Josh had been a total and utter prick earlier, *accidentally* wiping all Frankie's music from his iPod. I was pretty sure he'd done it on purpose because he'd caught Frankie listening to music at gone ten the night before when he should have been asleep. Josh said he'd been updating the software for him, but I wasn't that stupid. Luckily, my dad had backed every-thing up on his computer for Frankie, so after dinner I'd get him to reload it again. Unfortunately, the promise that his grandad would be able to do that, hadn't stopped Frankie from throwing a real temper tantrum at the time – earning himself another lecture from Josh.

"I take it Josh didn't want to come," Mum said, her voice tight and accusing.

I'd stopped defending Josh and lying that he'd made other

plans or that he'd been called into work, it wasn't as though they hadn't all seen through my lies over the last couple of years, each of them swapping furtive glances of disappointment in my boyfriend not wanting to be a part of the family.

"No, it's not his thing and to be honest, I think Frankie needs a bit of a break from him."

Mum looked at me quizzically, so I told her about the iPod. She adored Frankie, and Josh not so much, so all the way through the story her lip curled further and further into a snarl, until finally I actually thought she might bark at me.

"Dad will get it all back after tea," she said, a hardness to her voice.

"I know, that's what I told Frankie."

We continued to prepare our meal in silence, both of us stewing over what Josh had done. Animosity was positively bristling off my mother and I knew she was trying hard to keep her tongue. Neither she nor Dad particularly liked Josh, but as they said, he was my choice. They used to say 'he's good to you and Frankie and he's your choice, so that's all that matters', nowadays though it was simply 'he's your choice, Maisie'.

"You know," my mum finally said, breathing heavily. "It really concerns me how he is with Frankie. Doesn't it you? He never used to be like that, it's as though as time's gone on he can't cope with the fact that the poor child has a personality."

I paused peeling the potato in my hand and looked at her; the tears in her eyes shocking me.

"Mum." I threw the potato and knife into the sink and moved over to her, wrapping an arm around her shoulder. "He's not violent or anything like that. He just has quite strict rules about things, and you know Frankie, he likes to push the boundaries."

"And that's what makes him so wonderful," Mum said, gripping my hand. "Don't let him govern that out of him, Maisie. That child is bright and funny and yes he's a cheeky little beggar at times, but he's polite too, and he knows how to behave when it's important. His teachers love him."

"I know. They tell me all the time." I moved away from her and leaned against the counter, my back rigid. "Josh isn't a monster, Mum."

"I'm not saying he is, but the fire has gone out of your eyes too over the last couple of years."

"What fire?" I asked, feeling a knot forming in my stomach. "I'm the same as I've always been."

Mum shook her head. "No Maisie, you're not," she cried. "You used to be feisty and strong, but you just don't seem to have any fight left in you."

I felt as though she'd slapped me across the face. That my own mother thought that about me was as big a shock as when I'd found out I was pregnant.

"Well thanks, Mum."

"I'm not trying to be mean," she said, making a move toward me. "But I hear how he talks to you both and once upon a time you'd have told him to shove it, but now you just accept it. To be honest, once upon a time he worshipped both of you, now it's like he just wants to control you."

"I don't just accept things," I replied, knowing deep down Mum had a point. Josh had changed and I couldn't stand the arguments any longer.

"You don't have to settle you know."

My head shot up as I stared at my mum. "What? What do you mean, settle? I'm not settling for anything."

"I think you are, love, you're settling for Josh because you think Frankie needs a father and you want a partner."

"Of course I do," I snapped. "But I wouldn't settle just so we got those things. Give me some credit."

Her comments hurt, but they niggled too because I was scared she was right. I'd been wondering for a while whether I put up with Josh and his sniping at me and Frankie because I was scared of being alone. I had loved him a great deal when we first got together, he was fun and sweet, but the last year and a half, he'd made it pretty difficult to still feel that way about him.

"All I'm saying is, if he's not who you really want, then you will be fine on your own until you find the one."

"I'm fine with who I'm with now, Mum."

I turned back to the sink and continued peeling the potatoes, choosing to ignore the heaviness in my heart.

Dinner at my parents' house hadn't been the best of evenings. Mum and I barely spoke to each other, Libby did nothing but complain about having to eat pie, and Dad kept going on about Josh removing Frankie's music, and how it was a good job he'd backed it up on his computer. All this while Frankie went on and on about being cast as Grandpa Joe in the play. All in all I was glad when it was time to leave.

As soon as I walked through the door, I knew immediately that I probably would have been better staying at Mum and Dad's despite how crappy the evening had been. Josh was just coming out of the kitchen holding a bowl of cereal.

"Is that your dinner?" I asked, taking Frankie's coat from him so he could take off his shoes.

"Well you didn't leave me anything, so yeah."

Josh looked down at Frankie, who had his earphones in.

"I take it he whined to your dad to put his music back on."

I sighed inwardly, wondering what his bloody problem was. Frankie loved music and Josh for some reason found it irritating.

"Yes," I replied with a smile to try and calm his mood. "I asked him to."

Josh rolled his eyes. "You need to stop spoiling him."

"How is it spoiling him?" I asked, ushering Frankie toward the stairs. I pulled out one of his earphones and leaned down to his ear. "Go up and get your teeth cleaned and pyjamas on, I'll be up in twenty minutes to turn your light off."

"Light off straight away," Josh added. "And leave that iPod down here."

Frankie looked up at him through his long lashes and for one minute my stomach rolled when I thought he was going to argue back. Thankfully, he didn't, but without taking his eyes from Josh, turned off his iPod, took out his earphones and wrapped them around the silver music player before handing it to me. Josh's cheek pulsed as the two of them stared each other down.

"Frankie, go on up," I said, with a gentle tap to his back.

He turned and looked up at me and for an instant I saw sadness in his eyes. The sight was like a punch to my stomach. This was not what I wanted for my boy, to be sad because of the man I'd chosen to be in our lives.

"Night, Mum." He reached up on his tiptoes and kissed my cheek before racing up the stairs, adding an extra bang to his steps on each tread.

"Frankie!" Josh shouted. "Stop stamping."

I couldn't help the frustrated sigh escaping and immediately Josh's angry gaze landed on me.

"What the hell is that about?" he asked, the bowl of cereal dangerously close to losing its contents as it tipped.

"Nothing and be careful, you're going to spill your cereal."

He looked down at the bowl and then back up at me. "Can't have that can we?" With his narrowed eyes firmly fixed on me, he slowly tipped the cereal and milk onto the carpet. "Oops sorry."

"Josh!" I cried. "What the hell have you done that for?" I went to move past him to go and get a cloth, but he caught hold of my arm.

"I'm sick and tired of being the bad guy here," he snarled. "You spoil him and give me shit all the time."

I wrenched my arm from his grasp. "I don't spoil him, all I did was ask Dad to put his music back onto to his iPod, and all I asked you was *not* to spill milk and cereal on the carpet, but you had to act like a child didn't you."

"I fucking didn't."

"Well what do you call that?" I pointed in the direction of the spillage, still watching Josh closely. "I'll clean it up and then I'm going to bed."

"Now who's acting like a child? I'll clean it up and then I'm going to bed'," he said, mimicking me.

"Oh grow up."

Putting Frankie's iPod in my pocket, I moved toward the kitchen and before I'd taken three steps, the white bowl came whizzing past my ear and smashed on the wall above the door. As it landed with a resounding crash, I held a hand up to protect myself as china and milk sprayed everywhere and soggy *Corn-flakes* splattered on the pale grey walls. I felt a sharp jab against my forearm that was in front of my face and milk splashed over me.

"You stupid idiot," I screamed, turning to Josh who was standing behind me, his chest heaving. "You could have hurt me."

"I meant to miss you," he spat out. "I'm just sick to death of you fucking nagging me."

Shaking my hands out, to get rid of the residue of liquid, I heard a noise on the stairs. I looked up to see Frankie bowling down the stairs.

"Frankie, go to bed sweetheart," I said, giving him a soft smile.

"Are you okay, Mummy?" he asked, sounding small and frightened.

I nodded. "Of course I am."

"You heard your mum," Josh snapped, looking up. "Get to bed."

Frankie's eyes were tentative as he half turned on the staircase, hesitating.

"Go on Frankie," I urged as calmly as I could, "get on to bed. I'll be up soon."

"But Mum-."

As Josh stalked towards him with a hand raised, Frankie stopped talking and gasped as his eyes went wide with horror.

"Don't you damn well dare," I screamed, running at Josh, pushing him aside to get to my son.

"See, you're spoiling him again. A slap on the legs wouldn't hurt him once in a while."

"You will never put your hands on my son." I pushed Frankie behind me. "Frankie go up to bed."

"No," he sobbed. "Mummy no, I'm not leaving you."

"Oh stop snivelling," Josh groaned. "I'm not going to hurt her."

"Leave my mummy alone." Frankie's little hands grabbed the back of my t-shirt, clutching it tightly.

"Your mum told you to go to bed," Josh snapped. "Now go."

"No. I'm not leaving her."

I put an arm behind me to touch Frankie's arm. "I'm fine, Josh won't hurt me. He's leaving."

"*What?*"

"You heard," I replied, trying to stop my voice from quaking. "You're leaving. I want you out of this house."

"Over one bloody bowl of cereal," he scoffed, thrusting his hands to his hips. "You're fucking joking."

"No, Josh, I'm not. Things haven't been right between us for a while and that," I said, pointing at the mess on the wall, "is not acceptable. What is far worse though, is that you raised a hand to my son, so pack a bag and go."

"No way." He was shaking his head and sneering at me. "Not happening."

"This is my house, not yours, and I want you to go."

"You rent the fucking place, it's not *yours*."

"Exactly *I* rent it, not you, so unless you want me to call the landlord and the police, then get a bag and leave."

I moved toward the front door and pulled down the handle. I was about to pull it open when Josh slammed a hand against it.

"I'm not leaving," he insisted.

"Yes you are." I held my shoulders back and straightened my spine, trying desperately to appear brave and confident, but inside I was a quivering wreck, scared of what he might do to me or Frankie.

I couldn't believe how quickly things between us had evaporated. How he'd turned from a miserable, joyless man to someone who would throw things at me and threaten to smack my son. A man who in the space of a few minutes I'd become afraid of.

I pulled on the handle again and yanked at the door, managing to get it open. I had to get him out tonight, because this was the last time my son would be a witness to anything like this. I'd seen enough documentaries, read enough newspaper articles to know that this was merely the beginning and he would only get more violent as time went on. I loved my son too much to risk that, and I certainly didn't love Josh enough to give him an opportunity to either redeem himself or prove me wrong.

"Please Josh," I said, my voice low and strong. "Get a bag and leave."

We watched each other warily as a chill blew in through the gap in the doorway, all the time I had Frankie at my back, holding on tightly. Finally, after what felt like hours, Josh's nostrils flared and he pushed past both myself and Frankie and stomped up the stairs.

"Is he really going, Mummy?" Frankie asked, his voice quiet and timid.

"Yes sweetheart." I turned and picked him up. He was tall and broad for his age, but I didn't care how heavy he felt, he was staying in my arms until Josh had left.

After only a few minutes, he reappeared, now wearing a hoody and trainers with his joggers. On his shoulder was a sports bag, the zip only half closed as clothes spilled out. When he got to the bottom stair, Josh pushed everything inside the bag and pulled the zip fully closed.

"Don't think you can come running to me when you realise you've made a mistake," he said, pointing a finger right in my face. "Because I won't want to know."

"I won't," I replied, holding tighter onto my son.

"Fucking bitch," Josh hissed and slammed out of the house.

As soon as the door closed, I turned the key in the lock and let out a huge sigh of relief. I put Frankie down and ran a hand over his head.

"Go upstairs," I said. "You can get a book out for half an hour and I'll bring up some hot chocolate, okay?"

He looked at me warily, finally nodding his head and running up the stairs. Halfway up, he stopped and turned to look down at me.

"Mummy, can I sleep with you tonight?"

I didn't want him to be scared and think he needed to sleep with me, but if I was being honest, I needed it just as much.

I nodded. "Okay, just for tonight."

When he disappeared, I rushed into the lounge to peek through the curtains to make sure Josh had really left. His car was gone from the driveway, which made me let out a huge sigh of relief, but then I saw a man dressed in jogging gear. He was standing on the road next to my car and looking at it, before glancing up the street. When he looked up at the house, my heart thudded rapidly, knowing something was wrong. Not thinking about whether it was the right thing to do or not, I rushed to the front door, unlocked and opened it.

"What's the problem?" I called from my doorway.

The jogger looked up from my car and scrubbed a hand down his face. "I'm really sorry," he called. "But I think you need to see this."

"Tell me." There was no way I was going out there to stand next to a man who could turn out to be some sort of serial killer – although deep down I knew it was probably something to do with Josh.

"Some guy just smashed into your car," he said, walking towards the drive. "He was in a white Audi. I saw him pull off your drive and then ram yours. This is your car?" He nodded his head toward my little red car.

"Yes," I replied weakly. "It's mine."

The jogger continued up the drive and it was only as he stopped about three feet away that I recognised him. Of all the people to be jogging past my house when Josh lost it, it had to be Elijah Cooper, Sam's brother.

9

the present

"Hey, Eli," I said into my mobile, glad that things with my brother seemed to be okay again.

"Sam, you need to get here now," Elijah said, sounding a little uptight.

"Why and where is here?" I asked, pushing up from my sofa and walking into my bedroom.

"I'm at Maisie West's house."

My stomach bottomed out, landing with a thud. "Is it Frankie?" I asked, pushing my feet into a pair of trainers. "What the fuck's happened and why are you there?"

"I was jogging," he replied, his voice lowering. "I saw this guy pull off a drive and then ram a car on the road outside the same house. The woman came out and it wasn't until I walked up to the door to talk to her that I realised it was Maisie and that it was her car."

"What, he just rammed her damn car?" I grabbed my keys from a bowl on a shelf in the hallway of my apartment and let myself out, rushing over to the lift, stabbing at the button.

"Yeah. She's pretty shaken, but won't call the police. I don't really want to leave her, but I've been out for almost two hours.

67

Amy's told me to stay with her and make sure she's okay, but I don't know what I can do. Plus, Maisie pretty much told me to go home and shut the door on me."

"Not sure I can do anything either, and if she shut the door on you then go home," I replied, wondering what the hell he'd called me for.

"She needs someone to check she's okay, and that someone should be you."

"You do remember that I told you I have a kid with her? A kid I've had nothing to do with."

"Yeah," he huffed out. "Which is why I think you're the best person to be here."

"Eli, it's not right that I be there. She won't want me to be, I don't want to be."

"If you don't want to be then why the fuck are you, at this very moment, on the way here?"

My brother chuckled on the other end of the line and I truly wanted to punch him in the fucking bollocks.

"You sounded worried, but now I've had time to think about it, I'm pretty sure it's the wrong thing to do." I walked out of the lift and across the apartment block lobby. "Just get her to call the coppers." Pushing open the exterior door, I pointed my car key and beeped my lock open, the lights of my Range Rover flashing.

"So that wasn't your car I just heard beeping?"

I remained silent, sitting myself inside and resting my forehead on the steering wheel.

"Sam, you need to man the fuck up and get over here. It doesn't matter whether you're shit scared to look your kid in the eye, or too chicken to talk to the woman who told you to fuck off eight years ago, you need to do what's right."

"I'm not scared or fucking chicken," I protested.

"Yeah, you are. Put this address in your *sat-nav*, number twel-."

"I know where she fucking lives," I groaned, turning the key in my ignition.

Elijah's laugh rumbled. "Well, well, well, who would have thought it?"

"She lives a few doors from Hannah, Frankie is in the same class as Hannah's kid, Rosie."

"You fucking told Hannah about your child, but not me, your own brother?" he blasted. "Thanks for that Sam, I know where I fucking stand now."

"Eli," I growled. "I got pissed one night when I was out with her and Connor. So pissed, she insisted I stay with them, in case I choked on my own puke or some shit like that. The next morning, Hannah was going to give me a lift home and Maisie came out carrying Frankie. He was just a toddler and I froze like a damn idiot. I didn't know what to do, run, hide, or go over and speak to her. Hannah noticed and put two and two together – even then, if you knew, it wasn't hard to see the likeness between me and him."

"You could have told me then, once Hannah knew." Elijah sounded hurt, and there was I thinking we were back on track.

"I'm sorry bro. I didn't plan on telling anyone at all, but once she knew she kept me updated from time to time."

"On a kid you don't give a shit about," he said, somewhat sarcastically.

I let out a long breath. "Yeah, on a kid I don't give a shit about."

There was no point denying it, I'd been more than a little curious about my son, but it didn't mean I wanted to be in his life.

"Whatever," Eli ground out. "Get your arse over here, because I have a feeling it was her boyfriend that just smashed up her car on purpose, and it doesn't sit well with me at the end of the day, Samuel. Maisie's son is your fucking responsibility, I have my own family I need to be with. I'll wait until you get here, but hurry up.

I'm getting cold standing out here in shorts and a fucking running top."

With that the line went dead and I thrust my car into gear, speeding off to relieve my bloody brother of his duty as protector.

I surveyed the damage to Maisie's red hatchback and let out a long whistle. The fucker had certainly gone at it hard. The only consolation was that he'd probably fucked up his Audi prick wagon. All the driver's side was pushed in, the metal crumpled and scratched.

As soon as I'd got there, Elijah had growled something about me manning the fuck up and then jogged off back home, leaving me with the prospect of having Maisie give me another verbal pasting.

I ran my hand along the dented metal and with a long exhale, made my way to the front door. I knocked twice before noticing from the corner of my eye, the curtains move. It was dropped back in place and then a few moments later, the door was pulled open.

"He called you didn't he?" Maisie sighed, stating the bloody obvious.

"Yeah, he thought someone should be with you."

Thinking about it again, my brother's idea that it should be me was fucking ludicrous. Maisie and I had barely spoken in almost nine years and each time we had it'd been angry and agitated.

"I'm fine. I can call my dad if I need to." She looked back into the house and then pushed the door until it was almost closed. "I'll be fine Sam."

"Maisie, you don't look fine."

I looked at her hand that was clutching the door and it was shaking, she was also as white as the UPVC that she was holding onto for dear life.

"I'm not your responsibility."

At that moment, car headlights flashed onto us. Maisie gasped and moved to push the door closed.

"Wait," I said. "What the hell is going on?"

I turned to be momentarily blinded by the lights until they were suddenly turned off. The driver's door swung open and a guy about my height, with dark blond hair stepped out. Anger and animosity was steaming off him as he approached us, his hands flexing into fists.

"Josh," Maisie said, her voice shaking. "I asked you to go and I know what you did to my car."

"Who the fuck is this?" he asked, sneering at me.

This guy was a prick, someone who thought he was a big man, well he didn't fucking scare me.

"I'm a friend of Maisie's, now she asked you to go, so I suggest you do."

"What my girlfriend tells me to do is no fucking business of yours, now get out of my way so I can go into my house."

"No Josh," Maisie said. "I don't want you here."

"You can't stop me Maisie, I pay the bills here."

"Yes, and I pay the rent," she replied. "It's my name on the rental agreement, so go."

I watched as he tensed up and I was sure he was going to punch me, or at least attempt to. I moved back a pace, turning my back to the door, getting ready to retaliate or at least stop him forcing entry into the house.

"You heard her," I added, nodding toward his car. "So, get in your car and go before I call the police."

"Yeah and what for?" he asked, cocking his head on one side.

"Criminal damage to her car. We have a witness."

His smile faltered as he glanced at his own car.

"Yeah, the damage to your own car doesn't really help your case mate," I said, crossing my arms over my chest.

He opened his mouth to say something, but stopped when the door was yanked open and a dark head poked around it.

"Tell him to go." It was Frankie and his eyes were brimming with tears. "He threw a dish at my mummy and he was going to hit me. Tell him."

Bile rose in my throat as I watched big, fat tears fall down Frankie's ashen face. I swivelled back to the prick in front of me and when I saw him sneer, I immediately saw red. I grabbed a hold of his hoody dragging him to me and pulled back my other arm, my hand fisted and shaking with anger, ready to punch him.

"No," Maisie gasped. "Please, not in front of Frankie."

"Hit him," Frankie cried at the same time.

If I hadn't been so fucking furious, I'd have probably laughed, but instead I pulled my arm back again.

"No, Sam," Maisie's voice was pleading as she laid her small hand on my bicep.

The prick let out a hollow laugh and shook his head slowly. "So you're *him* are you?" he sneered. "No wonder the kid needs to be disciplined."

I tugged on his hoody bringing him so close, our noses were almost touching and snarled at him.

"You ever raise a hand to *my* fucking kid or Maisie ever again," I whispered menacingly. "I will fucking end you. I don't care if I have to do time, it'll be worth it to see a bully like you in the ground. In fact," I hissed. "I'll bury you myself and no one will find your worthless, piece of shit body. You hear me."

He tried to act the hard man for all of two seconds, but when I shook him, he nodded and relaxed his fists.

"Now fuck off." I pushed him so hard he landed on his arse on the driveway. "And don't come back."

Pushing himself up, he backed away until he collided with his car and got inside and screeched away.

I turned to Maisie who had Frankie tucked against her side.

"You okay?" I asked.

She nodded, but her bottom lip was trembling and her grip on Frankie must have been tight because he whimpered beside her.

"Okay, I'm coming in," I said, my tone uncompromising. "And you need to get these locks changed."

"I don't think that-."

"Maisie," I warned. "I mean it."

Maisie simply nodded and moving away from the door let me inside. As soon as I was, I noticed the stain on the wall above a doorway and there was a broken dish over the floor, mixed with what looked like soggy *Cornflakes*.

"He do that?" I asked.

Maisie nodded.

"Yeah, he threw it at Mummy," Frankie said, his bravado at wanting me to punch his mum's boyfriend suddenly gone. "He's not coming back is he?"

I shook my head. "Nope." Not tonight at least, but I had a feeling he might try again another day.

"You get Frankie to bed and I'll clean this up," I said to Maisie, who was staring at me bewildered.

"Can we have hot chocolate first?" Frankie asked.

Maisie looked down at him, running a hand over his dark brown hair, the exact colour of mine. "Okay. You want one?" she asked me.

I actually wanted to fucking run, get back in my car and never come back. I didn't want to be involved in their lives. I didn't want to care that some fucker had raised a hand to my son. I fucking didn't want to feel anything, but I did.

I nodded. "Yeah, that would be great."

10

MAISIE

the past

My mum and dad were watching me warily, why, I had no idea. I'd come to terms with being single and pregnant at twenty-two years of age, *they'd* come to terms with me being single and pregnant. After my scan today though, they'd barely taken their eyes off me.

"What?" I asked, the biscuit in my hand halfway to my mouth.

"We're just wondering how you feel after today," Dad said, glancing at Mum.

"Fine, why?" I took a bite of my biscuit, giving them a dismissive shrug.

"Well it's a big thing seeing your child for the first time," my mum said. "We wondered whether you felt upset that the father wasn't there."

I still hadn't told them who 'the father' was. I knew my mother and she wouldn't be able to stop herself from rushing around to Sam's parents and insisting that they make their son marry me or something equally as ridiculous. They'd argued with me, of course, but they'd eventually agreed it was my decision. I thought I might tell them at some point in the future, but for now I was happy to keep it to myself. The baby and I weren't what Sam wanted in his life, so I didn't want anyone rocking the boat and forcing him to make choices that he hated. Maybe I was being too generous and I should be thinking of my baby – was it fair to deny them of a father? If I was right though, Sam would be a great financial help, but it was doubtful he would provide any other form of support, and in my mind it was better for the baby to have no dad around than one that flitted in and out of its life, creating a lot of heartache for them. I actually didn't blame Sam. At least he hadn't told me stuff I'd wanted to hear and then let me down, and while I didn't want his money, I also realised that realistically I couldn't do this without some help. I knew my parents would help as much as they could, but they'd raised Libby and me and it wasn't down to them to raise my child too.

"No, I wasn't," I finally answered. "It isn't what he wants and I'm not forcing him. I can do this on my own. He's helping financially and that's it."

I thought about the solicitor's letter I'd received the day before, and I had to be honest, what Sam was giving me was pretty generous. I'd expected an offer of a hundred a month maybe, but it was way more than that. It would mean I could afford a decent place to rent eventually.

"Why can't you just tell us who it is?" Dad asked for the millionth time since I'd given them the news.

"I don't want to. I never want it slipping out and so it's just easier if I don't tell anyone."

"Will you tell the baby?" Mum asked. "When it's old enough to understand."

I shrugged. "I'll think about that at the time."

I hadn't really thought about it if I was being honest. I knew I'd got a few years before it would come up, so call me an ostrich, but

I'd worry about it then. Luckily, we lived on the other side of town to Sam, and it was a big enough place that we'd probably never see each other. My best friend from primary school only lived a ten minute walk away and I hadn't seen her for eleven years, so bumping into Sam wouldn't be an issue.

Dad shook his head in frustration and picked up his newspaper, evidently deciding he'd had enough of the conversation. Mum looked at him and then back to me before sighing and picking up the remote control to turn the TV over to one of the soaps.

As the theme music kicked in, my mobile buzzed on the arm of the chair. I picked it up and almost gasped out loud when I saw it was Sam. Even though we'd swapped numbers, I never thought for one minute that he'd ever contact me directly. I expected it'd be through solicitors, not that I thought he'd ever want to be in touch ever again anyway.

I glanced up, grateful to see that Mum and Dad were still occupied. Stupidly, I thought they may be able to read the text message from the other side of the living room. I then looked back to my phone, my heart racing as I did.

Sam: I just wanted to check the scan went okay today.

I was absolutely floored that he'd checked up on me, especially as it had been three weeks since I'd messaged him with the scan date. I'd told him I'd keep him informed, so had sent the scan date not expecting anything back, but I'd received a message that simply said – Okay, thanks for letting me know – even though I was pretty sure he wasn't thankful at all.

I quickly sent a text back, glancing up at Mum and Dad every couple of seconds.

Maisie: All good. Baby is healthy and growing well

His response was almost immediate

Sam: That's good. Take care

And that was it. Even though I kept one eye on my mobile for the next hour or so, no other text arrived and eventually I went to bed wondering whether Sam sending a text meant something, and hating myself for caring.

11

SAM

the present

I looked over at Elijah and decided that there was possibly no one less smug than my brother, and he was getting right on my nut sack.

"What?" I snapped.

He shrugged. "Don't know what you mean."

"You're looking at me with that damn stupid grin on your face – why?" I threw a pair of sliders into my duffel bag and zipped it up.

"What stupid grin?" He asked, looking at me with...a stupid grin.

"You're a knob head," I grumbled, picking up my car keys. "Now if you don't mind, I need to get to the Leisure Centre."

"Oh yeah, you're giving Frankie another swimming lesson aren't you?"

I rolled my eyes and pushed him toward the front door. "I'm giving a lesson tonight, but not to Frankie."

Eli stopped in the hallway and turned back to me. "Why not?"

"Maisie thinks it best they don't leave the house or go where her ex will be expecting to find them. Plus Stuart is going round there to look at her car."

I gave the last piece of information as a mutter, with my head down. Stuart was one of my best mates, so Eli would have guessed that I was the one who'd arranged for him to go and see Maisie.

"Didn't she know anyone who could fix it?" he asked, knowingly.

"Nope, plus why risk being ripped off when Stu will do her a good job at a reasonable price."

What my brother didn't need to know was that I'd asked Stu to do me a favour – a bloody big seventy percent discount favour, and even then I'd asked him to give me the invoice. I had no idea why I felt as though I wanted to pay, but something told me that Maisie didn't have spare cash to shell out on repairing the bodywork of her car.

"So, Frankie not swimming tonight, was it Maisie's idea, or a decision you came to together – you know as his parents?"

I threw him a frustrated look and pushed the door open to the stairwell, not wanting to be in the confined space of the lift with him, giving him a view of my face. The fucker always knew how to read me and after the previous night, what I did know about Maisie and Frankie was that they scared the living daylights out of me and I didn't need Elijah picking up on that and then going home and grassing to bloody Amy about it, because she'd give me shit for weeks.

I'd stayed at Maisie's for hot chocolate and then Frankie had got me talking about music and of course we had a lot to talk about. He knew his stuff and I couldn't help but grin like a loon when he popped an earbud in my ear and played me his favourite Northern Soul song – The Elgins', Heaven Must Have Sent You. I was pretty impressed, the kid had great taste in music, as far as I was concerned. After that Maisie had told him it was bed time and I left. As I'd been leaving, Maisie had told me that she thought it a good idea that Frankie missed his swimming lesson and I told her that I'd send Stu around to look at her car. She tried to argue, but when I put my foot on the door step, stopping her from closing the door, she finally nodded and said 'okay' and agreed to swap mobile numbers.

I was there a total of fifty-five minutes, nothing out of the ordinary had happened, we hadn't said anything about talking soon and neither had I told her I'd be back, yet somehow I think we both knew that I would be and that we would most definitely talk again soon. The fact that I didn't hate the idea of that, of them, made my fucking stomach ache with anxiety.

"Don't think this is anything more than it is," I snapped at my brother as we reached the apartment lobby. "You were the one who got me into all her shit."

"Because she needed someone," Elijah protested.

"Yeah and she could have called her dad. Just stay out of things Eli," I sighed, getting into my car.

"What, like you stayed out of my business when Amy and I needed a kick up the arse?"

"Totally different. You were meant to be together." Holding the door open, I pointed a finger at him. "I mean it Elijah, keep out of it."

I then slammed the door and drove out of the car park, hoping the next hour or so went quickly.

"What are you doing here, Sam," Maisie sighed, peering at me from around the front door that was only slightly ajar.

"Checking up on you both." I half-turned and nodded towards the drive that was empty. "Did Stu take your car?"

She nodded and reached up to tighten the messy bun on top of her head and as she did her t-shirt rode up, revealing creamy white skin in the gap between her top and the tracksuit pants that sat low on her hips. Her stomach was slightly rounded, but her hips were narrow, with the tiny hint of bone sticking out and I couldn't help but remember our night together all those years before. She'd been sweet and crazy all at the same time and definitely knew how to please a man, yet somehow I knew she wasn't very experienced. She'd been pretty much perfect if I was being honest.

"He was here about half an hour ago. Said I'd get it back in a couple of days. At least it's the weekend and I don't have to get to work or school."

"That's good."

"Yes, thanks for sorting it out. I didn't have a clue who to call and I didn't want to have to ask my dad."

"What've they said about it all?" I asked, pushing my hands deep into the pockets of my hoody.

She chewed on her lip for a few seconds and then sighed. "I haven't told them yet. I don't want to have to listen to the 'we told you so' lectures."

"Your dad didn't like him then?"

For some reason that gave me a sense of happiness because I'd been proved right; Josh was a wanker who drove an Audi prick wagon.

"Not really, none of my family did." She let out an empty laugh. "Not even Frankie did."

"Talking of, how's he been?" I asked around a cough, feeling self-conscious at talking about him.

"He's fine. In fact he's been happier today than I've seen him for a long time." Maisie sounded wistful and heaved out a heavy breath. "I should have realised before."

Her eyes were shining and I knew she was close to tears. Frankie may well have bounced back quickly from the previous night's nightmare, but Maisie was obviously struggling.

"Listen, can I come in for a bit?" The words were out of my mouth before I had chance to talk myself out of it. "I can see you're upset and I don't really want to leave you feeling like that."

Maisie leaned the top half of her body back and gaped at me. "Since when do you care, Sam?" she hissed.

"I'm not a total knob, and you were the one who said you understood that I couldn't offer you more."

"And I did, so why the hell are you suddenly worried about me?" She put her hands to her hips and I couldn't help but notice the way her tits pushed against her t-shirt.

"Because of what your dick head of an ex-boyfriend did last night. It must have been fucking scary as shit for you, and I can see you're still worried now, so just let me come in."

"And if I do," she said, glancing behind her, "what the hell do I tell Frankie, hey?"

I rubbed a hand down my face and groaned. "I don't know – I came to check up on him after missing swimming lessons. Does it matter?"

"Yes it matters. Oh my god," she cried. "You have no idea do you. He's a little boy who saw the man who was supposed to protect him like a father throw something at his mum and then raise a hand to him, so he's emotional and delicate. If you keep coming in for hot chocolate and bloody Northern Soul sessions, he'll grow attached Sam, and that's not fair on him."

I took a mental step back and thought about what Maisie had said and she was right. It wouldn't be fair to Frankie if I went in again. He was a little boy without a dad, as far as he was concerned, and if I stepped over that threshold again it was likely he'd think there was more to it. I'd scared the bad man away and it wouldn't take much for him to become attached to me.

"Okay," I said, now taking a physical step back. "You're right, but if Josh comes back make sure you call me." I watched Maisie's face morph into that of a stroppy teenager. "Or at least call the coppers," I added. "Don't try and deal with him on your own. Okay?"

"Fine," she said, moving further behind the door. "But he won't be back."

"If you say so, but if he does, I mean it Maisie, I want you to call me."

She nodded. "Is that all?"

"Yeah," I sighed out. "You've got my number."

"I do, but I won't be needing you. Thanks for calling, Sam," she said, her voice softening, "and for what you did last night and with my car, but I swear we'll be fine."

I nodded and turned down the drive to leave, thinking she was probably right – famous last words.

12

MAISIE

the present

Frankie had been asleep for about an hour when the banging on the door started.

Boom, boom, boom.

"Maisie, open this fucking door now."

I heard the flap of the letterbox as Josh's voice bellowed, loud and harsh, making my heart thump in time with his fist on the door. I flicked off the lamp next to my armchair and lifted up my feet, praying that he'd get bored and go away.

"I mean it Maisie, open up."

I then heard a key scraping against the lock and thanked god I'd payed out a huge amount of money for new locks. When Sam had suggested it I'd thought it a stupid idea, but the more I pondered about it throughout the day, the more I realised he was right, so I called a locksmith.

"You fucking bitch," he yelled. "You can't do this. I'm entitled to be in this house."

He went quiet and I held my breath, listening intently for any noise at all, jumping in my seat when he bellowed my name again. Tears started to roll down my cheeks as the fear intensified when the banging continued. It was then that I heard a thud above me –

85

Frankie had woken up. I got up quickly and rushed into the hall, heading for the stairs, desperate to stop him from coming down.

As I put my foot on the first stair, the letterbox was pushed open causing me to screech out.

"I can fucking see you Maisie, now open this door before I set fire to the damn house."

I gasped, pushing my hands against my churning stomach as I looked over my shoulder. Josh's hand was poking through, but was too big to get much more than his fingers in. When I caught Frankie out of the corner of my eye, I turned and ran up to him.

"Frankie, sweetheart," I said, holding out a hand to him. "Go back into your room."

"Mummy, he's going to get in," Frankie cried, rubbing at his sleepy eyes with his hands. His chest heaved in his Spiderman pyjamas and his bottom lip started to tremble.

"It's okay, he won't, I promise. Let's go to your room." I put a hand between his shoulder blades and ushered him along the landing to his room.

Once there, I held back the duvet and urged him to get in and then got in next to him, pulling him into my arms. He snuggled his face against my chest, his little body trembling as Josh's banging continued. When it stopped for a couple of minutes, I hoped it meant that Josh had got bored, but when the banging started on the back door I almost screamed.

"Mummy make him go. Call the policeman like Sam said."

I kissed the top of Frankie's head and slipped my mobile out of the back pocket of my jeans. As I keyed in my PIN, I had every intention of calling them, but before I realised what I was doing, I went to my contacts and pressed Sam's number.

He answered within seconds, sounding breathless.

"Maisie, everything okay?"

"I'm sorry, am I disturbing you?"

"No. What's wrong?"

I glanced down at Frankie and closed my eyes to stem the tears that were brimming at my lashes. "He's here, Sam. He's banging on the doors and wants me to let him in."

"I'm on my way, I'll call the police."

"Please hurry," I whimpered, hating myself for feeling so weak.

The line went dead and I hugged Frankie to me, waiting for Sam to arrive.

Just over ten minutes later, my phone rang and I saw it was Sam.

"I'm here," Sam's voice said as I answered my phone.

"He's around the back. Please be caref-."

I didn't have chance to finish before the line went dead and seconds later I heard Sam shouting.

"Frankie, stay here," I said, slipping out of the bed and pulling the duvet over his shoulders,

"Mummy no, don't go, please," he sobbed.

"I'll be right back, I promise."

As Frankie called to me again, I slipped out of his bedroom and down the stairs, into the hall and toward the kitchen. I could hear Sam shouting outside, but it didn't sound as though Josh was there. I rushed to the back door and listened carefully.

"Where the hell are you, you prick?"

I unlocked the door and flung it open to see Sam standing with his back to me, looking around the garden which was lit up by the security light.

"Sam," I called. "Has he gone?"

Sam turned and stalked toward me, his arms outstretched. "Are you okay? Is Frankie okay?" As he reached me, he took hold of my biceps and stooped down to look me in the eyes. "The truth, Maisie."

"He's fine," I croaked out. "We're both fine, just scared. He wouldn't stop banging on the door and shouting and banging and-."

"Hey, hey," Sam soothed. "Calm down, he's gone now. I think he jumped the fence." He nodded toward the fence where my garden bench was pushed up against it.

"He's definitely gone?" I asked, my eyes searching the garden warily.

"Yes, he's not here, I promise. Come on let's get you inside."

Gently he ushered me inside and when I moved over to the table I heard the door lock behind me. As I wrapped my arms around my stomach, I felt Sam's hand on my shoulder.

"Sit down and I'll get you a brandy or something. Do you have any brandy?"

I looked up at him and shook my head. "I've got some vodka in the cupboard over the fridge, but I don't want any."

"Just a shot," he said, moving away from me. "Just to calm your nerves."

"Mummy," Frankie's tiny voice came from the doorway.

I pushed off the chair and went to him, kneeling down in front of him and pulling him into a tight hug.

"It's okay sweetheart, he's gone. Sam checked and he's not here."

Frankie looked over my shoulder and I sensed that Sam was behind me.

"Has he really gone?" Frankie asked.

The next thing I knew, Sam was crouching down next to me. "Yes buddy, he's gone."

My gaze shot to the man next to me, and I felt my breath hitch as I saw how his eyes were full of warmth and comfort as he watched his son. This man who didn't want to be a father, who'd told me over eight years ago there was no way he could be a father, was looking at Frankie like a father looked at a son.

"But what if he comes back?" Frankie asked, bringing my attention back to him.

I drew in a jagged breath, my heart sinking at the sound of my little boy's fear. I released him slightly and looked directly into his eyes.

"You don't need to be scared, Frankie," I whispered. "I will never let him hurt you, I swear."

"Neither of us will," Sam added.

The sound of his deep voice and the words he said made my heart miss a beat. Having him here made me realise how hard it was doing this alone and how Josh had never really supported me. Sam's four words gave me more comfort than Josh had ever done in almost four years.

"Did you call the policeman?" Frankie asked.

I looked to Sam who gave Frankie a comforting smile. "I did, they said they'd keep a look out for him."

Sam gave Frankie's shoulder a squeeze and then looked at me. There was something off in his gaze as his jaw tightened.

"Hey," I said brightly, turning back to my son. "How about you go and get back into bed and read a book for a little while. There's no school tomorrow, so you can have your light on for half an hour, okay?"

He gave me a grin and nodded. "Can I have my iPod too?"

"I don't think so," I said around a quiet laugh. "Don't push it. A book and that's it."

Frankie sighed. "It was worth a try," he said, grumbling softly to himself.

I felt Sam laugh beside me as we both watched Frankie walk away. Once he was bounding up the stairs we stood up.

"What is it?" I asked. "What weren't you telling me?"

Sam raked a hand down his face and breathed out heavily through his nose. "The police said they'd try and get a squad car to drive past, but that was the most they could offer. Fucking idiots," he hissed.

"It's fine, Sam. He's gone now, that's the main thing."

"Yeah and what if he comes back?" He moved away from me back to the counter next to the fridge, where the bottle of vodka stood. He looked around the kitchen and then reached for a mug that I'd washed earlier. He poured in some of the clear liquid and then came back to me, holding out the mug for me to take. "Drink that."

With a wince, I swigged down the drink and handed the mug back to Sam. "Thank you. I'm sorry I dragged you into this. I should've just called the police."

"Yeah well, we've established they wouldn't have helped," he grumbled, turning to put the mug into the sink.

"I know, but I shouldn't have called you."

Sam swivelled around and glared at me. "Yes you should. I told you to."

"But we're practically strangers," I argued, placing a hand over my fast beating heart. "I should've called my dad if not the police."

"No you shouldn't. You should've called me and I'd have been pissed if you hadn't. It doesn't matter how well we do or don't know each other, I want to make sure you're both safe."

"Why though Sam, why would you want to get involved in all this crap?" I cried taking a step closer to him. "It isn't down to you."

"I want you to be safe, I want my..." He paused hanging a hand off the back of his neck. "Listen it's all irrelevant, you did call me and I'm here, so we just get on with it."

I knew he'd been about to mention Frankie, his pink cheeks

and the way he couldn't look me in the eye showed it. Even if I hadn't heard the word 'my', I would've known it was his son he was trying to protect.

I took a few breaths in the silence and then walked over to the cupboard that held my glass wear and took out two tumblers. I then went to the fridge, taking out a bottle of tonic water. Moving silently to the vodka, I then poured us both a drink, turning to hand one to Sam.

"Here you go. You probably need one too."

He gave me a small smile and took the glass from me. "Cheers."

We both took long swigs of our drinks, standing opposite each other, the silence echoing around us.

"Was his car here?" I asked, the thought suddenly striking me.

Sam shrugged. "It wasn't on the drive, or on the road. Maybe he was on the way home from the pub or something and drink made him brave."

"So you don't think he'll come back?" I asked, hopefully.

"Who knows, but what I do know is I'm staying here tonight."

My eyes widened as I stumbled back. "What? No, no you're not staying here. You can't."

"Um yes I can and I am," Sam replied, taking another swig of his drink. "I'll sleep on the sofa. Did you change the locks like I suggested?"

"Yes," I snapped. "God, bossy much."

"Maybe I am, but I was right when I said he'd come back. Did he try and get in?" he inclined his head, waiting for me to prove him right again.

"Yes, okay."

His lips twitched and moved to one side, so like bloody Frankie it was scary. He gave me a quick grin before he finished off his drink and turned to place the glass in the sink alongside the mug I'd used.

"Right, do you have a spare duvet or blanket?"

"Yes, but it's nine-thirty, you're not going to bed yet are you?" I asked, realising it was pointless arguing about him staying if the strong jut of his jaw was anything to go by.

"No," he replied, frowning at me. "I'm going to watch the footy. Lounge this way is it?" He pointed in the general direction of the hall and strode off leaving me standing with my mouth gaping open.

I'd slept fitfully all night, listening carefully and jumping at any noise outside. The last time I'd checked the clock on my phone it had been four-thirty, but I must have then dropped into a fairly deep sleep because it was the sound of rain outside that woke me at just gone six. I lay there for a few minutes with my eyes closed, desperately trying to go back to sleep, but it was useless. With a sigh, I kicked off my duvet and dropped my legs to the floor. Frankie would be dead to the world for another couple of hours at least, especially as he hadn't gone to sleep until almost ten-thirty the night before – I knew because I'd checked on him about forty times, mainly because it was better than sitting with Sam, feeling awkward while he watched football on *my* TV. It had been almost eleven when Sam started to yawn and I decided to go to bed myself. I'd have gone earlier but thought it rude after he'd dropped everything to help us. I'd started up the stairs and realised I'd left my mobile in the lounge, so had pushed back through the door to find a tattooed and topless Sam about to drop his jeans. I'd only seen the hint of '*Calvin Klein*' but it had been enough to make me blush, grab my phone, and practically run up to my room.

Deciding to get myself some breakfast, I yawned loudly and tying the belt of my dressing gown tight, decided to check Frankie was still asleep. When I walked into his room, I almost screamed when I found his bed empty and his duvet and pillow missing. My heart thudded erratically, as fear gripped me and I ran from the room and down the stairs calling his name.

I barrelled into the lounge and pulled up short, as a thudding ache took the breath from my lungs. Lying on the floor, wrapped in his duvet was Frankie. He looked peaceful with one earphone in his left ear. My gaze followed the line of the white wire to see the other earphone was in Sam's right ear. They were both snoring lightly, lying on their backs, both with an arm in the exact same position – cocked at an angle above their heads. That was enough to bring a huge lump to my throat, but what made the tears fall was when I noticed Frankie's left arm was reaching up and his tiny hand was resting on his dad's bicep, on the tattoo of an angel.

13

SAM

the present

I stretched myself out, trying to alleviate the back ache I'd woken with. As I did, the earphone dropped out of my ear, plopping onto the pillow next to me. It was then that I also noticed the little hand resting on my arm, and all sorts of shit started to rush through my head and my chest.

I turned my head to look at Frankie, holding my breath in case he woke. I just wanted a few minutes to look at him, without worrying that if my gaze stayed on him too long he'd recognise himself in my features. There was no denying he was a Cooper and I knew if anyone saw us together, it would be difficult to persuade them that we weren't related.

His nose was a smaller version of mine, his eyes were the same shade of brown as mine and even his *ears* were the same shape. He was the epitome of a mini-me, except for the smattering of freckles on his nose and they were most definitely Maisie. It all was all too weird, but it was fucking amazing too and the emotions welling up inside of me were ones I never thought I'd ever feel and were as alien as fuck. For eight years I'd denied myself of this kid, denied him of a father, and even though I still wasn't sure I was going to be any good at it, or even deserved it, I was beginning to think I wanted to try. I knew it was a big ask of Maisie to change her mind after just a couple of days of being around Frankie to let him and everyone else know that I was his dad, but she might at least let me be a friend to him.

Slowly I turned on my side, holding his hand in place on my arm and continued to watch him sleep, glad that he was and didn't seem scared, as he had done when he'd sneaked into the lounge at three in the morning. I'd been awake, listening for the prick coming back, when the door pushed open and a little voice said.

"I think the men should sleep in the same room, it'll be safer for Mum."

I'd wanted to laugh at him calling himself a man, but even in the dim light I could see his tiny shoulders shaking and could hear the quake in his voice.

"You want the sofa?" I'd asked, pulling back the blanket that Maisie had given to me.

"No thanks, I've got my duvet and pillow."

Frankie then moved further into the room, trailing his bedding behind him. He dropped it onto the floor, close to the sofa, and then moved over to the oak cabinet that the TV stood on. Kneeling down, he opened the bottom drawer and pulled out his iPod.

"I'm not allowed to have it at bedtime anymore," he'd said, pushing the drawer closed. "Now he's gone though, Mum might change her mind."

I'd lifted myself up on my elbows to watch him and grinned to myself when he walked back to me, his gait long and lazy, just like mine. Frankie had then wrapped himself in his duvet and lay down, popping an earphone into his ear. I started to settle myself back down when he poked me in the arm.

"Here you go." He handed me the other earphone. "Wigan Casino, forty Northern Soul tracks," he announced and settled into his makeshift bed.

I had no idea what time either of us fell asleep, but Frankie's humming stopped at track five, and I was pretty sure I only lasted another couple of tracks before I too fell asleep.

This was not what I'd expected to be doing on my Saturday morning, watching my son sleep, but I had to admit I was glad that Maisie had called me. The thought of what Josh might have done, had he got in, scared me. Even if I hadn't had a connection to Maisie and Frankie, I would have been worried and would have wanted to help them, but knowing it was my own flesh and blood in danger had made me crazy with fucking deep black anger. If I'd caught the stupid prick I was pretty sure I'd have ended up in a police cell for assault and battery. On the drive over my only thought had been how I was going to smash his face in for scaring my kid.

Each time I'd thought of Frankie as 'my kid' over the last few days, it'd been when he was being scared by Josh, and each of those times I was willing to kill for him. And what sort of knob of a dad did that make me, only admitting he was mine when there were thoughts of violence swimming through every vein in my body? Not a good one that was for sure.

I sat up, letting Frankie's hand fall against the sofa and then down onto the floor. He stirred a little, but turned onto his side and snuggled further under his duvet. Sighing heavily I dropped my feet to the floor and pushed up from the sofa, edging myself around Frankie's sleeping form. I reached for my jeans and t-shirt pulled them on and then pushed my feet into my boots and left the lounge.

When I got to the kitchen, I'd planned on getting a drink of water and then leaving, but was shocked to see Maisie standing at the hob. She was shaking her hips as she stirred something in a pan with a wooden spoon. The radio was softly playing some crap pop tune, but she seemed to like it, if the way she was dancing was anything to go by. She was swaying from side to side with the occasional thrust of her left hip to one side, with a quick shake of her shoulders.

"You like this crap?" I asked.

"Oh my god," she gasped, turning to me. "You scared me to death. I thought you were fast asleep."

"Just woke up," I replied, rubbing a hand over my face. "What're you making?"

All thoughts of cutting and running were forgotten as I looked into the pan to see scrambled eggs and my stomach rumbled as I sniffed them.

"It'll be ready in a couple of minutes," Maisie said, turning to the toaster and pushing down the three slices of bread in it. "You can get the plates out for me, don't bother with one for Frankie, he'll sleep for a while longer."

"He likes his sleep does he?" I asked, moving to the cupboard that Maisie was pointing to.

"Yeah he does. He's an absolute nightmare to get up in a morning if he hasn't had enough sleep."

"Is that why he's not allowed music at bedtime?"

I placed the plates next to the hob and leaned back against the counter, watching Maisie as she continued to stir the eggs.

"He told you that?" she asked, turning to me.

"Said Josh wouldn't let him, but seems to think you might be of a different opinion now."

We both laughed and Maisie rolled her eyes.

"Always spying his chance that one," she said. "I would never dare have asked for or said half the things he does."

"Is that right." I ducked my head and scratched my ear, trying to hide my grin.

"Hmm, it appears he may have picked up a few traits from his father."

Maisie's lips thinned, but I could tell that it was all in good nature and it made my chest feel a little tight. Standing talking about my son and how much he was like me was something I would never have imagined, would never have wanted – yet it felt right; strange but right.

"What you going to do about the prick?" I asked, feeling it best to change the subject before I started wailing and wafting at my eyes like some stupid teenage girl.

Maisie sighed and reached for the toast that had popped up. "Report him to the police, I suppose." She started to butter the slices, putting one on one plate and two on the other. "Although, it sounds like they won't be bothered, because what's he actually done except try to get back into his home."

"Yeah, but it's how he tried to get back in which is the problem," I growled. "He fucking scared both of you, shouting and banging in a violent manner, so they should fucking listen. You want me to come with you?" I asked without thinking twice.

Maisie stopped spooning egg onto the toast and looked up at me. "You don't have to," she said. "You've helped enough."

"I told you, I don't mind."

Maisie then handed me the plate with the two slices of toast on it. "Knives and forks are in the drawer on the right. You want some orange?"

I nodded and watched as she went to the fridge. Her dressing gown stopped mid-thigh and her long legs looked smooth and silky and seeing as I'd not been laid in a while since I was too busy and it was morning, my dick decided it might want in on some action. When she leaned into the fridge and the tops of her thighs and a pair of skimpy pink shorts were revealed, I had to adjust myself, repeating in my head 'it's just morning wood, it's just morning wood'.

I quickly moved to the table, grabbing two sets of cutlery as I did, placing Maisie's on the other end of the small rectangular table to where I sat myself.

"This looks great," I said, cutting into the toast and adding a forkful of eggs.

"I'm not the best cook," Maisie said, placing a glass of orange in front of me, "but I can do the basics well. Frankie loves my sausage and mash."

I got the sense that she was trying to offer me snippets of my son's life, without having to admit it. It was an olive branch of sorts and I just had to decide whether I wanted to take it or not.

"He's got a good appetite?"

Maisie nodded as she chewed on her food. "Hmm," she finally said around a swallow. "Really good. My mum reckons he's got hollow legs."

I laughed. "My mum used to say that about me. I think it was the swimming, it made me hungry all the time."

Maisie looked at me over the rim of her glass, her eyes studying me.

"What?" I asked.

"Why did you take on the swimming lessons? Did you know Frankie was in the class?"

I was surprised that she'd think that, knowing how adamant I'd been about not being in his life. Yet, my recent actions – threatening Josh, rushing over here, insisting I stay the night and sharing his damn iPod with him, kind of contradicted that, so I supposed it was a natural conclusion to jump to.

"I had no idea he was," I replied. "It was Amy hounding me for days about it. Bella, her and Elijah's little girl, is in the water babies' class and if I hadn't stepped in their teacher would've had to and nooo waaay was Amy allowing that to happen." I grinned, thinking about the force of nature that was my sister-in-law.

"I can't believe they're back together," Maisie said. "After everything that happened. I mean I didn't really know them that well, but it was all anyone in that social circle we were in could talk about."

"Yeah it was a pretty shit time," I sighed. "It impacted on us all."

Maisie's face coloured slightly and I knew she was thinking about why I'd called things off with her.

"They're good now though," I replied, moving the conversation on. "Brilliant in fact."

"I know it's nothing to do with me, but did he cheat? I mean I can't imagine it, but for Amy to just leave like that."

I shook my head. "Nope, he never would've done that to her. Lauren Procter set it all up at that party we were all at, plus she'd fucked with Amy's head for years, trying to take Elijah from her and coming on to him all the time."

"What a bitch." Maisie said, her eyes wide in shock. "How did they find out she set them up?"

"Yeah she was and they don't actually know."

"What?" She put her knife and fork down and settled back in her chair.

"I bumped into Lauren a few years back, not long after they'd had Bella. She told me everything." I carried on eating, watching the look of shock develop on Maisie's face.

"You've never told them?"

"Don't see the point in raking it all up. They'd sorted themselves out and were happy. Knowing she cost them five years of a life together won't change anything, it might just make them feel like shit again. Amy knows now she was wrong to run and should have listened to him, but like I said, Lauren had pecked at her head for years *and* Amy was grieving, so I guess her actions were understandable to a point."

"She was grieving?" Maisie's eyes were bright with emotion as she placed a hand over her heart.

"They lost a baby a few months earlier."

"Oh my god, that's awful, I didn't know that. Poor Amy and Elijah." She leaned forward and placed a hand on my forearm. "No wonder he was in such a state and then I come along and lay my news on you. Shit, Sam, your head must have been battered by it all."

I shrugged, realising that there was some truth in what she was saying, but my actions toward Maisie were purely based on what had happened to me when I was eighteen; but that was something I couldn't talk about to her.

"It was hard like I said, but honestly Maisie, how I was with you was all on me – I was a selfish prick."

"*Was* a selfish prick," she said, grinning and removing her hand from my arm. "Does that mean you're not now?"

I considered her question and really wanted to give her an answer that wouldn't disappoint, but wasn't sure I could. Spending one night listening to music with Frankie and sleeping next to him to make him feel safe didn't really make me unselfish or father of the year.

"I'm trying not to be," I replied and put the final forkful of breakfast into my mouth.

"I suppose that's something," Maisie muttered as she stood up. "Would you like a coffee or a tea?"

"Tea would be great."

As Maisie picked up my plate, I sat back and rubbed at my full belly.

"Hey," a voice called from the doorway. "You didn't wake me."

I turned in my seat as Maisie looked over her shoulder to see Frankie standing there rubbing at his sleepy eyes. His hair was sticking up in about seven different directions and one pyjama leg was pulled up over his knee.

"Sorry buddy," I said. "You were well away and I didn't want to disturb you."

"It's really early Frankie." Maisie walked to him and pulled him into a hug. "How come you're awake?"

Frankie pulled away from her and came and sat at the table. "I'm hungry and when you're keeping watch you only sleep for a little while. You've always got to be alert." He tapped his temple close to his eye and nodded sagely. "And I needed a wee."

Maisie and I both snorted out a laugh.

"Can I have porridge and toast please, Mum?" Frankie asked, seemingly unaware that we found him amusing.

"Both?" I asked. "Wow that's some breakfast."

"Yeah well," he said, looking at me as though I was stupid. "I need my energy for when you take me swimming."

"Swimming?"

"Yes, Mum, swimming. I didn't get to go to my lesson yesterday, so Sam can take me today. Can't you Sam?"

He looked at me with his head tilted to one side and the look on his face was pretty much daring me to say no. My gaze turned to Maisie who shrugged.

"It's up to you, but we've really taken up enough of your time."

Ah, fuck it.

"Yeah, of course I'll take you buddy. Eat your breakfast and then we can go, with a quick detour to my place to pick my gear up. That okay?"

I asked Frankie, but looked at Maisie who gave me a small smile.

"Hey, I know," Frankie cried. "Mummy can come too. It'll be great, she can do laps while you teach me how to do the crawl."

Maisie's eyes widened and a blush touched her cheeks. I on the other hand, couldn't help but wonder whether she'd wear a bikini or an all in one swimsuit.

14

SAMUEL

the past

It didn't matter how often I tried not to, my thoughts were constantly on Maisie, wondering how she was doing, was everything okay with the baby, how much of a twat was I being by letting her do it all alone?

The trouble was, I still hadn't changed my mind. I didn't want to be a father, so why I kept thinking about her, I had no idea.

We hadn't seen each other for months and had only had contact via a couple of text messages, but she seemed fine with the way things had ended up. Okay, it probably wasn't what she had planned for her first kid and maybe deep down she hated me, but all in all she seemed pretty amiable and now only had a couple of weeks left before the baby arrived – boy or girl I had no clue. I'd chosen not to ask and Maisie hadn't volunteered the information.

Trying to clear my head, I had decided to nip into town and get myself a couple of new shirts. I hoped some retail shopping would distract me for an hour at least. Throwing my sandwich wrapper into a bin, I turned to make my way over to my favourite menswear shop. It was then that I spotted her and my mouth went dry. She was just three feet away from me and everything I'd thought I'd feel didn't happen.

My heart didn't pound.

My mouth wasn't dry.

My legs didn't feel like jelly.

The world hadn't stopped turning.

"Sam," Alison gasped as she saw me.

I looked beyond her to see Roger holding hands with a little girl with tight ringlets of curls and cute pink glasses on the end of an upturned nose – Abigail.

"Oh my god," Roger cried, stooping to pick up his daughter. "Sam, how you doing man?"

I allowed him a small smile and looked between him and Alison.

"Great. How about you two – sorry, three?" I asked, choking back the venom which I really wanted to spit out.

Alison shifted from one foot to another and nodded. "Yeah, we're great too."

Abigail stared at me over her glasses and I could see her striking resemblance to her mum. Apart from the skin tones, they were practically identical.

"So, what you up to man? Roger asked, running a hand over Abigail's head.

"I, um, I work for a recruitment company. Hoping to buy it actually," I replied, avoiding Alison's gaze. I knew they probably weren't interested in my plans, but I wanted her to know that she hadn't left me broken and pathetic – well not in every sense at least.

"Really? Cool." Roger bobbed his head looking suitably impressed. "That's great, isn't it, Ali?"

"Yes," Ali croaked. "Fantastic."

An uncomfortable silence followed and as I watched each of the family members standing in front of me, I knew things were definitely not perfect in this garden of roses.

Ali's hand clung to the strap of her bag as her gaze drifted to the side, while Roger looked at me with dull eyes, his daughter's arms firmly around his neck.

"You still swim?" he asked.

I glanced at Alison, wondering whether his question would pique her interest, but there was nothing – no indication that she was even listening.

"No," I responded, suddenly desperate to get away. "Haven't done for years."

My response was short, even though I knew I could have said much more like; no your wife took my love of swimming away from me when she seduced me, when I was too young to know any better. Or maybe; no I can't bear the thought of it since the smell of chlorine reminds me too much of losing my virginity in a fucking changing room surrounded by life buoys and rusty lockers. Nope, there was nothing else I could say.

Weirdly, Roger didn't ask why or mention whether or not Ali still coached. He glanced at her and I wondered if he knew, if maybe she'd done it again and this time been caught. I didn't care though, looking at her now I realised I had no feelings whatsoever for her.

Hah – how ironic was that? She'd ruined my fucking life, blackened my heart, and I felt nothing for her – no love, no hatred, no pity, nothing.

"I'd better go anyway," I said, half-turning. "Need to get back to the office."

"Well great to see you, Sam," Roger said.

Alison finally looked up at me and gave me a thin lipped smile. "Bye, Sam."

I didn't reply but simply raised a hand and walked away. As I did, I felt a little lighter knowing that even though she'd already changed me and my life, Alison no longer had a hold over me. I was done. My hatred was gone after one innocent little meeting. That's all it had taken and I wondered if we'd met up a few years earlier if things might have been different with Maisie and me.

It didn't matter though, there was no point thinking it because the deal was done – I had a hard heart and nothing was changing it.

15

MAISIE

the present

I was such a stupid, stupid idiot. What the hell had made me think it was okay to agree to Sam giving Frankie one on one swimming lessons? What planet was I from that I could possibly think Frankie spending more time with Sam was a great idea?

I'd been grateful to Sam for coming to my rescue the night before and while I knew it probably wasn't the best idea, him staying over, I did feel much safer knowing that he was in the house. Which was ridiculous in itself. I'd allowed a practical stranger to sleep under the same roof as my child. A child that I cherished more than life itself.

I knew he'd have had all the appropriate checks done, other-wise he wouldn't be allowed to give swimming lessons, but if I was being honest, that hadn't even entered my head when he'd told me he was staying over. When I saw Frankie sleeping on the floor next to him, my only emotion had been happiness for my son. There was no fear, anger, or resentment, just pure joy at seeing them together.

I should have screamed with fury that he thought it was okay to waltz into Frankie's life, eight years too late. Any normal mother would have told him to back off the moment she realised he was her son's new swimming coach – but no, not me, Maisie West who lived in fairy tale land and thought that unicorns and mermaids existed and that fairies granted bloody wishes.

All I could think was 'oh my god, Frankie is with his dad'.

Now to top it all off, the damn man was concentrating all his efforts on showing Frankie how to do the front crawl, and with each movement the hard, contoured muscles in his back stretched and pulsed liked a perfectly timed machine. Each sinew and muscle working with the next and creating perfection.

Sam was tall and sculpted and stood out among the rest of the men in the pool. His broad shoulders and slim waist, typical of a swimmer, despite the fact that I knew he hadn't swum competitively for years. Frankie had inherited a similar shape, but whereas my boy still had a little chubbiness at his waist, Sam was lean. As for his tattoos, he had many more than the single one he'd had all those years ago. Now his arms, chest, and back were a myriad of pictures, each one moving fluidly whenever he stretched or flexed a muscle. He was magnificent, and I hated him for it because I couldn't take my eyes off him when I wasn't watching Frankie.

It pissed me off that after all the years that had passed Sam still had an effect on me. Years where I should have hated him and taught Frankie to hate him too, but I'd never been able to because he'd never lied to me. Okay, the day I had Frankie, Sam had acted like a pure, unadulterated prick, but he'd never given me false promises and had always provided for his son, up until Josh had insisted we stop taking the money. Part of me always wondered if I hadn't insisted on the secrecy around Frankie's DNA, whether Sam might have come around eventually, but deep down I'd known he probably wouldn't have. That was why I'd insisted that no one ever knew, that way I would never be disappointed or spend my life hoping and Frankie would never feel let down that he didn't have the relationship with his father that he deserved. It was also why I'd always told my son his dad went away before he knew about Frankie and I had no idea where to find him. One day when, or even if, I told him the truth, Frankie would probably hate me for it, but I hoped above all else he'd understand that I was protecting him.

I continued to watch the pool from my seat in the café and almost screamed when I saw Frankie flying through the air.

"Oh my god," I gasped, causing a lady who was knitting to look up.

Halfway out of my seat, I paused as Frankie landed with a splash in the water. I held my breath waiting and watching, only releasing it when seconds later he appeared with a huge smile on his face. I could see that he was laughing as he swam toward Sam. I let out the breath and plopped back into my seat, placing a shaking hand over my thudding heart.

"Your partner seems to enjoy giving you a heart attack, love," the knitting lady said. "But your little boy is loving it though."

I glanced at her and then back to the pool, watching as Sam launched Frankie once more.

"They're having a whale of a time," she said, dragging my attention back to her.

"Yes, they are." The lump in my throat was huge and I wasn't sure that I wasn't going to cry.

"Fathers and sons, eh." She shook her head and then went back to her knitting.

My eyes moved back to the pool and I wished I'd not been so adamant about not joining them.

———

"Mum," Frankie cried as he barrelled toward me, arms and legs flying around. "Sam says my front crawl is one of the best he's seen. Did you see?"

His eyes were bright with excitement as he thrust a towel and wet swim shorts at me.

"I did, you were brilliant," I replied, holding the shorts and towel out in front of me. "Where's your bag?"

I started to fold the towel as Frankie smacked his forehead with the heel of his hand and raced off, passing Sam who was on his way out.

"Where's he going?" Sam asked, looking behind him at Frankie's retreating figure.

"He forgot his bag."

I rolled the swim shorts up with the towel, not looking at Sam, afraid that if I did he'd realise I'd been lusting after him for the last hour and a half.

"Shit, I should have checked," Sam groaned. "But I let him get changed on his own. I didn't think I should go in with him, so I took the cubicle next to his."

I looked up and could see Sam's uncertainty and a little discomfort and yet again, I wanted to kick myself. This all seemed so natural and normal that I hadn't considered it might be wrong to leave Frankie to get dressed with Sam in charge. I knew there was always a member of staff stationed inside the changing rooms, but was I being neglectful of Frankie? Sam was a member of staff too and Frankie's dad, so maybe it was just me trusting my instincts – shit this was all too bloody complicated.

"It's fine, Sam," I found myself saying. "He dresses himself every day and he should know to bring his bag out, but so you know I wouldn't have minded if you'd helped him."

Sam didn't reply, but simply gave me a single head nod. Before there was time for any awkwardness to grow, Frankie reappeared at my side, still minus his bag.

"Where is it?" I asked, looking down on him.

He looked at me with wary eyes and shrugged.

"What does that mean?"

"I don't know," he replied. "It wasn't there."

"Did you ask Dave?" Sam asked, placing a hand on Frankie's wet head. "He's in the changing room office."

"Yeah, but he just said he'd look for it."

"Frankie," I groaned. "It can't have gone missing already. You've only been out of there for five minutes."

The way he looked at me, I knew something was worrying him. His nose was wrinkled and his shoulders hunched, the usual tell when he had a problem.

"Frankie, what is it?"

He sighed and blurted out, "There was a big boy in there and he had my bag, but when I asked him for it back he said it was his and that he'd had it for ages, but I knew it was mine, it had the piece of blue string that you tied to the zip so I wouldn't mix it up with Nathan's at school."

As Frankie took a breath, Sam made a growling noise and when I looked up at him, I could see his jaw was set tight.

"What does the boy look like?" he asked, stooping down to look Frankie in the eye. "And what's the bag like?"

"He's got black hair and looks mean and the bag is a Man City bag."

Sam's eyes glinted quickly with pride before morphing back into a scowl. "I'll get it."

Frankie grinned as Sam turned and stomped back to the changing room.

"Sam," I shouted after him, not entirely sure why.

He held up two fingers. "I'll be two minutes."

"Do you think he'll shout at him?" Frankie asked his eyes shining brightly.

I chewed my lip and shrugged, feeling uncomfortable. This all seemed like too much of a 'dad' thing for Sam to do and after everything else over the last twenty-four hours it was a little weird.

True to his word Sam appeared a couple of minutes later, dangling the pale blue bag from his long fingers.

"Here you go," he said passing it to Frankie. "And good choice of team, buddy."

Frankie smiled widely as he took the bag and gazed up at Sam. "Wow, thanks. Did you tell him off?"

"Something like that," Sam grunted.

"Oh god, what did you do?" I asked, worried about the prospect of dealing with an irate parent.

"Nothing," he replied, watching Frankie as he took his swim gear from me and started to put it into the bag, unravelling it all as he did so. "I just told the little fu-fool who it belonged to and I gave Dave a mouthful for not sorting it out like he should have."

"Sam," I groaned. "You didn't have to."

"Yeah I did, now are we going to get food or not?"

I looked at him with my mouth open. "What?"

"Sam's taking us for burgers, Mum," Frankie cried excitedly, as he grabbed my hand. "Come on."

Before I had chance to argue or question, I was being dragged out of the leisure centre, worrying about what all of it meant and what it would do to my son if it all went wrong. I had to speak to Sam and as much as I didn't want to deep down, ask him to keep his distance.

16

I had no idea why, but I'd told Frankie he could call me if he wanted to go swimming again before the lessons. After having spent the day with him and Maisie, it felt like the natural thing to do, but as soon as I'd dropped them back home and seen them into the house, I'd started to wonder if I'd done the right thing. If I'd been doing the right thing for the last twenty-four hours.

My Saturday night should have been spent down at the pub with my mates, but instead I'd stayed home, watching some crap action film, just in case Maisie needed me. My interest had only been half on the film as I'd had my eye on the phone willing it to ring, but dreading it at the same time. Now it was burning a hole in my pocket as I spent time having lunch at my parents' house.

"What's wrong with you?" Amy asked as she came back into Mum and Dad's lounge after putting Bella down for her post lunch nap.

"Nothing, why?" I moved the cat, Biggins, making room for my sister-in-law on the sofa.

"Either you're thinking too hard about something or you've got a stomach ache."

She giggled and nudged me, prompting me to give her the finger.

"Charming."

"Well you get on my nerves," I replied, not really meaning it.

"So, tell me what's wrong." Amy reached for Biggins to pull him onto her lap, but he batted a paw at her and stalked off, probably to beg for food from Mum who was tidying up the kitchen, while Dad got Elijah's advice on some bush in the garden which he thought might be dying.

"There's nothing wrong," I sighed, rolling my eyes.

"Samuel," Amy warned.

"Oh for fuck's sake," I cried. "I spent all of yesterday with Maisie and Frankie, okay."

Amy's eyes went as wide as saucers, her mouth opening into the perfect 'o', as I realised it hadn't taken much for me to spill my shit.

"Oh my god," she eventually gasped. "How did that happen?"

I shrugged, not sure what to tell her, unsure whether Maisie would want her to know. Amy pulled her legs up onto the sofa and edged her body closer, her face full of expectant excitement.

"Tell me, Samuel, because last time we spoke she'd given you shit for being his swimming teacher, so what the hell happened to make her want to spend a whole day with you?"

"And night."

As soon as the words were out of my mouth, I winced.

"Fuck."

"*Night*! God, Sam."

"It's not what you're thinking," I exclaimed, pointing a finger at her.

"So what is it then?" Amy moved even closer. "Because it sounds like exactly what I'm thinking."

I sighed and ran a hand down my face. She wasn't going to let it drop, so I spent the next few minutes telling her about Maisie, Frankie, and Josh.

"What a bastard," Amy hissed when I finished. "And the police just said they'd keep an eye out?"

"Yep."

"And how do you feel about that?" she asked. "Him being a threat to your son."

"I don't-."

I didn't finish my sentence because of the gasp that sounded from the doorway, pulling my gaze to it.

"Your son?" My mum drew in a breath and placed a shaking hand against her chest. "Samuel?"

"Shit." Amy closed her eyes, without turning her head. "Please tell me your mum isn't here."

"Nope, she's here."

I got up from the sofa and walked toward my mum, her face devoid of any colour. Her eyes were sparkling with tears and her chest was heaving.

"Mum," I said, pulling her into a hug. "I'm sorry I didn't tell you."

"I have a grandson," she whimpered against my chest. "You have a son."

Guilt stabbed at my chest, knowing I'd kept something so precious from her for so long. My mum was a woman who always had a cause to fight for, someone who wouldn't take shit from anyone. I'd seen her argue with executive directors of fuel companies and go toe to toe with hardened politicians, yet put Bella in her arms and she turned to mush, smothering her granddaughter with kisses and enveloping her with love, and I knew she'd be exactly the same with Frankie given the chance; but I'd taken that opportunity away from her.

"It's complicated, Mum," I said, taking a step back from her.

"How complicated?" she asked. "Tell me."

I shrugged. "It wasn't what I wanted. I was honest with her from the start and we agreed that no one would know."

"Why? Surely the poor child deserved to know his family?" Mum wrapped her arms around her waist and strangled out a sob.

"Yvetta," Amy said softly. "Come and sit down."

She led Mum to a chair, guiding her down onto it.

"Maybe he does deserve a family," I continued, watching my mum intently. "But he doesn't deserve a father who really doesn't want the job."

"And does he have someone he calls 'dad'?" Mum asked as Amy perched on the arm of the chair and gently rubbed Mum's back.

I drew in a breath and then very slowly exhaled, trying to rid the tension in my chest and shoulders.

"No." My voice sounded flat and as soon as I said the word more guilt hit me. "His mum did have someone, but recently kicked him out."

"But you've been spending time with him, from what I heard you say to Amy?" She sounded hopeful and I really wished she hadn't heard us.

I nodded. "I have, but it's a long story."

"Well I want to hear it. I want to know about my grandson. How old is he? What's his name? Can we meet him?"

Panic hit me as she blurted out each question and I felt my chest tighten as my gut roiled.

"No Mum, no, it's not possible."

"But why not?"

I could see the desperation in her eyes and this was exactly what I'd been wanting to avoid all these years.

"He has no idea I'm his dad," I cried. "Maisie and I agreed that he'd never find out."

"But why?" she pleaded, reaching out for my hand. "Why can't he find out?"

"Because it's not what I want."

"Why don't you? He's your son, surely you want that?"

"No, I really don't," I implored.

"But Sam-," Amy started.

"No, no way, Amy. Just don't." I held my hand up and retreated from them. "You both need to stay out of this and listen to me. He is to never know and you need to forget about him. I mean it."

"What the hell is going on in here?"

We all turned to see Dad standing and watching us.

"What's the shouting about?"

Mum stood up and almost ran to Dad, wrapping her arms around his waist and laying her cheek against his chest.

"James, talk to him," she sobbed.

"What about, love?" Dad asked, lifting her chin.

"He has a son James. He has a son and he doesn't want the boy to know."

Dad stared at me and the way he looked at me, I'd never felt like such a disappointment in my whole life.

17

SAMUEL

the past

I don't know how I was expecting to feel once I knew that Maisie was in labour, but fear was the one emotion that surprised me.

Gut clenching fear gripped me as I stared down at the text on my phone.

Maisie – You asked me to keep you informed. Am in labour and just off to hospital.

I didn't know whether to reply or throw my phone away and pretend I had no idea who Maisie was and why she was texting me.

"What's wrong?" Hazel, my boss, asked. "You've gone a pale shade of green."

My head shot up and as our eyes met, I swallowed the huge fucking lump in my throat.

"Nothing," I replied, putting my phone to the back of my desk. "Just something I forgot to do."

Hazel eyed me warily, one eyebrow raised.

"You sure you're okay?"

"Yeah, positive."

I cleared my throat and went back to checking the CV that was on my computer screen.

"You can go now, Sam, if you need to. You're here until seven most nights, so I really don't mind you taking the afternoon. Eve can check these CVs when she gets back from lunch – she needs to have a little more responsibility."

My eyes darted to my phone. I wasn't planning on being at the hospital, or even seeing the kid, but I knew I'd be restless and agitated all afternoon waiting for Maisie's next text – I wanted it to go well for her. Just because it wasn't for me, didn't mean that I didn't want it all to be okay.

"You wouldn't mind?" I asked, already closing down my PC.

"No Sam, now get off and do what you need to do," Hazel replied with a smile. "We won't crumble without you for the afternoon."

When she laughed, I rolled my eyes and pushed up from my desk. "Thanks, Hazel. See you in the morning and try not to ruin the place."

It was no secret that I thought the business would go to shit without me, and to be fair Hazel often agreed.

A half hour later and I was changed into grey sweatpants and a t-shirt, pacing the apartment waiting and wondering. Elijah had called me and I'd ignored his call, letting it go to voicemail. I knew it wouldn't be urgent – he was just starting up a gardening business and I'd put him in touch with a few contacts, so it would probably be about that or the fact he wouldn't be home for dinner again. I just knew I couldn't speak to him, or anyone else for that matter – I was too wound up, even the gentle hum of the central heating was annoying me.

To keep myself occupied, I put in a load of laundry, washed

and dried mine and Elijah's breakfast dishes and even cleaned two pairs of shoes – it was fucking stressful just waiting.

Finally, at almost nine pm the text came.

Maisie: Frankie James born at 745 weighing 7lb 3oz.

That was it, nothing else. I had no idea how she was feeling, whether it had all gone well. The one thing that did strike me was that he had my dad's name as his middle name – how was that for a coincidence?

I looked down at my phone again and reread Maisie's text. Seeing the words made my skin itch and my fingers twitch. I curled them into my palms and then stretched them out again and edged my index finger toward the screen. I pulled it back, and ran my hand through my hair, trying to use it as an act of distraction.

I could almost hear my heart beating, it was thumping so hard. My lungs felt tight and I was confused by the feeling of excitement – or was it trepidation – which was swilling around in my stomach.

Looking over at the clock on the cooker, I knew what I had to do – what I wanted to do. I swiped up my keys and rushed out of the apartment with only one destination in mind.

18

the present

It had been two days since I'd heard or seen Sam and even though I knew it was totally a bad idea that he be involved in our lives, I was kind of hoping he'd call around or even text me. I did think he might have checked up on us, but I couldn't blame him, I'd been adamant I'd be the one to call him if I needed anything. Sam had also made me promise to call the Police if Josh turned up again, but thankfully there'd been no sign.

Thinking of Josh I shuddered inwardly, thinking about his behaviour and how he'd scared both me and Frankie. Hopefully he'd realise what an idiot he'd been and that would be the last we'd see of him. I knew my mum and dad would be worried, when I finally decided to tell them what had happened, but they'd also be glad I'd finally dumped him; neither were his biggest fan in the past few years. They were picking up Frankie from school for me, but I'd made him promise not to mention anything until I got there – I just hope he remembered, because I didn't want to be hit with a barrage of questions as soon as I walked through their front door.

I was making my way to the estate agents where I worked part-time doing the administration; not the greatest job in the world, but when I'd gotten pregnant with Frankie I couldn't keep up with the hours acting as PA for the very demanding Finance Director of an Investment Company. When Frankie was just over a year old I began my job with Angela. She'd just started up her own estate agency and while the pay wasn't brilliant, she was good to me, letting me do additional hours if I needed some extra money – something that I was probably going to be asking for quite a bit in the future, seeing as Josh was gone. I wished that he'd never persuaded me to tell Sam we didn't want his money, but hindsight was an amazing thing.

Walking into the office, I was surprised to see Angela sitting at one of the desks talking on the phone. I waved a hand and frowned. Angela rolled her eyes in response and carried on her conversation.

I expected to find Denny, the other girl that worked in the office with me, in the kitchen but there was no sign of her. When I went back into the office with two mugs of coffee, Angela was finally off the phone.

"Where's Denny?" I asked, placing a mug in front of Angela.

"Don't mention her name to me," she growled, picking up her mug. "The little bitch has dropped me right in it."

"Why, what's happened?" I asked, turning on my PC.

"Left me a message to say she's not coming back. She's got a job with Turner Rentals."

"She can't just go like that, surely?"

"Well any normal person would give notice, but not her. No, that little madam thinks it's perfectly okay to leave via a sodding voicemail."

Angela sighed and punched at the keyboard.

"Any idea what her password is?" she asked.

"Try Jason Momoa without a space."

Angela screwed up her brow.

"He's this month's sexy hottie on her calendar." I nodded at the small desk calendar in front of Angela.

She tapped at the keys. "Bingo. Right, let's see where she's up to with the rental collections."

"Do you need me to do anything specific?"

Angela carried on typing. "Yep, you can call Temploy Recruitment and see if they can find me someone permanent and maybe a temp in the meantime."

The air rushed from my lungs. "Temploy? Not A1 like we normally do?"

"No, those bastards tried to rip me off last time, so let's try Temploy." Angela flashed me a smile and then carried on typing.

I coughed nervously, wondering if I could somehow persuade her to do it herself, because Temploy was Sam's agency. It was the one he'd taken over a few years before, the one that had been more important to him than becoming a father.

I hadn't spoken to him in two days and suddenly the thought of hearing his voice made me feel nervous and excited and like a teenage girl with a crush.

I clicked on my PC to our contact list to find the number and then tentatively picked up the receiver of my desk phone. I stared at the computer screen for a few seconds before reaching out a finger to dial the number. When a female voice answered after a few rings, I visibly relaxed back in my chair, relieved but a little disappointed that Sam hadn't answered. My relief was short lived though when she took the details and told me either Sam or Eve would call me back because I knew that when Sam saw my name on the enquiry I'd be getting my call back from him.

Almost half an hour later, I was proved right.

"Hey, it's Sam," he said when I answered the call. "I hear you're looking for a new member of staff."

"Hi Sam," I replied, feeling a heat creep up my neck and hoping Angela hadn't noticed. "Our other admin girl just up and left, so we need someone pretty quickly." I'd offered to do some extra hours, but I couldn't do the two late nights or the Saturday, not without putting on my parents for extra childcare time with Frankie and they already picked him up from school three nights a week.

"Why didn't you call my mobile," he replied. "You didn't have to call the office."

"Well, I didn't want to bother you. I didn't think, to be honest."

"Next time just call me, it's fine. Anyway, I think we have someone suitable. She could pretty much start straight away if Angela likes her. I think she will though, she's really good and I wouldn't have any problems placing her."

"Really? That would be amazing, thank you."

"That's the perks of knowing me," he said, laughing softly. "I'll send her round at nine tomorrow. Just call me if that doesn't suit Angela, okay?"

"Yes will do, thanks Sam."

The line went silent for a few seconds and I wondered if he'd ended the call. I was just about to say his name, when he spoke.

"How have things been since Saturday? I take it you haven't heard anything from *Josh*."

The way he said Josh's name made me smile, he sounded just like Frankie when he didn't like something – or I supposed Frankie sounded just like Sam.

"No, nothing. All quiet."

"That's good, yeah really good."

Sam's voice was quiet and he sounded a little unsure and I knew it was probably because he didn't know how to tell me he wouldn't be contacting me again. I evidently didn't need him and he was feeling awkward on how to tell me that we would be going back to being virtual strangers, and he'd go back to simply being

Frankie's swimming coach for the next few weeks and then...well then, like a puff of smoke, he'd be gone permanently.

"Anyway," I said, taking a deep breath. "I'd better get going and I'll let Angela know that...oh sorry what did you say the girl's name was?"

"Bernadette Wright. I've emailed it all over to Angela's email address that you gave to Christy."

"Great, I'll check with Angela that she's okay to see her in the morning, but I'm sure she will be."

"Great," Sam replied.

I chewed on my lip, having no clue what to say. As Saturday had gone on, I'd felt comfortable with Sam, but now the silence was practically static with the discomfort that we both felt. Sam because he didn't know how to say 'goodbye and enjoy your life' and me because in a matter of twenty-four hours I'd become used to him being around us and I wasn't really sure I wanted that to end.

"Okay, I'll probably see you at swimming," I said, giving him a get out if he needed it.

"Yeah, about that," Sam replied with a loud exhale.

Here it was. This was where he told me he wasn't going to be doing teaching any longer.

"Yes, what is it?" I slumped in my seat, disappointment washing over me.

"Well, I was wondering if you and Frankie would like to go out for pizza tomorrow night."

SAM

What the fuck was I doing, asking her if I could take them out for fucking pizza? I was an idiot, a complete moron and wanted to stab myself in the balls, yet the words had come out as naturally as they would when I asked a girl on a date.

This was not a fucking date. No way, not even close.

"Pizza?"

At the sound of Maisie's soft, surprised voice, I dropped my forehead to my hand and shook my head at my own stupidity.

"Yep," I ground out.

When there wasn't a response, every bit of my hesitancy disappeared and worry gripped me that she might say no.

What the hell was going on with me? I'd quite clearly told my family the day before that there was no way I wanted to be a father to Frankie, and absolutely no way in this world they'd be getting to know him, leaving my mum in tears and my dad almost spouting angry steam from his ears. Yet, here I was asking Maisie for more and feeling shit scared that she'd turn me down. I was playing a damn dangerous game with not only their emotions, but mine and my families too, yet I didn't have it in me to worry about what spending more time with them might result in. All I wanted in that moment was to take them out for pizza and spend time getting to know them both.

"Yes," Maisie responded. "Pizza would be great."

I groaned inwardly at my stupidity, yet somehow couldn't stop the fucking huge grin that was spread across my face.

19

SAM

the present

As Frankie tucked into a huge triple cheese pizza, I couldn't take my eyes off him. It bloody amazed me how much he was like me. He had the same colouring as me and looking at his eyes was like looking at my own in the mirror, but it was more than that, it was his mannerisms too. The way he closed his eyes on that first bite of food, how he rubbed his eyebrow when he was thinking and how he couldn't hide it in his face when he found something amusing – we both twitched our lips to one side. Not to mention his taste in music and his swimming ability – it was all kind of freaky.

I shouldn't have been surprised, we Coopers had strong genes. Elijah and I were a mirror image of each other and there was no doubt who our dad was, and they both did the eyebrow thing too and all three of us had the exact same laugh. As for Bella, she was a much prettier, cuter version of my brother, so no wonder my son looked like me.

The words 'my son' tumbled around my head, banging against my brain, reminding me with every hit about the strange situation I'd found myself in. It was strange because I'd been adamant that this was in no way what I wanted, but in a matter of days I'd found myself entwined in Frankie and Maisie's lives and it wasn't as shit as I'd always thought it would be.

To be honest, it amazed me that Maisie hadn't punched me in the bollocks and told me to fuck off after the way I'd treated her all those years ago. I wasn't stupid enough to think she'd been thinking of me all that time, or us being a family had been what she'd wanted for all those years. I knew that, but for *Josh* being a dick head and a twat, and Elijah sticking his damn nose in, she may well have taken Frankie to a different swimming instructor and told me to drop dead. I'd helped her, she'd been grateful and it just so happened I'd enjoyed doing it and felt good about something I'd done for the first time in years.

"You were right about his appetite," I said, looking over at Maisie who was taking a bite of her own pizza.

She giggled and held a hand in front of her mouth.

"God, sorry," she replied, swallowing her food. "Yeah, I know. He'll scoff all of that down, no problem."

Our gazes fell onto Frankie who was studying a piece of crust intensely, then silence fell around the table again as we all continued eating. It wasn't an uncomfortable silence, yet it didn't feel right to me. I wanted to talk to Maisie and to Frankie. I wanted us to discuss our days, get to know each other and chat, but I was also conscious that I was still telling everyone that this was exactly what I didn't want and it would not be happening. Shit, on the day that Frankie was born I'd told Maisie in the most fucking cruel way possible that there was no way she'd be getting a nice little family – so I had no clue why she'd even want to share the same airspace as me, never mind chit chat around the dinner table. Truth be told, the whole fucking thing was messing with my head.

"Bernadette is starting full time next week," Maisie said, pulling me back from the shit storm in my head.

"Yeah, Angela called to let Eve know."

"Of course you'd know." Maisie rolled her eyes. "You're the big boss man after all."

I shrugged. "It took a while, but I got there in the end."

"I think it's great you achieved what you set out to do." Maisie reached over to Frankie and handed him a paper napkin. "You've got tomato sauce all round your face. What on earth have you been doing, washing your face with it?"

Frankie took the napkin and scrubbed it across his face, only managing to increase the spread of the sauce. There was even some on his earlobe.

"Come here," I said around a laugh as I leaned closer to him and with my own napkin wiped at his face and ear.

Once he looked a little more presentable, I turned to Maisie. "Better?"

She exhaled slowly and nodded. Her eyes were a little glassy and the sight of her made my heart jump. She stared at me without saying a single word and I held my breath as I watched the slight tremble of her chin. I didn't know what was happening, but in that moment, I knew we were sharing something. We watched each other closely, words that I knew I shouldn't speak forming in my head. My nerve endings were sparking off each other and I felt the urge to reach my hand out for Maisie's.

All I'd done had been to wipe my son's face with a paper napkin, yet my heart had expanded as though it was so much more. The way Maisie's face had softened told me I wasn't wrong.

"I'm sorry," I said, glancing at Frankie.

Maisie's eyes widened. "For wiping his face?"

I shook my head. "No, for so much more."

Maisie inhaled and her head shot toward Frankie who was making slurping noises with his orange juice. He was totally oblivious of the tension between us, or that he actually had both his parents at the table. The only concern he had was whether he could suck hard enough to make a piece of ice stick to the bottom of the straw with the suction.

"Maisie," I said, tentatively reaching a hand out.

Her gaze shot back to mine and her back straightened. "I don't...Sam I..." she shook her head slowly and absent-mindedly screwed up her napkin and threw it onto her half eaten pizza.

"It's fine. I'm sorry. I just..." I blew out my cheeks. "This is all so surreal. I have no idea what I'm doing, or why."

"Um aren't you eating pizza, because you're hungry." A little voice piped up.

We both turned to Frankie and I forced out a smile. This was not the time or the place for me to suddenly get a come to fucking Jesus moment about being a damn father. I wasn't even sure that was what had happened, all I knew was I suddenly felt the guilt clutching at my throat and stopping me from breathing easily.

"Yeah, of course I am buddy. I was trying to be funny."

Frankie screwed up his nose. "Well, it wasn't really was it? I mean I'm not laughing and neither is Mummy." He shrugged and went back to his game of catch the ice cube.

I looked at Maisie to gauge her reaction, but her face was impassive. Gone was the glassy eyes and the soft smile, now there was nothing, she was simply watching Frankie before flashing me a false smile.

"We should get going soon," she said, clearing her throat.

"Muuuummm," Frankie groaned. "Do we have to?"

"Yes, we do. You have school tomorrow."

"But we haven't had ice cream yet. We can have ice cream, can't we Sam."

I had no clue what to say. Either way someone was going to

think I was a prick. When I didn't answer, Frankie sighed and placed a tiny hand on my forearm.

"Don't worry, Sam. I know you said you'd pay, but if you don't have enough money for ice cream too, my mummy will help out, won't you?"

He looked expectantly at Maisie, giving her what I guessed was his best puppy dog look. I knew it had to be, because at that fucking minute I'd have given the kid my left kidney if he'd asked.

"Frankie," Maisie scolded. "Don't be rude."

"It's okay -."

"I'm not," Frankie interrupted me. "You always say you should be honest and I honestly want some ice cream and I honestly know you'll pay if Sam can't."

My mouth twitched and I almost pulled Frankie against my chest when I saw the exact same expression on his face.

"I'll go to the toilet and let you chat about it," he said, pushing away from the table. "So Sam doesn't get embarrassed."

Before either of us could stop him, he ran off dodging a waitress with a tray full of drinks.

"I'm sorry, Maisie," I rushed out. "I have no idea what the fuck is going on in my head. I just know I'll never be able to apologise enough."

Maisie laid her palms flat on the table and took a deep breath. "I understand that spending time with him might have confused you, Sam, but you can't just decide that you want to be his dad after all this time." Her voice was a little shaky and her eyes kept darting toward the toilet, watching for Frankie coming back.

"I don't want that."

When Maisie gasped I shook my head.

"Shit, I'm cocking this up. What I mean is, I have no idea if that's what I want, Maisie. I spent all of Sunday afternoon telling my fucking parents that they should forget they have a grandson because they wouldn't ever be meeting him, but-."

"You told your parents," she hissed, leaning across the table. "Sam, what the hell were you thinking?"

"Shit," I groaned. "I was going to tell you. They heard me talking to Amy."

"Amy knows?"

Maisie's face had paled and her hand trembled as she lifted it to place against her chest.

"Oh my god," she whispered. "We agreed. What if Frankie finds out?"

Her words punched me in the gut making my lungs feel as though they'd just deflated like a pricked balloon.

"What if he does?"

Maisie's mouth dropped open, in silent shock.

"Maisie I-."

"You were the one," she snapped. "The one who didn't want him to know. We agreed. I agreed with you because it was better he had no dad than be constantly hurt that the one he did have didn't want him."

"I know, I know, but spending time with him, with you both, I don't know how I feel any more. I'm not sure that's what I want."

Maisie looked away momentarily.

"Well I'm sorry, Sam but you *have* to be bloody sure. You can't mess with his heart like that. If that's what you want then you have to be sure, because that boy is my life and if you hurt him, I'll...I'll fucking kill you."

I opened my mouth to retaliate, but didn't when Frankie dropped back into his seat.

"So, are we having ice cream or not."

Maisie forced a wide smile. "Yes sweetie, we are, but Sam had a phone call, he has to go."

I looked at her and almost disagreed, but when I saw the fire and anger in her eyes, decided better of it.

"Really?" Frankie groaned. "Oh no, I brought my Football Top Trumps with me." He turned in his seat and reached into the pocket of his coat, hanging on the back of his chair. "Grandad got them for me."

Frankie slapped the pack of cards on the table and gave me a look I recognised from Bella when she was struggling to make herself understood.

My emotions were a fucking mess as I looked at him. I wanted to laugh at his consternation at not being able to play cards with me, my damn heart was aching that I had to go, but I also had a sudden urge to run as fast as I could.

"Sorry, Frankie," I managed to say while trying to hide the quake in my voice. "But I'll pay for the ice cream on my way out."

His face brightened slightly and then he nodded. "Can I go and get some, Mummy?" He looked over his shoulder at the 'ice cream factory' a couple of feet away.

Maisie nodded. "Say goodbye to Sam first."

I looked at her, hoping she might change her mind, but her gaze never left Frankie and her jaw was tight. If I felt confused before, as soon as two little arms were flung around my neck, any semblance of understanding of what was going on in my heart and my head totally disappeared.

"Night Sam," Frankie said against my ear. "Thanks for the pizza and ice cream. Maybe we can play Top Trumps another time."

"Yep," I managed around the ball of emotion that was almost choking me. "That would be great."

"Yes, bye Sam," Maisie said. "And thank you."

I glanced at her over the top of Frankie's arm that was still wrapped around my neck, but she was searching in her bag.

Finally, Frankie let me go and raced off to get his ice cream.

"I am sorry, Maisie," I said as I pushed up from my chair. "But we do need to talk some more."

She nodded. "We do, but not until you've really thought about what you want, because you only get one chance at this Sam. You let him down just *once* and *that* is it."

Her voice was determined and I knew she was right; I had some serious thinking to do.

20

SAMUEL

the past

As soon as I reached the door to the maternity ward, my palms started to sweat and bile rose in my throat. If I thought I was over what Alison had done to me, I was getting a huge wake up call. I might not have cared about her any longer, but the fucking shit trick she pulled on me had obviously embedded itself into my soul.

As I stood in the corridor with my hands hooked at the back of my neck, I felt a continuous stabbing pain in my chest – the knife point of anxiety reminding me that this could all just be a pile of lies and I wasn't sure I could go through that again.

"You want to go in mate?" a guy carrying a flower patterned duffle bag asked. "Have you pressed the buzzer?"

My gaze shot to him, taking in his huge smile and tired looking eyes. "Yeah," I muttered.

"Yeah you've pressed the buzzer?" He turned and looked through the viewing panel in the door. "No one's coming. I'll try it again."

I shuffled closer to him, still not sure that I was doing the right thing.

"You look a bit shell shocked, mate." He landed a hand on my shoulder and gave it a squeeze. "Your first is it?"

I nodded, looking at him blankly.

"I was like that with our first, but this time around it doesn't seem so scary. You'll be fine mate. Just think of your poor missus, what she's gone through."

He laughed again and shook his head as I stood there dumb.

"Oh here we go." He nodded to the viewing panel.

"Hiya Stuart," the nurse who opened the door said. "We've just moved Carly to the first bay, second bed in."

"Great, cheers."

With that, the guy Stuart pushed past her. "Good luck, mate," he called over his shoulder.

"Can I help you?" The nurse gave me a knowing smile as I rubbed a hand down my face. "Who you here to see my love?"

I cleared my throat. "Maisie West. She's had a baby."

"Most people have on this ward." She lifted the small watch that was attached to her uniform. "It's a bit late for visiting love. We only allow partners or a family member, if necessary, at this time of night."

"Does she have someone with her?" I asked, fearful of someone in Maisie's family finding out I was the father.

"No, her mum went about a half hour ago. So, unless you're her partner, I can't let you in I'm afraid."

I let out a sigh of relief and dropped my hands to my knees, but the nurse must have misunderstood and took it as a response for disappointment.

"Are you the father?"

My head shot up to look at her as I tried to swallow down the huge lump that had formed in my throat.

"W-what?"

"Are you the father? You've got that look of a man who's been floored by the realisation that he's become a dad."

I nodded. "I don't know if..."

She inclined her head, waiting for me to finish, but when I didn't she smiled and evidently thought I needed her to take pity on me.

"Okay, I tell you what. I'll go and ask her if she wants to see you and if she does, as you're the father, I'll let you in. What's your name, sweetheart?"

"Sam, but it's fine. I don't want to put you to any trouble," I burst out, feeling that I'd made totally the wrong decision in even thinking about visiting Maisie and the baby.

"It's no trouble, Sam. We have this a lot, couples who split up before the baby gets here and then dad has an urge to visit. It's nothing new. Just wait here and I'll check what Maisie wants to do."

Before I had chance to argue, she was gone. I considered running – sprinting out of the hospital and never coming back, but my feet wouldn't move. They were rooted to the spot with my desire to know; to check whether it was true and wanting proof that Maisie wasn't the same sort of cruel bitch as Alison.

Within a couple of minutes the nurse was back wearing a big smile. "Come on," she said, beckoning me with her head. "There's a little boy who wants to meet Dad."

My heart drummed in time with every step I took towards Maisie and the baby and even as we rounded the corner and the nurse pointed to a bed with a curtain around it, I was still thinking of running – if I didn't have a heart attack first.

The ward was quiet, except for the soft whispers of parents and quiet gurgling of babies. The lights were low and everything seemed remarkably calm, the total opposite of how I was feeling with the typhoon of emotions whirling around my head and my heart. It was all too surreal and I was sure it was all just someone's idea of a sick joke – me standing in a maternity ward waiting to see my son.

As I took a hesitant step forward, the guy who I'd seen outside in the corridor appeared from behind a curtain, holding an empty glass.

"Alright, mate," he said, holding up the glass. "The wife wants a drink. You see your nipper yet?"

"I-I'm just going in now," I stammered.

"Best thing ever. Better go, and good luck."

As he disappeared, I heard Maisie quietly call out my name, so taking a deep breath, I pulled back the faded blue and yellow curtain and step into the peaceful cocoon that she and the baby were in.

"Hi," she whispered, looking up at me shyly, the baby cradled in her arms. "I never for one minute thought you'd come."

I stared at the tiny bundle sleeping against her chest desperately trying to see something of me in him.

"Sam?"

I looked at her and shrugged. "I wasn't sure I would. I don't even know whether I've done the right thing even now."

Maisie watched me carefully and must have seen something in my face because she shook her head and sighed.

"Maybe you shouldn't have. I know it doesn't mean anything, but if you haven't changed your mind, it seems pretty pointless."

"No," I said, my eyes wide with shock. "I haven't. I just needed to see."

"To see what," she replied before looking back down at the baby. "It's a baby that you don't want anything to do with, so what's to see."

I didn't answer, but continued to stare at her.

"I knew I shouldn't have let you come in," she muttered, pulling the baby's blanket closer around him. "But when the nurse said you were here, I just thought..."

She trailed off and I noticed her chin tremble.

"Don't think anything, Maisie. I just wanted to check you were okay and see him."

"Frankie," she said around an empty laugh. "You wanted to see Frankie."

I didn't respond, because I didn't want to say his name. If I said his name, it meant he *had* a name which meant he was real and I really didn't want to think of the fact that I was a dad. Shit, I might not be. I'd been here before, it wasn't my first time around and look how that ended up.

"Do you want to hold him?" Maisie asked tentatively.

I shook my head. "Nope."

"Okay, but you could at least look at him."

"Maisie, don't," I groaned out.

"Why the hell have you come here then?"

She dropped her head back against the mountain of pillows behind her and closed her eyes. The baby roused slightly and opened its eyes and I'll swear it looked right at me, blue eyes boring into me and judging me.

"He has blue eyes," I said, gripping at my hair.

"And?" Maisie's curious gaze went back to the baby. "All babies have blue eyes."

"We both have brown eyes. Why does he have blue eyes?"

My pulse started to quicken as I stared at Maisie, demanding answers. This couldn't be happening. No way should he have blue eyes if we both had brown.

"Sam, what's wrong?" Maisie asked as I started to breathe heavily. "Are you okay?"

"Why the fuck does he have blue eyes?" I snapped. "What aren't you telling me?"

"I've told you, most babies are born with blue eyes."

"I'm a quarter Greek, so why the fuck doesn't he have brown eyes?" I spat out, pointing a finger at Maisie

"Stop it," she cried, the noise disturbing the baby again. "You're being stupid."

"No, no I'm not. I'd be stupid to think that its mine."

"He's not an 'it'. He's your bloody son."

Tears slowly crawled down Maisie's cheeks and her arms were trembling as she pulled the baby closer to her. I didn't care though, all that mattered to me was that I wasn't made a fucking fool of again.

"I don't know that though, do I?" I snapped. "He could be anyone's. We were careful and then after one night you tell me I'm the father."

"You are. We talked about this."

Maisie swiped at her tears and looked at me, devastation written all over her face.

"I know what you told me, but you could be lying."

"I wouldn't lie about something this important. You prick, how dare you?"

"I dare because you're a fucking woman and women lie and cheat about things like this."

"What's going on in here?" The curtain was pulled back and a nurse popped her head in. "There are new born babies and exhausted new mums on this ward and you are disturbing them."

She looked at Maisie who was obviously distressed.

"Do you want me to get him thrown out?" the nurse asked her.

Maisie shook her head. "No," she said defiantly. "He's going anyway."

"Well do it quietly, or I *will* call security."

"You're a bastard," Maisie said when the curtain fell back into place.

"Yeah, just like that."

I pointed at the baby and Maisie gasped.

"Get out," she hissed. "I never want to see or hear from you again."

"Get a DNA test, Maisie," I snarled. "And if its mine I'll pay what's due, but I don't want anything to do with him. I never want him looking for me, or turning up on my doorstep in eighteen years' time, you hear me?"

"I don't want your bloody money and don't worry, I'll never tell him about the twat he has for a father."

"You'll have the money if he's mine. I don't want to be taken to court or have some bloody government department on my back for years of back pay if I don't provide for him."

Maisie shook her head and heaved in a ragged breath. "What the hell has got into you? I can't believe you're being like this. I didn't ask you to come here, I didn't ask you for anything."

"Like I said, I wanted to be sure and seeing as I'm not, get the fucking DNA done. In fact, I'll sort it."

"No," she said, shaking her head and looking at me with narrowed eyes. "I don't want anything from you. I'll speak to a solicitor and get him to deal with it, now go and don't bother ever coming back."

"I won't," I replied, grabbing the curtain ready to disappear. "And if you've lied to me, I'll make sure everyone knows what you tried to do."

"Just get out, Sam," she sobbed. "Get out."

I pushed through the curtain and practically ran from the ward, just about reaching the car park before I puked.

As I wiped my mouth with the back of my hand, a couple walked toward me, the woman nudging the guy as they both looked at me sideways. It didn't appear to occur to them that I might need help, despite the pile of vomit at my feet.

Coughing and with an acid burn at the back of my throat, I stumbled toward a metal bench where a few smokers were gathered and sank down onto it. My hands were shaking and the adrenalin rushing around my body was making my heart thud an erratic beat.

"Fuck," I whispered, dropping my head into my hands. "What the hell have I done?"

The thought of Maisie's devastated face when I'd accused her of lying about the baby being mine, was torture. This was supposed to be one of the best days of her life and I'd ruined it for her because I was selfish and fucking scared; but I was preserving my own heart too.

"You alright?"

I looked up to see a security guard looking down at me, a nurse standing at his side.

"Sorry?"

"Someone said you were being sick out here," he replied.

"Do you need to come inside and let us have a look at you?" the nurse asked.

"No I'm fine, thanks."

I lifted my shaking hand to run it through my hair.

"Have you taken something?"

The nurse stepped nearer and looked closely into my eyes, the light from the overhead lamp disappeared as she moved forward, shrouding us in darkness.

"Fuck no," I cried.

"So why do you think you were sick?" she asked, standing straight again, her eyes examining me closely.

"Eaten a bad sandwich," I said curtly, wishing she'd just fuck off and leave me with my self-hatred.

She frowned and glanced at the security guard. "Okay, but if you need any help just go to A&E."

"I'm fine," I sighed, pushing up from the bench and starting to walk away. A little more self-loathing hit me and I paused and turned around. "Thanks for asking though."

She nodded and said something to the security guard that I didn't hear and then they both turned to go back inside the hospital. As the door swished closed, I made my way back to the car park, emotion pricking at my throat with every step.

Sitting in my car, I stared up at the floors of windows of the hospital, wondering which one Maisie and my son were in, wondering if I should go back and apologise. I had no clue what to do. I was so fucking scared of going through the same shit as I had at eighteen – of being made a fool of again. I didn't want to be a dad, I didn't want to be responsible for another human being, yet I felt like the biggest shit at the same time.

I picked up my mobile and scrolled through my contacts until I found Elijah's name. My finger hovered over the thumbnail of his face, but I couldn't do it. I couldn't tell him because he'd hate me, especially as he would give anything to be in my shoes. His disappointment would kill me.

Staring through the windscreen it hit me that I had no one to talk to, no one to ask for help, to tell me what to do. No one to tell me I was wrong, no one to even tell me I was fucking right and as guilt and fear clawed at me in equal measures, I felt wetness on my cheeks.

The breath I dragged in turned to a sob, everything I'd holed up inside me from the age of eighteen beating its way out of me as a pained cry.

"I fucking hate you," I screamed, beating my hand against the steering wheel. "You've fucking ruined my life, I hate you."

No one heard or saw me. No one stopped to check if I needed anything.

I had no one and I never would because my heart was black and hard.

21

the present

"So, what's this about?" my dad asked as he and Mum sat down. "Why the big secret and why did Libby have to take Frankie out for tea?"

I took a deep breath and passed them both a mug of coffee, giving myself time to try and calm my nerves.

"Well?" Mum asked when I finally sat opposite them.

"I needed to talk to you, about Josh and about Frankie's dad."

I'd lain awake most of the night after we'd got home from pizza, thinking about what had happened and what Sam had said and I knew if he decided being a dad to Frankie was what he wanted, I'd have to tell my parents. They'd been the ones who'd supported me from the minute I'd told them I was pregnant and was doing it alone, so I owed it to them to tell them all about Sam.

"What about them – he isn't Frankie's dad is he?" My mum looked and sounded horrified, but when Dad growled her name, she quickly checked herself. "I mean, I'm sure you'd have told us before now if he was."

"No, Mum," I replied. "He isn't, but you should know we broke up."

149

Neither of my parents could hide their relief, both of them sagging back against the cushions on the sofa in a synchronised move.

"What happened?" Dad asked.

"He showed me that he really isn't the sort of man I want around my son."

Mum opened her mouth to speak, but suddenly snapped it shut, obviously deciding against the 'I told you so', that she was evidently going to blurt out.

"Did he do something specific?" Colour rose in my dad's face and I knew that he had an idea at what Josh might have done.

I told them everything about his behaviour that night and about him coming back and trying to get into the house, but I didn't mention Sam.

"Why the hell didn't you call me," Dad cried, leaning forward and clasping his hands together in front of him. "I would have come around and got rid of him. Neither of you should have been scared like that."

"It was fine, Dad."

I blew out a breath and straightened my shoulders. This was the time to tell them everything. To explain how Frankie was being coached by his father and how the man that they probably hated for abandoning us had come to our rescue, and how he'd started to spend time with Frankie.

"How can it be fine?" Mum cried. "The man scared you. He threatened to hit my grandson. You could have both been in real danger with a man like that. I knew he'd changed, but to turn violent, what if he had hurt you?"

"Well he didn't and we weren't in any danger because once I threw him out, Sam arrived."

They looked at me blankly and then at each other, their brows furrowed in confusion.

"Sam?" Dad asked.

"Who's Sam, lo-?"

My mum clamped her mouth shut abruptly, realisation hitting her right between the eyes.

"So Frankie's father is called Sam." Dad looked at me expectantly. "And Frankie knows?"

I shook my head. "No. He just thinks Sam is his swimming coach."

"What? I thought he was called Danny. Your mum told me he was a young lad called Danny."

"He was."

I went on to explain how Sam had become Frankie's coach and all about the first time that I'd seen him in years. I told them about Elijah seeing Josh smash my car and how Sam had turned up and why I'd called him the next night when Josh came back to the house.

"So what, you're a couple now?" Mum asked incredulously.

"God no," I cried. "He's just spent some time with us, making sure we were safe. I think he feels bad about the years he ignored the fact he had a son and now he knows Frankie, well he's enjoying his company."

"Well how very big of him," Mum snapped, flouncing back against the sofa. "And you've just let him waltz into Frankie's life as though he'd only missed a couple of weeks of it."

"No, I haven't. It just happened. I had no idea he was Frankie's swimming coach, I even told him he had to quit."

"Yet he's ended up spending time with you both as soon as you've ended your relationship."

"Yes, Mum, but only because of the *way* my relationship ended. It was his brother who called him, not me."

"So his family know about Frankie?" Dad asked, placing a palm on my mum's vigorously bobbing knee.

Shit, how did I tell them that they were the last to know about it all? I decided that a little white lie wouldn't' hurt.

"Only his brother knows, but now Sam's going to tell his parents too."

"So it's serious then?"

"What?" I asked my mum. "What's serious, him wanting to spend time with Frankie?"

"You and him."

"I've told you, there is no me and him. This is all about him wanting to get to know Frankie."

"Calm down, Jen," Dad soothed. "Just let Maisie explain."

"She's explained," Mum scoffed. "The father is back in their lives and spending time with them, and she just so happens to have ended her long term relationship."

"Which you've been wanting me to do for ages," I added.

"Not the point Maisie and you know it."

Mum crossed her arms over her chest and moved her head to look out of the window, into the garden. Her gaze intently fixed to Frankie's swing, blowing in the wind.

"Listen," I said with a long exhale. "You should know he stayed the night but -."

"And you're telling me there is no you and him."

Mum's angry eyes were back on me and the hardness of her stare made me feel about ten years old again.

"Jen," Dad warned.

"Well I'm sorry Michael, but she needs to realise it's not good for Frankie for her to be moving from one man to another, even if the latest one is his dad."

"I'm not moving from one man to another," I cried, agitated by my mother's refusal to understand. "He's been making sure we're safe, *that is all*. He slept on the sofa the night Josh tried to get in.

There's no hint that he wants anything more than to be in Frankie's life. Which is the only reason that I'm telling you this. He took us for pizza last night and pretty much asked if he can start being Frankie's dad."

"Pretty much?" Dad repeated. "What does that mean?"

I was beginning to wish I hadn't bothered telling them until I was sure what Sam wanted to do. I knew that if Sam decided fatherhood wasn't for him, my parents would be on at me for the rest of my life about how all of this would affect Frankie. Somehow though, something was telling me that Sam was ready and he just needed a little more time to be sure.

Maybe I should have told him to take a running jump, but while his uncertainty scared me, I didn't want to dismiss him immediately in case I was denying Frankie the opportunity of knowing his dad.

Sam could just as easily say he wanted to be in Frankie's life and be an amazing dad as he could turn around and tell me it wasn't what he wanted, but as long as Frankie didn't find out until I could trust Sam's decision, then I had to give him that time.

"It means, Dad, that I've told him to go away and think about it. To be one hundred percent sure before we take it any further. I won't have my son hurt, so Sam needs to be aware once he tells me he wants in then he has to be fully in, because if messes up just once, then I'll make sure he regrets it and he'll never get a second opportunity at this."

My dad nodded and looked to my mum who didn't seem half as calm as him. She was looking up at the ceiling muttering wordlessly to herself. Dad gave her thigh a squeeze and smiled at me.

"Do what you have to do, love," he stated. "Your mum and I will stand by you, but if he messes up just once, I'll punch his bloody lights out."

I allowed myself a little smile, not really fancying my dad's chances against the six feet of tattooed muscle that was Sam Cooper. He'd have to get in line behind me anyway, because I would not allow him to hurt Frankie and get away with it.

"You know this might all be immaterial," I sighed. "Sam might decide it's not what he wants."

"Whatever, we're right behind you, aren't we Jen?"

"I'm worried about both of you," Mum said, leaning forward and reaching for my hand. "You obviously liked him once, enough to sleep with him, so what if you fall for him again but it's only Frankie he wants."

"Mum, nothing is going to happen between me and Sam."

I felt my skin heat, because I'd be lying if I said I didn't find him attractive and think about that night we'd had together, because I did, but I couldn't afford to let my judgement be clouded by lust for Sam. I needed to be on the ball and making sure he was doing right by our son. It didn't matter how sexy or good looking I thought he was, Sam and I were a thing of the past. We'd had our time, one night, almost nine years ago.

"We'll see," she replied and gave me a small smile. "I suppose we should meet him."

I shrugged. "If he wants to be a dad to Frankie then, yes, you will."

"And Frankie?" Dad asked. "When are you going to tell him?"

"That," I breathed out heavily, "is something I'll need to consider very carefully. I want him to get to know Sam first. He already likes him, but they need to spend more time together, just the two of them."

I saw worry whisper across my mum's pretty features and knew she was going to find it difficult, letting go and allowing *another* man into mine and Frankie's lives. She'd always been protective of Libby and me, but her instincts to safeguard Frankie's safety and security were much more intense.

"Everything will be fine, Mum," I whispered getting up to hug her. "I promise, I won't let him hurt Frankie."

"I know love," she replied. "But who is going to make sure he doesn't hurt you?"

22

the present

There so many thoughts swimming around in my head I couldn't concentrate on any one thing. I had a half painted bathroom, thinking doing something with my hands would keep me occupied and stop me from calling Maisie, but it hadn't helped. All I could think about was Frankie and ended up making a fucking mess of the paintwork so I gave up, putting it off for another day.

I understood why Maisie had told me I needed to think things through carefully, it was a huge decision to make, embedding myself into Frankie's life couldn't be a three day wonder – it was for life. Plus, there was the guilt I felt at having not been around for the last eight years, especially how I'd treated Maisie at the hospital on the day she'd given birth to him. I'd practically called her a slag as well as a liar. Accusing her of passing off someone else's baby as mine had been fucking mean as shit, and knowing that she was simply not that sort of person made it worse – it certainly wasn't my finest moment.

I was pretty sure I knew what I wanted to do, but there was a part of me that was still shit scared, which was why my little brother had decided to call around and give me the benefit of his fucking wisdom. According to him, he'd been sick of me looking as

157

though I'd been kicked in the nuts with a stiletto shoe for the last couple of days.

"I know you want to give me another lecture, Eli," I said leading him into the kitchen. "But I'm not in the fucking mood. I've been dodging calls from Mum all week wanting to know what I've decided. Talking of which you can tell Amy she's in trouble next time I see her."

Eli grinned. "You should know better than to have told her. You know she can't keep her mouth shut."

"Yeah, but to tell Mum that I'm thinking of becoming a dad to Frankie – *really*?"

I opened the fridge and pulled out a couple of bottles of beer, flipped the caps, and passed one to my brother.

"She said it just slipped out."

"It's not fucking funny," I grumbled. "She knew I'd get a fucking ton of calls. None of you are going to force my decision on this, it's too fucking important."

"Yeah, we know that. What I don't understand though, Sam, is why you're even having to do this. Why the hell did you decide that you couldn't be in his life? It's not like you to shirk responsibility. Look how you looked after me when Amy left. I'd have never got through that without you."

I looked down at my feet, wanting to dodge the subject of the shit that was going on in my head at the time of Frankie's birth. I'd let Alison's actions cloud my judgement. I'd let the heartbreak I'd felt at losing her and what I thought had been my child turn my heart hard and unfeeling. I'd been stupid and selfish only thinking about myself and not once considering that Maisie might have needed me for something more than money.

"Sam," Eli said, nudging my arm with his beer bottle. "What's going on in your head, tell me."

I lifted my head slowly and shrugged. "I have no idea."

"Yes you do, otherwise you wouldn't be second guessing everything. If you really didn't care you'd have called Maisie by now and told her you were out, but you haven't. You've spent the last couple of days thinking and worrying that you're doing the right thing, which pretty much tells me you're ready to be a dad to that kid."

I rolled my eyes. "What made you so wise, bro?"

"I've always been fucking wise," he scoffed. "You're the doer and I'm the thinker."

"Whatever." I let out a long breath and scrubbed a hand down my face. "I do want it, I do, but what if I let him down, or what if I'm shit at it?"

"You'll make mistakes, every parent does."

"Yeah, but she told me I had one chance. What if I blow that chance and she tells me to fuck off, but by then I'm in so fucking deep with him that I can't leave?"

"I don't think she meant you'd blow it by getting him the wrong Xbox game or by feeding him ice cream for breakfast. I'm pretty sure she meant you can't say 'yay Frankie, I'm your dad' and then decide it's not for you." Eli took a long swig of his beer, keeping his eyes on me at all times.

"What?" I asked.

"What aren't you telling me," he replied. "There's something more to this. Don't get me wrong, I'm fucking happy that you've finally decided to step up to the plate, but it's only taken a couple of weeks for you to get to that point, so what the fuck happened when he was born for you to just tell Maisie you weren't interested, and don't give me the crap about looking after me and wanting to concentrate on the business. I know you, I know there's something else."

My guts flipped over as I watched my brother carefully. I'd kept so many secrets from him, Frankie being one of them and he hadn't reacted well to finding out. Maybe I was being a coward, but if I told him now about Alison, would it fracture our relationship beyond repair. We'd gotten over me not telling him I had a son, but maybe another secret would be one too many for him.

"There's nothing," I replied, my face devoid of any expression, hoping he wouldn't be able to read me.

"I know that's a damn lie. You can't fool me, Sam, but if you don't want to tell me then don't, but I'm really struggling here with the realisation you may actually have been a prick when Frankie was born. You're my big brother and I've always looked up to you, yeah you talk shit from time to time, but you're not a coward, or a poor excuse for a man. You're a good man Sam and the brother I know wouldn't have abandoned his child for no reason."

His words felt like a punch on the jaw and I was glad I was leaning against a cupboard, otherwise I think I'd have stumbled with the despair at disappointing him. He was everything to me and he was the best man I knew apart from my dad, and the thought that he might think less of me made me feel sick. I wanted to be the one he looked up to, always had been from the moment he was born, but I was beginning to see *he* was the one *I* should be looking up to and I knew in that moment that Frankie deserved this man in his life.

"I had an affair with my swimming coach from the age of sixteen and when I was eighteen she got pregnant. She let me believe the baby was mine, but on the day she was born she finally told me it was her husband's, even though she'd told me she wasn't with him for the last eleven months we were together."

I tried to say the words in a quiet, measured way, but the enormity of what I was finally admitting to someone was too much. The relief at revealing a secret that had plagued me and shaped my life for years was immense. My voice cracked with emotion and I slowly slid down the cupboard until I was crouching down.

"What?" Elijah asked, dropping his beer bottle onto the floor.

I looked up at him and swallowed hard. "Alison had a baby that I thought was mine but it wasn't. We had an affair for two years, from when I was just sixteen." I let out a hollow laugh. "If you can call it that, basically we shagged in the changing rooms at the pool, apart from one time when her husband was evidently away."

I sat down on the floor and felt a wetness seeping around my backside as Elijah's beer flowed slowly toward me. I glanced down at the pale amber liquid but didn't have it in me to move, staying there until Eli flopped down beside me with a muttered 'fuck'.

"She was your coach and you were a kid," he said looking totally bewildered. "That's fucking sick, Sam."

"Yeah, I know that now, but at the time I thought I was god's fucking gift for bagging her, having someone like her wanting me." I thought about it for a few seconds. "She was thirty-three, same age as I am now."

Eli blinked slowly and then shook his head. "That's just wrong."

"But like I said, I didn't realise that at the time because I wanted it as much as her. As soon as my hormones kicked in I tried everything to make her see me as more than a bit of a kid who was pretty good at swimming. Then, when I hit my sixteenth birthday and got a bit of stubble on my chin, bingo, she noticed me."

I had no clue why I was almost defending her, she'd been so fucking wrong in what she'd done. Apart from it probably being illegal, her actions had made me do something that I wasn't proud of – I'd denied my son.

"So that's why you didn't want anything to do with Frankie?" Elijah asked. "Why you told Maisie you weren't interested?"

"Pretty much, although now that I think about it, it's a pretty shit reason. I'm supposed to be an intelligent man, yet I couldn't see that Maisie was a different sort of person. She's kind and generous and so fucking forgiving bro, it's unbelievable. You know when he was born, I accused her of doing what Alison had done, all because Frankie had blue eyes when he was born."

"All babies have blue eyes."

"I know that now, but I told her to get a DNA test. No, not asked, *told*."

"You twat," my brother groaned.

"I know, which is what makes it even more astonishing that Maisie even let me speak to him. Yeah, she told me I had to quit coaching Frankie at first, but since I helped her out she's been nothing but amazing. Letting me into their lives and even considering letting me be a dad to Frankie is more than I deserve."

"Like you said, you did help her out. Maybe she's just showing her gratitude and maybe she'll actually knife you in the bollocks one day when you least expect it."

I grimaced and cupped my balls, flashing a pained expression at my brother.

"Shit," he said, raking a hand over his head. "You told Mum and Dad?"

"No!" I snapped. "And I don't want you to either. This is one fucking secret that stays between you and me."

Elijah frowned.

"You can tell her, but I mean it Eli, if Amy tells them I'll never forgive her, I fucking swear."

"Okay," he sighed. "To be honest, I agree. It would fucking kill them knowing she did that when you were her responsibility."

"I was sixteen, bro. It's not like I wasn't legal," I reasoned.

Eli shook his head. "Only just, even so, she had no fucking right. She did wrong. She violated her position, she fucking violated you. How would you feel if that was Frankie?"

I pushed my back off the cupboard door, clenching my hands into fists and stared wide-eyed at my brother.

"I'd fucking kill them."

"Yeah," he said, grinning. "You're ready to be his dad."

My heart halted, missing a few beats at Elijah's words. "You think I can do this?" I asked.

"I know you can. Do not let what happened with that woman shape your life any more than it already has. We had a conversation about regret a few years ago, which I know for definite now was about Frankie, am I right?"

He paused waiting for me to respond with a nod.

"You regretted it then, so don't let us be having this same fucking conversation in another three years, because by then, Sam, it might be too late."

I knew then what I wanted to do, what I was going to do and do it to the very best of my ability. I would no longer be shrouded by the guilt and shame of what I'd done as a kid, because that's all I'd been, a kid who had been steered in the worst possible way.

I knew I'd make mistakes along the way, but I was determined to make my son proud of me.

23

the present

I'd tried to call Maisie about three times on my way around to her house, to tell her I was on my way, but each time it went straight to voicemail. At least she wasn't dropping my call, so hopefully she'd be okay at me just turning up.

After I'd changed out of my beer sodden sweats and pushed my brother out of the door, I'd jumped into my car to go to Maisie's house. I probably should have left it until I'd had a chance to speak to her first and possibly organise about going around there on the weekend, but I couldn't wait. I'd made my mind up and didn't want to waste any more time.

When I pulled up at the bottom of Maisie's drive, I was surprised to see the door fling open and her come rushing out. She had her phone clutched to her chest and was sobbing.

"What the fuck?" I opened my door and jumped out, meeting her half way. "What's wrong? Is it Frankie?"

Maisie's chest was heaving as huge, fat tears rolled down her cheeks. Her hair was falling from its plait and there wasn't a hint of colour in her cheeks – she was deathly pale.

"He's taken him, Sam," she screamed, grabbing hold of my bicep. "Mum went to pick him up from the school play rehearsal

165

and he wasn't there the teacher said his dad had picked him up Mum rang to ask if it was you but I knew it wasn't I just knew I-."

Everything was blurted out in one sentence, without any pause and every word felt like a knife stabbing at my skin.

"Maisie, sweetheart," I soothed, trying to keep the panic from my own voice. "Take a breath. Come on, breath."

I stooped down to look her in the eyes, breathing slowly and encouraging her to copy me.

"Sam...we...have...to...find...him," she gulped in between sobs. "They said it was his dad. I forgot to tell them that Josh wasn't on the approved list any more. This is all my fault."

"No Maisie, it's not. This is all on Josh. Have you called the police?" I asked, steering her back to the house.

"I-I-I only just got off the phone from Mum. I need to c-c-call them." She moved away from me and started to stab clumsily at her phone. "Maybe the school did. I don't know, Sam."

"Hey, let's get into the house and I'll do it." Gently I prised the mobile from Maisie's fingers and taking her hand led her into the house.

"You should be out there looking for him," I snapped at the copper taking a statement from me. "Not damn well questioning me about my whereabouts. We know who took him, the fucking teacher said it was him."

"Mr. Cooper," the copper started, holding out a hand. "We know what we're doing. We are taking this very seriously, seeing as he isn't the child's father and Miss West has already made a complaint against Mr. Brent, we've sent a squad car to his address and I'm just trying to get a clear picture so we can rule things out.

"You don't need to rule me out because I shouldn't have been bloody ruled in in the first place." I was about to push up from the sofa when a large palm landed on my shoulder. I looked up to see Maisie's dad standing over me. He was a tall, balding man and as soon as he'd walked into the house he'd created a presence – this man was the one I had to thank for making sure my son had a great role model, so it was with respect for him that I didn't brush his hand off me.

"Just calm down, Sam," he said quietly. "They're just doing their job. They know you're not involved, but without realising it you may give them some information that helps."

I relaxed back in the chair and nodded. "Sorry, but can I at least go to Maisie?"

The copper looked down at his notes and nodded. "Yeah, I think I've got everything I need. I'll get on the radio and see if there's any more news."

As he left, I stood and looked around the room searching for Maisie.

"She's in his room," her dad said. "Jen is making her some tea, would you like one?"

Pinching the bridge of my nose, I nodded. "Please."

"Okay, I'll bring them up to you both."

As soon as he'd gone, I rushed up the stairs two at a time to find Maisie. She was sitting on the end of Frankie's bed, staring through his bedroom window into the darkening street outside. It was almost six o'clock and Frankie had been with Josh for almost two hours and it was too fucking long.

"Hey," I said softly. "How you doing?"

She looked up at me with tear filled eyes, chewing on her bottom lip. "Have they found Josh yet?"

"No, nothing yet, but they will. Have you tried his number again?"

Fuck knows why, but I'd been encouraging Maisie to give him

the benefit of the doubt, suggesting that he'd had a long term plan to take Frankie out for tea or something and forgotten the time. When she told me that Frankie hated Josh and would never go out with him, my veins started to itch and I had an innate desire to kill the fucker.

Maisie nodded and glanced down at the mobile clutched in her hand. "Nothing," she replied.

I sat down on the bed and without thinking took her hand in mine. I felt like a fraud feeling so anguished about Frankie going missing. I didn't have a right to be upset, but I knew it was helping Maisie me being here. For some reason I'd been able to calm her and when the police arrived and said they were looking for Josh, it was me she ran to and wrapped her arms around.

"How's Mum?" she asked, leaning her head against my arm.

"Making tea."

I breathed in deeply and momentarily placed my cheek against the top of her head. Although it was a brief connection, she calmed me too and I was glad we could be there for each other.

"It wasn't her fault," Maisie said breaking the silence. "She was on time, early in fact, but Josh had already taken him."

"I know, sweetheart. No one is blaming her."

"She is."

"Well she shouldn't." I rubbed the back of Maisie's hand with my thumb and looked over the top of her head through the window. "You have any idea where he might take him? Does he have a special place or anywhere they went to together."

"No, I can't think of anywhere and like I said, Frankie didn't like him, so he wouldn't go anywhere with him." Maisie suddenly let out a sob. "Do you think he'll hurt him?"

"No, he wouldn't do that."

I had no idea whether he would or not, but the fucker could bet his last penny that if he did I'd hunt him down and kill him with my bare hands. I was fucking petrified at what might happen to my son and I knew I'd kill for him if I had to.

Maisie's shoulders started to shake and her hold on my hand got tighter, my heart squeezing with the same intense grip. I couldn't believe this was happening, just as I'd got my head from up my arse and decided to get to know my son, he might be snatched away from me. Why the hell had I been such a selfish prick and stayed away all this time and maybe I didn't deserve to have this fucking time with him, but not at Maisie's expense.

"You okay?" I asked, once Maisie had stopped crying.

She nodded. "Sorry, but I'm just so scared, Sam. Josh hates Frankie just as much as Frankie hates him and Frankie winds him up, what if he lashes out at him?"

The rage inside of me boiled up and I clutched at Frankie's duvet to steady myself. "He lays one hand on him and I'll make him wish he'd never lived. I'll fucking kill him slowly."

"What were you doing here anyway?" Maisie lifted her head from my shoulder to look at me, tears still brimming at her lashes but no longer falling.

"It doesn't matter," I replied, shaking my head. "We'll talk once Frankie is home."

"No, go on."

I took a deep breath and slowly let it out. "I was coming to tell you I'm sure I want to be a dad to him."

Maisie sat up straighter. "Really? You've decided eh?" Her tone was hard and while it surprised me, it wasn't anything I didn't deserve.

"Yeah. I'm so sorry Maisie for the way I've treated you both. I should never have spoken to you the way I did at the hospital on the day he was born, I was a real twat. I'm not that man, the one that doesn't own up to his responsibility. I knew you weren't the

169

sort of woman who'd lie to me, but I was just so fucking scared, Maisie."

"So was I," she replied, letting go of my hand. "I had no idea how to look after a baby and I would never have expected anything from you, just a little support now and again. You know, take the strain and listen to me when I wanted to cry because I thought I was messing everything up and was being a crap mum."

"I don't think anyone could ever accuse you of that." I looked at her puffy eyes and knew I'd done her a total disservice all those years ago, thinking she'd be like Alison. "He's an amazing kid and that's all down to you."

She gave a slight shrug. "Thank you, but I've done plenty of things wrong with that boy. So, what's changed, Sam? Why now?"

"Spending time with him, I've seen how great he is and what I've missed out on, and I've realised a few things."

"Such as, because you have to understand this from my point of view, you don't want to know and then a few days of spending time with him and tah dah you're cured of being a twat."

"I know how it looks, but like I said, I swear I'm not that man."

"Yes and like I said, this isn't something you can pick up as and when you feel like it, Sam. If we tell him you're his dad then that's it, you're his dad."

"I know that and I'm ready."

"Okay, so tell me what you've realised, what's this great dawning light you've had?"

I paused wondering whether to spill my guts to her about what had filled my heart with blackness, what had turned me into a coward. Telling Elijah had lifted the blanket of cloud that had shrouded me for years and he'd reinforced what I already knew, I wasn't the one to blame. Alison had a duty of care and she'd disrespected that. Maybe it was time to pull the last vestiges of my shame away and start afresh, learning to be the sort of man a boy would be proud to call dad.

"When I was sixteen, I had a two year affair with my swimming coach. She was older and married and when I was just eighteen she told me she was having my baby."

Maisie's eyes widened as she reared back to look at me. "*What?*"

"I had a thing with my coach. She told me she'd left her husband and that *we* were having a baby, but when I went to the hospital on the day she gave birth, she admitted that she'd never left him and the baby was his."

"She was *your coach?*" Maisie's hands went to her mouth in shock. "You were a child, Sam."

"Yeah, I know and I was ashamed and felt stupid that she'd tricked me for so long and I guess I carried all of that with me and let it cloud my judgement when you got pregnant."

"That's awful Sam, but it's no excuse," she whispered wrapping her arms around her waist. "You spoke to me like I was shit. I was okay that you didn't want to be a dad, you stepped up financially and you never told me a pack of lies and then let me find out the hard way, but you should never have tarnished me with the same brush as a woman who cheated and lied for her own needs."

"I know that," I sighed feeling the shame rise within me. "And I regret treating you so badly. The least I should have done would be to help you take care of Frankie, taken my turn."

"Yeah," she scoffed. "That is the least you should have done. You have missed out on so much with him. He's an amazing little boy and you don't even know the half of what he's capable of. I get that what happened is a reason for you behaving that way, but don't use it as justification. You were a grown man who should have lived up to his responsibility, no matter what happened in the past."

"Well you didn't take it quite like Elijah did." I gave an empty laugh.

"Of course he's going to be sympathetic, he's your brother and so am I to a point, but I have Frankie to think about. He's my priority Sam, not you."

Leaning forward, I rested my forearms on my knees, wishing I hadn't mentioned anything about wanting to be in Frankie's life. I should have waited until he was home. Shit – time wouldn't make any difference, if I told her today or in a week's time, I'd still been a prick allowing my past to rule me.

"I'm sorry, Maisie. You're right, I know you are, but I just hoped it might explain why I did what I did."

I glanced over and watched as Maisie got up and moved to the window. She kept her back to me and I could see her shoulders tense under her thin t-shirt.

"I'll think about everything you've said, Sam," Maisie said without turning around. "And I won't keep you from Frankie, if that's what you want, but to say I'm disappointed that you forfeited time with him because you thought I might do the same to you as some bitch who should have known better, well that's an understatement. I know we didn't know each other that well, but you should have handled things so differently than you did."

She slowly turned around to face me and the disappointment in her eyes was almost as devastating as when I saw it in my brother's. I cared about her because she was a good person, and much more forgiving than I deserved, and maybe this was a step too far for her.

"I don't hate you, Sam."

Her words surprised me, because I was pretty sure I'd hate me if things had been reversed.

"I'm glad that you want to be Frankie's dad, but I'm scared too and I know you were young, but if you can make a huge decision of not to be in his life because a woman lied to you, well it worries me what you'd do to him if something else spooked you."

"It won't happen," I replied, shaking my head. "When he gets home you can dictate the pace and when we tell him, but it's what I want. If I'm honest I regretted everything three years ago when we met to talk about the money I was sending to you. I should've said something then, but didn't and then lectured Elijah about regret like the biggest hypocrite ever."

"So what stopped you saying something then?"

"I thought he had a dad in Josh? I didn't think I deserved it? To be honest I have no fucking idea, all I know is that I want this now, but I understand that you're in charge."

Maisie nodded and then turned back to the window. As I stood up to join her, she let out a cry.

"Maisie, what is it?" I asked, rushing to her side.

"More police are here. It's bad news, Sam, I know it is."

I looked down as two sombre looking officers walked up the drive and dread thundered around my body, knowing she was right.

24

the present

I rushed down the stairs, getting to the bottom just as the two officers were walking through the door.

"What's happened?" I cried, as I rushed toward them.

The woman officer turned and gave me a small smile. "Maybe you should go and sit down, Miss West."

"No, tell me. What's happened to Frankie?"

Sam appeared behind me and placed a hand on my shoulder. Even though I was angry with him, I was also glad he was there. I knew that if I crumpled through all of this he'd be there to catch me. He'd proved over the last week how supportive he could be, it was just a pity he hadn't been like that for the last eight or so years.

"Have you found him?" Sam asked.

"Please come and sit down, both of you." The male officer stood to one side and ushered us into my lounge where Mum and Dad were already sitting; Mum clutching Dad's hand.

"Tell me." My hands were trembling as I looked at the two officers, waiting for the words that I knew would change my life.

"We found Brent," the WPC said. "But I'm afraid he doesn't have Frankie. We picked him up at a petrol station and there was a scuffle when he resisted our request to talk to him, but your son

175

definitely wasn't with him. Because we know he took Frankie, and because he lashed out at my colleague here, we have him down at the station. We-.

I didn't hear anything else, because my legs buckled and the air rushed from my lungs as I let out a pained cry. Sam's arms came around me and I was lifted from my feet as he pulled me against his chest, rocking me slowly backwards and forwards, desperately trying to comfort me.

"It's okay," he whispered in my ear. "I've got you. I've got you."

I reached up and put my arms around his neck, holding on tightly as my world swayed on its axis.

"Where is he, where is he?"

It was a chant that no one answered, the only response being Sam's soft whispers of comfort as he carried me to an armchair and sat down, still holding me tight as I sobbed into his shirt.

"What has he said?" Sam's deep voice sounded in my ear, as he tried to make himself heard over my cries.

I didn't hear what the officers said, but startled when Sam roared.

"I'll fucking kill him. The bastard, he can't do this."

"W-what?" I hiccupped looking up at Sam. "What has he done?"

I pulled at Sam's shirt, desperate for him to look at me.

"*Sam.*"

My mum was suddenly kneeling in front of me, rubbing her hand up and down my back, but I could hear that she was softly crying too.

"Mum," I said, turning to her. "What's Josh done?"

"He wants to talk to you, love. He won't comment further until he's seen you."

As I gasped I felt Sam's arms tighten around me.

"You don't have to," one of the officers responded. "But it might help us find Frankie a lot quicker."

"I'll speak to the fucker," Sam growled. "Let me."

"I'm sorry Mr. Cooper, but it's Miss West he wants to talk to. We've arrested him on assaulting a police officer and Child Abduction."

"So fucking make him tell you where Frankie is."

"Sam," Dad warned. "Calm down."

The male officer looked at Sam with some sympathy. "We know this is hard, Mr. Cooper, but he's making no comment until he's seen Miss West, even though we have him on the school's CCTV taking Frankie off the premises."

"I swear to god, I will fucking end him," Sam growled. "He has to tell you, surely?"

"Sam no." I shifted on his lap and dropped my feet to the floor. "I don't care. I'll do it. Take me now. Take me to speak to him."

"Maisie, are you sure?" Sam asked, taking hold of my hand.

"Yes, I'm sure. I want my son back."

We arrived at the police station and were ushered into a reception area with a row of hard chairs and a high desk. The officer behind it gave us a sympathetic smile as we all sat down. I had Mum on one side of me and my dad on the other, both gripping my hands, while Sam prowled up and down like a caged lion.

"We'll get an interview room set up," the female officer I now knew to be called Tracy said. "Just give us a few minutes. Dan will stay with you."

She nodded to the uniformed officer who'd questioned Sam at the house and then she and Clive, the policeman she'd arrived with disappeared.

"This is ridiculous," Sam hissed. "He's holding you to damn ransom, how can they allow it?"

"Mr. Cooper." Dan went over to him and placed a hand on Sam's shoulder. "We are still looking, checking the CCTV from around town to try and track his movements and we're also questioning Mr. Brent's father, so if we can manage to avoid Miss West having to speak to him, we will."

"No," I cried. "I want to speak to him as soon as possible. I need to know where Frankie is."

Dan nodded. "We know and we will do whatever possible to make that happen. I promise."

We sat in silence for a few minutes, Sam's thudding footsteps the only sound, that and the crackle of anticipation at when I would be face to face with Josh.

I could tell Sam was getting more agitated with each passing minute, so I wasn't surprised when a door opened and two policeman came through guiding a cuffed Josh in front of them that Sam erupted with rage and went for him.

"You fucking bastard. Where is he? Where's our boy?"

He lunged for Josh, but Dan was too quick for him and with an arm around Sam's waist dragged him back.

"Sam, no," I cried pushing up from my chair.

"Mr. Cooper, leave it. Get back," Dan grunted as he tried to drag Sam away from getting himself into trouble.

As they struggled, with Sam throwing punches at Josh, a door swung open and Tracy came rushing out.

"What the hell were you doing bringing him through here, you pair of idiots," she yelled at the two policemen. "Get him out of here, *now*."

"I'll fucking end you, Brent, if you've harmed my boy in any way, I swear down I'll kill you."

The whole time Josh didn't say a word, but unflinching at the blows thrown his way, he watched carefully, his eyes on Sam the whole time.

"Sam." I wrapped a hand around his wrist and pulled on his arm. "He's not worth it."

"He's a fucking psychopath. Why would he do this to you?" His voice was strained with the pain that he was feeling as much as the rest of us.

"I'll talk to him," I whispered as Sam staggered back against my chest. "I'll find our son."

Sam swung around and let out a jagged sob. When I saw his eyes were filled with tears and his chest was heaving with emotion, I pulled him to me and wrapped my arms around him, feeling his anguish pulsing from every pore in his body.

"We'll find him, Sam."

"I'm so fucking sorry, Maisie," he whimpered against my neck. "So, so, sorry."

As we embraced, sharing our emotion, Tracy reappeared and gently touched my arm.

"I'm sorry about that," she said. "Some people just don't listen to instruction."

I pulled away from Sam, who wiped at his face and gave Tracy a small smile.

"It's fine."

"No it's not, but anyway, we're ready for you now."

"You sure about this?" My dad asked, appearing beside me.

"Yes. I want Frankie back."

I took a step toward Tracy when Sam pulled me back. He didn't say anything but hugged me tightly and kissed the top of my head before letting me go.

25

MAISIE

the present

Walking to the interview room, my hands began to shake and my heart beat picked up its pace. I hated that I had to sit in front of Josh and listen to whatever crap he wanted to say, but I wanted Frankie back more. I wasn't sure I wouldn't jump across the table and try and kill him, but I knew I had to stay calm if he was going to tell me where my son was. Tracy had said I didn't need to do it, and they would question him alone, but if there was any chance I could get my baby home then I'd take it.

"You okay?" she asked, placing a hand on my back. "You still sure?"

Biting my bottom lip I didn't hesitate and nodded.

"Right, well try and stay calm. Let him speak and don't rush him into telling you where Frankie is."

My face crumpled and Tracy sighed.

"I know, but we don't want him to clam up and if you don't let him speak, he may just do that. Like I said, we can't keep him much longer once we've put the charge through."

I managed a smile and nodded. "Okay."

"Good girl. I'll be in there with you and the duty solicitor, so you've nothing to worry about."

She pushed open a door and stood aside to let me into the small square room that held nothing but a table, four chairs, and one of the huge tape recorders that I'd seen countless times on TV police shows.

Josh's eyes met mine as I walked forward and I drew in a breath. I had to curl my fingers into my palms, my nails digging into the skin to stop myself from lashing out in his direction, especially as the look on his face was one of smug arrogance. He was dressed in a t-shirt that was torn at the neck and I wondered whether Sam had managed to do that when he'd lunged for him.

As I sat down I tried to keep my eyes off Josh, but it was difficult to ignore him when he was only a foot away from me. Tracy sat next to me and while she completed all the official procedures, Josh slumped back in his chair, his hands deep in his jeans' pockets.

"Okay," Tracy said, clearing her throat. "Do you want to start Mr. Brent, seeing as you were the one that asked Miss West to come here?"

Josh shrugged. "Just want to know why she threw me out."

"You know why." I rubbed my temple beginning to think this was a total waste of time. It was not only stupid, it was cruel of him to put me through it when all I wanted was my son back.

The tears I'd been trying to hold back started to creep down my cheeks as the pain gripped at my stomach. I wanted to get on my knees and beg him, but that would be what he'd want. He'd be loving having power over me; he always had to be in charge. I guessed over the last couple of years that was why he'd demanded I stop taking money from Sam for Frankie, because without it he was in control. I only wished it hadn't taken a bowl of cereal being thrown for me to realise it.

"It was one argument," he replied leaning forward. "One argument and you threw me out without one shit whether I had anywhere to go."

"You have your dad." I tried to keep my voice steady as I swiped the wetness from my cheeks and chin. "You raised your hand to Frankie and threw a dish of food at me, so I had no choice. Anyway, it wasn't just one argument and you know it, but it doesn't matter, you raised your hand to my son once too often."

Tracy placed a calming hand on my knee that was bobbing up and down. "You okay?" she asked quietly.

I nodded and turned back to Josh, waiting for him to continue.

"So you shagging him now, the kid's dad?"

"Mr. Brent," Tracy said with a sigh. "Is that really relevant? You asked to see Miss West, you've seen her so maybe you should tell us where Frankie is."

"I said I wanted to talk to her," Josh snapped. "And I haven't finished." His eyes were narrowed onto me as he tapped a finger on the table. "So answer me."

I straightened my shoulders and looked him in the eye. "No, I'm not. He wants to have a relationship with Frankie, but there is nothing at all going on between me and him."

Josh studied me for a few seconds and then whispered something to his solicitor.

"Mr. Brent would like it be known that he was still down as an authorised person on the pickup list at school and has been like a father to the boy for four years. Giving him guidance and providing for him financially."

My heart dropped because he was right – anyone on the outside of the nightmare would probably agree he hadn't done anything wrong. He was simply a man wanting to see the boy he had raised as a son.

"You shouldn't have taken him, Josh." I couldn't help the sob that came with my words, for all I was trying to appear strong in front of him, I wasn't and I would feel empty and lost until Frankie was in my arms. "You don't care about him, you don't even like him."

"Just catching up with him," he replied nonchalantly. "Are you going to let them have a relationship?"

I leaned forward, shocked that he would even care. "Yes, he's his father." I said the words without even thinking. Even after what Sam had told me and the latent anger I had at him not wanting Frankie, even questioning he was his, I had no doubt that I would let him have a relationship with his son. After a few short days I already knew he would be better for Frankie than Josh had ever been.

"So everything I did for him counts for shit. I raise my hand once and that's it, all the money I spent feeding and clothing him, the time I had to listen to that shit music he likes, take him to damn parties and swimming club, it's all for nothing because I'm not his father. Whereas his *father*," he said with venom, "can swan into his life after eight fucking years and do no wrong. Which kinda leads me to fucking believe you were already shagging him."

I shook my head breathing heavily through my nose as the anger rose up in me. "No, I wasn't. I haven't seen him for years, not until he took over coaching at the swimming club and you resented every single thing you ever had to do for Frankie, so don't pretend to me that you're hurt."

His eyes went dark and he shifted uneasily in his seat.

"Whatever," he scoffed.

A cloying silence fell over us as we watched each other warily. It was almost a battle of wills, but I wouldn't give him the satisfaction of seeing me break in front of him.

"Where is he, Josh? My son that you don't care about, where did you take him?" I kept my voice strong and looked him directly in the eye. "You're on the school CCTV taking him off the premises, so you're not going to get away with it, so just tell me where he is because I know you only did this to get at me, to upset me. Well you've managed that, so tell me where Frankie is, *now*."

Finally Josh curled his lip at me and spoke.

"He's with Marie and Carl Roberts, he's a guy I work with. Frankie is playing with their kids."

"Address?" Tracy demanded.

"Seventy-nine, Primrose Avenue and Marie and Carl have no idea we split, so don't even think about dragging them into this."

Tracy looked up at Clive who had come into the room without me realising. "Book him for the assault and Child Abduction."

"He hit me first," Josh bellowed. "And I was on the fucking list."

"You took a child out of the unlawful control of his parent, so it's abduction," Clive snapped.

Ignoring Josh's protestations Tracy got up, scraping her chair on the floor. "Okay, Maisie, let's go and get your son."

26

the present

The minute Frankie ran into Maisie's arms, I knew I would do whatever necessary to protect him in the future. He was fine at Josh's friend's house, playing with their kids, but he was obviously confused and worried and as soon as we got him outside and into my car, leaving the police behind to question the couple, Frankie burst into tears.

"Hey, come on," Maisie soothed, cradling him against her chest. "You're okay."

"You're not mad at me for going with him?" he sobbed.

"No, not at all. He was the one who knew he shouldn't have taken you." Maisie's voice cracked and she looked at me over the top of his head.

"But he said you'd said it was okay because you were at work and Nanna couldn't pick me up."

When Frankie let out another shuddering cry, I pushed my arm through the two front seats to the back where he and Maisie were huddled together. I placed my hand on his back, feeling the rise and fall of his sobs and I had to force myself not to push over the seats and wrap them both in my arms. I hated seeing my boy so

187

upset, and I hated seeing how much pain Maisie had been in – I wanted to protect them both with my life.

As I tried to regulate my breathing and remember that he was safe, a soft, warm palm cupped my cheek.

"He's okay," Maisie whispered. "We have him back."

I nodded and swallowed hard. "I know."

As we both stared at each other, Frankie lifted his head and sniffled.

"Can I have ice cream when I get home?"

His voice was quiet and timid, but the glint in his eyes was one I recognised from myself, and I let out a laugh.

Maisie rolled her eyes, holding Frankie away from her body and looking into his face. "You can't trick me Frankie James West. It's bed time when you get home and you know it," she said, with a little smile tipping her lips up at the corners. "Maybe tomorrow."

"Okay," Frankie sighed and snuggled back against her.

I watched them both and felt something in my world shift. My heart had never felt so full and despite the absolute fear that we'd experienced for the last few hours, I didn't think I'd ever felt more content. This kid was working his way into my soul. Every day he claimed another little piece of my heart, and with each piece he took, my guilt grew at a rapid rate. He had no idea I was his dad and that was all on me for being stupid and selfish, for being pathetic when I should have been strong and supportive.

Clearing my throat, I pulled my hand away from Frankie's back and started the car.

"I told the police if they need to question him, they can't do it until tomorrow. Is that okay?" I looked at Maisie through the rear view mirror, wondering if I'd over stepped the mark when she didn't answer immediately.

"Yes," she finally breathed out. "That's fine, Sam."

I waited to see if she was going to say anything else, but when her head dropped to rest against Frankie's, I put the car in gear and drove them home.

———

Frankie had been in bed for almost an hour and I was still finding it difficult to leave. I was fucking scared beyond belief that Josh would be let out and make his way back to the house. Every little sound had me jumping up from my seat on the sofa and going to the window, or standing in the hallway and listening.

"Do you think they'll let him out?" Maisie asked, worrying her bottom lip.

"They'd better fucking hadn't," I growled. "But I doubt it."

"So why are you so edgy then?" She managed a small smile, but I knew she was just as worried.

"I think I should stay again," I said firmly. "Until we know for sure what's happening with him."

I was surprised when Maisie didn't argue, but nodded. "Don't know about you, but I fancy a drink. You want one?" she asked.

"When you say drink, you talking about alcohol, because I've got to be honest Maisie after tonight, I could murder one."

"Alcohol it is then," she replied. "I think we both deserve one."

———

After almost half a bottle of vodka between us, my gut was warm and my head light. In fact, *everything* felt warm and relaxed. Maisie's cheeks were also pinker than usual and she was laughing loudly at pretty much everything I said. She was currently giggling as I told her the story of when Elijah and I were fourteen and sixteen and went skinny dipping on holiday and our clothes floated out to sea.

"So what did you do?" she asked, leaning closer.

We'd somehow both ended up on the sofa, at opposite ends, and Maisie had her legs up with her tiny feet almost touching my thighs.

"What else could we do? We ran to the hotel and scared half the resort to death as we streaked through with our white arses on show. Mum and Dad went ballistic with us when we got back."

"How did they find out?"

"They were waiting in reception for us because we'd forgotten to take the key to our room. Mum pointed toward our dicks and shouted 'I haven't seen those things for years and I don't want to see them now'."

Maisie doubled over laughing, giving me a great view of her cleavage and a hint of pink lace and I suddenly felt hot. The curve of her creamy white tits was perfect, her skin looked soft and smooth and when I got a waft of her delicate perfume my dick twitched in my jeans.

Clearing my throat, I reached for the bottle of vodka and held it up to Maisie. She nodded enthusiastically and held her glass toward me.

"You're really close then, you and Elijah," she said as I poured the alcohol.

"Yeah, there's only twenty-two months between us, so we've always been best mates as well as brothers. I lost touch with a lot of my mates when I decided I wanted to buy the business, they were out every night and I was saving my money, but Eli has always been there for me."

"You were there for him too."

Maisie lay back against the cushion, resting her glass on her stomach and I was momentarily mesmerised by the rise and fall of it along with her chest, with each breath she took.

Shit, how had I not remembered just how good her tits were?

As Maisie poked my leg with her toe, I looked up.

"Sorry, um, yeah I was there for him when Amy left. I couldn't not be, he was a fucking mess."

"I think it's beautiful that they got a second chance," Maisie sighed. "How many couples who break up manage to get that?"

I shrugged, feeling my jeans get a little tighter as she raised an arm behind her head, causing her t-shirt to rise and show me a flash of her stomach. A tiny bit of skin didn't normally make my dick hard, but I was mellow with booze and couldn't stop thinking about what might be beneath her clothes.

"So," I said, coughing and edging away from her. "How about you, you still see your mates from back in the day?"

Maisie curled her lip. "Nah, not really. When I got pregnant they were all busy going out. Hey," she said laughing and reaching up to slap my arm. "Maybe they were out with your mates."

"Yeah, maybe." I grinned at her, liking the way her happiness made me feel. "You've just had your family then for the last few years."

Guilt hit me again, knowing that I should have been there to help out too.

"I've made a couple of friends with the mums from school, Hannah from a few doors down has been great. She's had Frankie after school for me for a few times. Her little girl is in Frankie's class."

I looked down, avoiding Maisie's gaze, hoping she wouldn't see by my expression that I already knew. Hannah was my friend and had been the one who'd given me bits of information on Frankie for years. I glanced at Maisie and then up at the ceiling, toward where Frankie was sleeping. I'd kept too many secrets over the years and it was probably time I stopped before I really fucked my life up.

"I um, I know Hannah," I said tentatively.

Maisie shot up into a sitting position, and props to her, didn't spill a drop of her vodka that was clutched in her hand.

"You do?"

I nodded and exhaled. "Yeah, we used to be really good mates, but like I said I haven't seen much of my mates since I bought the business. She's told me a couple of things about Frankie over the years."

"Like what?" Maisie asked indignantly.

"Nothing major. Just that he was a great kid and was in Rosie's class."

Maisie's eyes went wide. "Have you slept with her?"

Her question surprised me, but her bottom lip jutted out sulkily making me smile.

"Shit, no," I replied. "We are strictly mates, have been since primary school. I don't look at her like that, apart from which I like Connor, her fella."

Then as if I *hadn't* told her I'd been practically spying on her and Frankie for years, she flopped back down and huffed.

"It doesn't matter," she said, taking a long gulp of vodka. "It's quite nice that you asked about him. Shows you actually cared when you didn't think you did."

I looked at her and watched carefully, wondering whether it was a joke and in any minute she was going to go mad and kick me out for having the nerve to ask about my son, but not having enough nerve to step up and be his dad. She didn't though, she took another sip of her drink and then sighed.

"You ever wonder what would have happened if your coach's baby had been yours?"

A little shocked by her question, I squirmed in my seat and swigged back the rest of my vodka.

"Well?" she urged.

"No, I tried to put her out of my mind as soon as I left the hospital. She ruined my life as far as I'm concerned – or was." I shrugged. "I guess a lot of that is on me for not having the balls or the brains to realise that what she did shouldn't have affected how I lived the rest of my life. Her actions shouldn't define me, and I let them, like a dick head."

Maisie's face was soft as brown eyes watched me and she let out a sigh.

"It was bound to affect you, Sam. I'm sorry I wasn't more sympathetic but you have to understand that Frankie is my main and only priority."

"Yeah I do," I replied, placing a hand on the top of her foot. "I totally get it and I didn't want your sympathy. You were right it should never have been an excuse, but it was a reason, that and the fact that I'm a prick."

Maisie laughed quietly and pulled herself into a sitting position. "Do you wish it had been your baby?"

The question was tentative and her eyes were wary as we stared at each other in the lamplight. She looked so damn pretty with her pinked cheeks and messy bun, and wearing just sweat pants and a t-shirt, and I felt a burn in my chest as she licked her plump lips, waiting for my answer.

"No," I said, shaking my head. "Because then I might not have Frankie and he's starting to mean everything to me. He's my main priority now too."

Maisie inhaled sharply and before I even had chance to blink, she slammed her glass down and threw herself on top of me.

27

the present

I couldn't help myself, I just had to kiss him. The alcohol helped, the emotion we'd been through contributed also, but the need was all me. He seemed so sad and genuinely sorry for what he'd done, but more than that, it was evident he cared a great deal about Frankie. Maybe he even loved him, because what had happened with Josh seemed to have caused him so much pain. I'd seen the look of distress on his face during the hours we'd waited for news and he didn't look like a man who didn't care.

I knew I should have kept my distance and I knew that if I started something, I'd probably end up regretting it, but I just couldn't not take the risk. All the reasons I'd found him attractive all those years before came flying back, like sand in the wind.

"Maisie," Sam groaned as my mouth left his to move to his neck. "We shouldn't do this."

"You don't want to?" I asked, with my fingers tangled in his hair. "Because how hard you are tells me you actually do."

"Fuck."

The next thing I knew, Sam had me flipped onto my back one hand cupping my face, while his other gripped my bottom. His hips took up a natural rhythm as he kissed along my jaw making a path to my earlobe which he pulled between his teeth.

"You have no fucking idea," he groaned.

"Idea...about...what?" I gasped, arching my back, desperate for friction to ease the ache my whole body was feeling.

"Every fucking thing."

Taking hold of my hands, Sam pushed them above my head, capturing both wrists and wrapping his fingers around them. His soft lips kissed down my neck and his free hand pushed my t-shirt up exposing my stomach. As he moved down my body, goose bumps broke out across my skin and hardened my nipples. My clit started to throb and everything he was doing wasn't enough. I needed so much more.

"So fucking beautiful," Sam said letting go of my hands and pushing my t-shirt over my head and throwing it onto the floor.

"Sam, please."

He nipped gently at my skin and hooked his fingers into the waistband of my sweat pants, slowly dragging them down my legs. Each second was torture as he pulled them down, laying gentle kisses on my skin as inch by inch it was revealed.

When he finally had them all the way down, he sat back on his haunches and pulled them off throwing them to land with my t-shirt. He stared down at me, a sexy grin lifting the corners of his mouth. Thinking of the thin lines of stretch marks, silvering across my skin, I laid my arm across my stomach, hoping to hide them. Sam shook his head and lifted my arm.

"You're beautiful."

"But-."

He leaned forward, a soft kiss halting my words.

"The things I want to do to you," he whispered against my ear, before sitting up and unbuttoning his shirt, slowly and deliberately.

The anticipation was almost enough to make me come as Sam revealed his beautiful toned body, his tattoos moving with each ripple of his muscles. I thrust my hips forward trying to entice him to do all those things he was thinking about and he knew I was desperate and gave me a knowing smile as I whimpered with need.

"You sure about this?" he asked as his hand went to the button of his jeans.

I nodded. I was more than sure. I knew it wasn't going to be the love affair of the century, it would be one night and that would be all, but in that moment I wanted it. I wanted *him* more than anything. More than the pain I would feel when he acted like it hadn't happened. More than the jealousy I would endure when he moved on with someone else. More than the shame I would feel when it hit me how rash I'd been. More than anything I needed him to fuck me. Help me to forget about the fear I'd felt for those hours that Frankie had been missing.

His eyes looked over every inch of me as I lay there in nothing but my underwear, waiting expectantly for him to undress. Finally, he unzipped his jeans and lowered them over his slim hips revealing his magnificent abdominal V. I'd seen them on guys in pictures before, when Denny had been lusting after them on the internet in the office, but never had I seen one in the flesh. I'd caught a hint of it when he'd taken Frankie swimming, but up close I simply needed to lick my tongue along it, appreciating it as if it was the best ice cream I'd ever tasted.

While I admired him lustfully, Sam climbed off the sofa and dropped his jeans to the floor, stepping out of them and toeing off his socks. He stood over me, giving me time to stare at his amazing body, his definition perfected from his years of swimming and his hard muscles perfected from I had no idea how. I licked my lips and as Sam prowled toward me his desire for me was evident in his hard, smooth dick and memories of what he was capable of in bed poked at my desire, making me wetter.

My eyes followed his every move, watching him bend forward and grab my ankles. He swung my legs around and pulled me gently so that my bum was on the edge of the seat and my feet on the floor. As I pushed into a sitting position, he kneeled down in front of me and spread my legs.

"Get rid of the bra, Maisie."

His voice was deep and full of meaning so swallowing hard, I reached behind me and unclasped it, letting the straps fall down my arms. The pink satin and lace dropped onto my lap and with the look of wonderment in Sam's eyes, I let out a gasp of excitement.

"Now the knickers," he commanded.

Mesmerised by his voice, I lifted my hips and slowly dragged my underwear down, and with every inch I kept my gaze on Sam who was fisting his rock hard cock. The sight of his hand wrapped around himself made my breath quicken and evoked a need in me that I'd never experienced before.

I knew at that moment I would do whatever he asked of me. I was relaxed from the vodka, but drunk on him. I was frantic for his touch, to have his mouth on me, to have him inside of me.

Keeping his eyes fixed on me, Sam bent forward and kissed along the inside of my thigh while his large hands covered mine as they gripped the sides of the seat cushion.

"I'm going to make you come so hard," he whispered against my skin. "So fucking hard."

I couldn't formulate any words, I was too engulfed by the need and desire that Sam evoked in me and when his tongue reached my clit and gave it one long lick, it took my breath away.

"Sam," I gasped, thrusting my hips upwards.

He moved his hands to my thighs, pulling them wider so he could edge forward and take my tiny bundle of nerves into his mouth and suck on it. When I let out a throaty moan, he inserted two fingers inside of me and moved them with a steady rhythm. I felt as though my body was on fire as waves of pleasure swelled inside of me. With each thrust I moved my hips forward, desperate for more, threading my fingers into his hair and pushing his head against me.

When I thought I was going to explode, Sam moved back and in one swift move pulled me from the sofa and down, hard, onto his dick, the shock and pleasure causing me to cry out. My legs wrapped around his waist, my arms around his neck and I clung to him as he used his strength to move me up and down. His fingertips dug into my waist as a slick sheen of sweat formed between us, our low moans mixing with the noise of our naked bodies as they slapped together.

"Fucking hell." The words fell from Sam's mouth. Breathing heavily, his strong, corded muscles continued to do all the work.

It was fast and hard and every time he went back inside of me, his dick caused a ricochet of pleasure. Every part of me was sparking. I was a tinderbox getting ready be set alight.

"*Sam.*" My orgasm hit me and stripped me of air, of logical thinking, and my senses.

I had never come so hard in my life. Never felt so much, been so consumed – ever.

As I cried out, Sam began synchronising his hips with the driving force of his arms, slamming me down onto him. Another wave mingled with the first that had still not ebbed away and the pleasure of the pain was too much to take.

"Oh my god."

Sam groaned loudly and called out something indecipherable as he came inside me. His hands moving to the small of my back to push me closer to him as he drove his hips up in the final throes of his own orgasm.

With both of us breathing heavily, I linked my arms around his neck and dropped my forehead to his shoulder that was damp with the sweat of his exertions.

"Wow," I said, my body heaving and rubbing my sensitive nipples against Sam's chest.

"You're not joking," Sam replied, wrapping his arms around my waist and kissing me softly underneath my ear. "Absolutely fucking perfect."

We sat joined and entwined for what could have been hours, I had no idea because at some point my eyes closed and I fell into a peaceful slumber. I wasn't totally asleep because I felt it when Sam lifted to his feet and carried me to the sofa. I heard when he gave a quiet groan as he pulled out of me and I snuggled closer to him when he laid us both down and pulled one of the blankets I'd brought downstairs for him, over the top of us.

When I felt him reach to turn the lamp off, I thought momentarily about the need to move, to go upstairs to my own bed, but my limbs were heavy, I was totally sated and was paralysed and spent.

"Just a few minutes," I muttered, making myself comfier on top of Sam's body.

I felt the kiss to my forehead and heard him whisper about being a fool and then I fell asleep.

28

the present

I was already in the kitchen making some tea and toast, when I heard her footsteps on the stairs. It had to be Maisie because it was too early for Frankie. I'd come to realise in the last couple of weeks how much my son enjoyed his sleep. The steps were also hesitant, another indication it was Maisie. Not only would Frankie have been thudding down the stairs, but I knew Maisie would be second guessing what we had done the night before.

As far as I was concerned there was nothing to think about – we'd had amazing sex; twice, and I wanted to figure out what that meant with her; I know I had my thoughts and hoped she was on the same page. After the first time, Maisie had snoozed on my chest for a while but then she'd woken up and wanted round two and I certainly wasn't going to disappoint her. She took control that time and with her on top, had made me come harder than the first time, which had been fucking epic. I then carried her up to bed, wrapped around me like a sleepy pider monkey. I hadn't wanted Frankie to find us sleeping naked on the sofa together, or even fully dressed, because even I knew it was a sensitive situation that needed to be handled with care with a kid of Frankie's age – and that was even before we told him about me being his dad.

When I'd tucked her under the duvet and moved to leave her there to grab a perch on the sofa, Maisie had grabbed my hand and given me a soft smile and if I hadn't have been knackered, and worried about Frankie wandering in, I may well have jumped into bed and spooned her all night. That thought made me take a mental step back, because when had I ever spooned anyone, or even wanted to spoon them, and how the fuck did I *even* know about spooning?

When I heard bare feet slapping on the kitchen tiles, I turned and gave her a smile, holding up the tea pot.

"Cuppa?" I asked. "Toast is already in the toaster."

Looking around tentatively, Maisie pulled her hair over to one side of her neck and the sight of her soft skin made my dick stir. She was dressed in denim shorts and a cotton vest, and without make up, looked as beautiful a woman as I'd ever seen.

"I take it Frankie's still sleeping," I said, turning back to finish making the tea and hide the bulge that was starting in my jeans. "I put all the cereal out, wasn't sure which one he'd want."

"He, um, he's hooked on *Coco Pops* at the moment," she replied in a barely audible voice.

Having poured tea into a mug, I turned to hand it to Maisie, who was staring at me, open mouthed.

"What's going on in your head?" I asked.

Maisie looked down at the mug and then back up to me. "I-I, I think we need to talk about last night."

"Okay. I'll get the toast, you take a seat."

I busied myself putting the slices of toast on a plate and getting butter from the fridge, all the time sensing the tension building up behind me. I'd known that she would feel strange so I'd already got my speech ready. I'd done nothing but go over and over it in my head while I'd lain wide awake on the sofa for half the night.

I put the toast in front of Maisie and sat down. "What do you want to say?" I asked, taking a piece of toast and buttering it, trying to make things as light as I possibly could. "I know what I think about it, but you're obviously feeling a little worried."

"A little worried. Sam, we had sex," she hissed.

"Yeah I know, twice." I gave her a grin and I didn't give a shit that it probably wound her up a little more.

"I am aware and I'm not saying I didn't want to, or that I was too drunk to know what I was doing, but you have to agree Sam, it wasn't sensible."

Maisie pushed her mug away, still not having picked up any toast, while I took a huge bite of mine and enjoying her discomfort a little bit, if only because her breathing was heavy and the vest top she was wearing was pretty tight. Also, I kind of liked the blush that was creeping over her skin as it reminded me of when she'd been about to come the night before.

"You're sitting here as if everything is perfectly normal." With both hands, Maisie pushed her hair away from her face and groaned up at the ceiling. "I know you've probably had a lot of one night stands, Sam, but I haven't – unless you count us all those years ago, and even then I didn't think that was what it was going to be."

"No, if things had been different and I hadn't got my head up my arse, it probably wouldn't have been, and neither was last night."

Maisie reared back in her seat. "You can't be serious?"

"Deadly. You sure you don't want any of this, I'm not a brilliant cook, but I do make great toast."

She shook her head and stared at me as though I had two heads and I knew I had to say what I wanted to say and I knew I'd have to give her time. I wasn't that much of an egotistical prick; I knew I had a lot of making up to do.

"I like you Maisie, I like you a lot and I'd like to see where things can go between us. I know it'll take time for you to trust me after everything I said and did in the past, but I swear I'm a different person now. Being around you and Frankie has made me see that I can't let my past spoil my future."

"That's all very honourable," she replied, rubbing her temple, "but just because you want to be a dad to Frankie, it doesn't mean that we should be together. You don't have to have me to have Frankie, as long as he's really what you want."

"You know it is." I tried to keep my voice steady. I had a lot to make up, but I'd been adamant I wanted to do better by my son, and after what had happened the day before, I thought she'd realise how serious I was.

"Okay," she sighed. "Maybe you do want Frankie, but that isn't dependant on you being with me. I'm not part of the deal."

"What if I want you to be?"

Maisie's hands flopped to her sides, dangling as though she'd been knocked out cold in her chair.

"I mean it Maisie, I want to see how things go between us. I've lain awake all night thinking about it and watching you in so much pain yesterday made me realise how much I care about you. I wanted to take it all away. I know it's a lot to think about, but I actually think we'd be good together."

"And what if we aren't?" she protested, startled back to life by my words.

"We won't know if we don't try."

"No! I can't do that to Frankie." Her voice was high pitched and more redness was spreading up her neck. "Do you have any idea how it's going to affect Frankie, when we tell him you're his dad? Which means we can't then force a relationship on him that might fail. Can you imagine what it would do to him to think he's getting a family and then to find out it's not going to happen because you decide you and me isn't what you want."

"I've changed, so don't judge me by my past behaviour." I let out a long, exasperated exhale. "I was a dick, I admit it, but I know now what I want. I know now that I should never have let what happened with Alison affect me in the way it did. I've missed eight years of my son's life because I was a stupid, self-centered cock who acted like a victim when I should have been braver and realised what my responsibilities were. I have done so many things wrong, Maisie, the biggest being letting my son down, but the other thing I should never have done was let you go."

"And what if I'm pregnant again?" she asked, jutting her chin forward in defiance. "What then, will you run away again?"

I had to admit, the idea was fucking terrifying and not something I was ready for, but what the hell could I say to her, except be honest about it.

"I admit it wouldn't be ideal and probably the worst thing possible at this point, but I wouldn't run. I wouldn't do that to you again – I swear."

That I did know to be the honest truth, I wouldn't; *I couldn't.*

Maisie swallowed hard and shook her head. "I can't do it, Sam. I've only just ended my relationship with Josh, the man who I lived with. What sort of person would it make me if I jumped into something with you?"

"You'd be living your life and being happy, because I'd work fucking hard to make sure you were Maisie, both you and Frankie."

The more I thought about what Maisie and I could be, the more I wanted it. I'd had a taste of it over the last couple of weeks and the night before I'd felt a shift in my feelings. Not just because I was buried inside her, feeling all the amazing sweetness and light that she had to give, but because I saw a glimpse of my future.

Me holding her.

Me giving her anything she wanted to take from me.

205

Me being the best man I could be for her.

I saw all those things and I wanted them. I wanted them with Maisie and I wanted my son. I wanted a life I knew I was worthy of.

"Could you be pregnant?" I asked as the thought popped into my head and hoping I didn't sound petrified. "We didn't use a condom."

"I'm aware how bloody irresponsible we were, Sam," she huffed. "But you're in the clear, I'm on the pill and clean."

I held in the breath of relief, knowing it would only serve to prove Maisie right in her misgivings about what I was asking for.

"I'm clean too. I had a health check a few months ago. If I wasn't sure, I'd have insisted and not put you at risk." I took a long drink of my luke-warm tea, watching Maisie carefully over the rim of the mug.

"I haven't had a check, but Josh always used condoms as well," she said with a scowl. "I think he hated the idea of having kids more than you do, so he wanted to be sure."

The sound of the prick's name sent the hairs on my arms on end. I still wanted to kill him for what he'd done and just wished I'd been able to get my hands on him. He'd have been begging for fucking death when I'd finished with him.

"I'm nothing like that prick. Well not any more. Told you, I know what I want now."

"Sam, you really are just having a gut reaction to what happened yesterday," she sighed. "You don't really want me. I promised you we'd tell Frankie, if it's truly what you wanted and I think you do, so in a couple of weeks, when you've spent more time with him, then that's what we'll do, but you and I," she paused, watching me carefully, "we aren't happening. I'm sorry, but deep down you'll be glad I didn't agree."

"No I won't, Maisie, but I'll give you some time. I'll prove to you that I've changed and that I'm worthy of both you and our son."

Maisie's chin wobbled and it took everything in me not to get up and pull her into my arms, but I knew she needed time to process what I'd asked for. I knew I'd kind of landed it on her, but I didn't want to live a life of regret any longer. It was time to give her some space, so I stood up and reached into the back pocket of my jeans and pulled out my wallet. The crinkled piece of paper had been in there a couple of days, but the day before hadn't been the best time to give it to her.

"What's this?" Maisie asked as I handed it to her.

I didn't answer, but let her unfold it and smiled when I heard her gasp.

"I can't accept this," she cried, the cheque shaking in her hand. "No way. Take it back."

She shoved the cheque at me, but I took a step back.

"It's yours and Frankie's. It's all the money that you never took from me after that prick Josh stuck his nose in. I had it put into a bank account. I thought maybe I'd give it to you when he went to Uni or got married, or bought his first house, but the time seems right now. And just so you know, I'll be going back to giving you regular payments."

I folded my arms over my chest, daring her to disagree but she didn't speak and just stared down at the cheque.

"Thirty-two thousand pounds, Sam," she whispered. "You can't afford this."

"I told you, it's what I was paying, plus some interest. I just had my solicitor pay it straight into a bank account instead, so I've never missed it. At the moment he's the only one that can draw from it, but we can change that if you'd prefer to leave it there and draw from it when you need it. Personally I'd prefer you take the cheque and pay it into your account, mainly because I know you won't use it otherwise."

"No I won't," she snapped. "Really Sam I can't take it."

"It's for Frankie, Maisie," I whispered leaning closer to her, getting in her space. "So take it."

Her breath hitched and I knew then that I affected her and I might have a chance.

She looked at me warily, her eyelashes fluttering as I knew she was working through everything that I had said.

"If I take it, I want it to go into an account in Frankie's name and for us to be co-signatures on it."

I nodded. That I could live with, even if I'd wanted it to provide her with some security too.

"That's it though, Sam. When the time is right, we co parent Frankie, but you and I isn't happening."

My eyes studied her carefully, taking in the heaving of her chest, and the blush and goose bumps on her skin.

"We'll see," I said. "Because by the time I'm finished, you'll wonder how you ever thought we wouldn't work."

Maisie's mouth dropped into a perfect 'o', and before I did anything too stupid I dropped a kiss to the top of her head.

"Tell Frankie I've gone home to change but I'll be back to take him to school." Maisie opened her mouth to protest, but the tilt of my head must have told her not to bother. "I want to be sure he gets in safely and you and I need to talk to the school about who is allowed to pick him up, because I'm going on that authorised list."

Leaving her staring at me and gripping the cheque tightly, I let myself out feeling a new determination to be the best dad I could be for my son and the best man I could be for the woman who I wanted to be mine.

29

the past

I looked down at the letter in my hand and read the contents again. No way was it fucking happening, I was not going to be accused of not providing for him. We'd agreed that I'd send money every month and if I was happy to stick to it then so should she.

Maisie's solicitor had contacted mine to say she didn't want my money any longer, because apparently her partner had insisted he would provide for her son. He sounded like a controlling knob to me and while I might have been just as big a knob in the way I'd abandoned my responsibility of him, I wasn't totally heartless. I knew kids cost money and just because Maisie wasn't single any longer, it didn't mean she shouldn't take the cash. She didn't have to spend it, she could save it for Frankie and I was going to try and make her see sense.

A flash of red caught my eye and screwing up the letter, I stepped out of my car.

"*Maisie!*"

I'd been waiting outside her office for around an hour, waiting to talk to her and there she was. I hadn't seen her for a few years, we lived on opposite sides of town and I suppose we'd both actively avoided each other, and I couldn't help but notice how good she looked. The red coat she was wearing was pulled in with a belt, showing off her slim waist, her long blonde hair hung down her back in loose curls and when she swung around to see who was calling her, questioning, big brown eyes stood out from beneath her fringe.

"Sam?" She took a half step back, her bag falling from her shoulder.

I walked toward her, still gripping the ball of paper in my hand.

"W-what's going on?" she stammered.

"You know why I'm here, Maisie. Why don't you want my money?"

"Sam, this is being dealt with by our solicitors, you shouldn't be here."

"As far as I'm aware you don't have a fucking restraining order on me, so I'm not doing anything wrong."

I stopped in front of her, noticing the tiny freckles scattered over her nose, remembering how I'd counted them during out night together. There were nineteen if I remembered correctly.

"If you've read the letter then you'll know why I don't need your money anymore."

She pulled her bag back onto her shoulder and straightened her back, but the little quiver of her top lip gave it away – she felt nervous and unsure.

"Listen," I sighed, moving back a couple of steps to give her space and shoving the paper in my pocket. "I know what it says in the letter but I'm not happy about it."

A noise behind me took Maisie's attention prompting me to look over my shoulder. A girl with short black hair was coming out of the estate agents where Maisie worked and was looking our way.

"My car is over there." I nodded toward my black Mazda sensing she felt uncomfortable. "I'll drive you home."

Maisie's eyes went wide with shock. "No. You can't do that."

"Do you have a car, because we obviously can't talk here?"

She looked over my shoulder again and sighed. "The bus stop will be fine."

Moving quickly, Maisie scurried past me to the car, darting a quick look over her shoulder.

"I take it you know her," I said, nodding through the windscreen once we were inside.

The girl was taking her time walking away, stopping every couple of yards to turn and look at my car.

"She works with me and is nosey as hell. Can we just go please?" Maisie pulled the seat forward, stuck her head down, and started searching through her handbag.

"Coast is clear," I said with a laugh as we pulled out of the main street onto a side road.

"Just pull up over there." She pointed to the bus stop.

"Well that was hardly worth it. Why don't you let me drive you home?" I slowed down but didn't stop. "We can talk on the way."

"Nothing to talk about Sam, you don't need to send the money any longer."

"But I want to." I pulled up and turned off the engine, determined to get her to see sense.

"Why? You didn't want him, so why insist on giving him money?"

"Because I don't want to be accused of not supporting him and I'm not that much of a twat. I might not have wanted to do the hands on dad thing, Maisie, but I do want to help."

She rolled her eyes. "We don't need your help."

She looked so damn defiant, with her little chin jutting out, her brown eyes shining with anger, I didn't find it difficult to remember what I'd seen in her. I'd liked her for a while before the party, but always thought she was too quiet and I'd be too much for her, but I'd been very wrong. She was funny and interesting and fucking hot in bed. She was pretty much perfect, it was me that had the damn issues that made me act like a prick, but I couldn't help how I'd felt about the prospect of fatherhood.

"You know the money is for F-Frankie," I said, stumbling a little over his name. "Not your partner."

"Of course I know," she snapped indignantly. "And so does he, he can provide for him, for us and doesn't want you to have to give us anything anymore."

"Controlling prick," I muttered.

"What did you say?"

I groaned and ran a hand down my face. "You know, you're just like my brother."

"Elijah?"

"Yeah, Elijah," I sighed. "His ex-wife is back and he still fucking loves her, but is too stubborn and too proud to tell her and is insisting on being in a relationship that doesn't fulfil him, with a woman he thinks he loves just 'cause she's *nice*."

"I'd say that makes him loyal."

"No Maisie, it makes him stupid."

"So, I'm stupid now, well thanks for that."

She reached for the door handle but before she could open it, I put a hand on her shoulder.

"Please Maisie, just take the fucking money."

She stopped and turned in her seat. "I have a picture of Frankie in my purse, do you want to see it?"

I didn't hesitate. "No."

To her credit, Maisie didn't falter. My words didn't seem to shock or hurt her.

"Didn't think so, well we don't want your money."

This time I didn't stop her, wincing the only movement I made when she slammed the card door.

"Fuck."

I dropped my head back against the headrest and let out another curse at the way I'd handled it. Maybe if I apologised, she'd see sense and take the fucking money. I wanted him to have it. I needed him to have it because the guilt I'd feel if he didn't would be in danger of choking me. I'd left the kid without a dad, the least I could do was help financially, plus my own damn ego didn't want that label stuck to me for the rest of my life.

When I looked back through the windscreen, Maisie was nowhere to be seen, all that I could see was the back end of the bus disappearing up the road.

With regret and anger, I pulled out my phone and stabbed at a couple of buttons, bringing up my gallery of photographs. Finding the one I wanted, I opened it up and sighed. It was a picture of my friend Hannah's kid, Rosie. It was her birthday party and she was wearing a pink tutu and tights and was holding a fairy wand. She looked cute, but it wasn't her I'd asked Hannah to send me the picture for, it was for the boy in the background wearing a Super Man costume with earbuds in and an iPod in his hand – that boy was my son.

30

MAISIE

the present

My eyes shifted sideways to catch a sneaky glimpse of Sam, wondering what the hell was going on in his head. He'd done exactly as he'd said he was going to do – got changed and then came back to take Frankie to school. Frankie was delighted, but when he looked at Sam through one squinted eye, I knew he was trying to figure out *why* it was happening and *why* Sam had been with me when we'd picked him up from Josh's friend's house. The night before he'd been too upset, or maybe too tired to ask, but when we'd got into Sam's Range Rover to go to school I could see the cogs working in my son's brain. The time was definitely getting closer to when we would have to tell him who his dad was.

"Something you want to say, Maisie?" Sam asked, drumming his fingers on the steering wheel in time to the music he was playing.

"Nope."

I had plenty to say, plenty that I wanted to ask him, but I didn't. Instead I sighed and looked through the side window watching the clouds that were gathering and darkening the sky.

"Play that one again, Sam," Frankie chirped up from the back seat. "It's really good."

"I can't believe you haven't heard that one before," Sam replied.

"I don't think I have. What's it called?"

As the song started to play again, Frankie began to sing along to it, tunelessly.

"Soul Time by Sarah Ellis."

Sam joined Frankie's sing-a-long and it suddenly became obvious why Frankie was tone deaf – so was his dad.

I looked between Sam and Frankie and shook my head. "You two are awful."

"I think we sound good," Sam quipped, a huge grin on his face. "Don't you, Frankie."

"Yeah Mum, we sound excellent."

Frankie giggled as Sam held up a hand to high five him and after what had happened the night before, that was one sound that I didn't mind listening to.

With Sam and Frankie singing along to each song that played, we carried on to the school and as we got closer, I began to feel more and more emotional. It was stupid, but the thought of being at the place from where Josh had taken my son was making my stomach churn.

"Stop worrying." A large hand landed on my thigh. "He's locked up and the school won't cock up again."

My eyes were pinned to his profile as he carried on driving; trying to soak up his confidence and composure. I couldn't afford to crack up and needed to stay calm for Frankie's sake – to see me losing control would only serve to upset him.

"I was so scared," I whispered, failing at holding the words and emotions in.

Sam briefly took his eyes from the road to flash me a sympathetic smile. "I know, we all were, but he was safe and he's home now."

His hand on my leg squeezed gently and I felt my heart beat faster. My eyes widened with surprise as a whole host of feelings rushed through me, while pictures of the night before danced before my eyes causing my skin to heat up.

"Are you okay, Mummy?" Frankie's voice sounded small and scared and I felt guilty for worrying him.

"I'm fine sweetheart," I said brightly, looking between the seats. "Just being silly."

"I promise I won't ever go with Josh again," he replied, his chin lowering to his chest. "It was because he said Nanna wasn't coming."

"I know," I soothed, reaching to rub a reassuring hand up and down his leg. "It was not your fault, so don't ever think it was. Josh did a bad thing lying to your teacher and he only did it because he was mad at me. So, don't you worry, okay?"

His long lashes swept against his cheeks as he closed his eyes and nodded slowly.

"Good, now let me hear you singing again, it was actually pretty good."

Frankie's cute little face broke into a smile, his freckled nose screwing up and his teeth showing.

"I told you we were good."

With that, he and Sam continued singing until we reached the school.

"I can't apologise enough, Miss West," Mrs. Rowntree, the headmistress said. "But Mr. Brent was still on the authorised list."

"I understand," I sighed. "I should have let you know, it's just all happened so quickly, I forgot to call and tell you."

Sam sat silently, listening to our exchange and with every word of apology from Mrs. Rowntree and Miss Carmichael, the teacher who had let Josh take Frankie, his jaw had tightened along with the grip he had on the coffee mug in his hand.

We had been in the office for over half an hour and he'd barely uttered two words and I was beginning to wonder if he'd changed his mind about the whole parenting thing. I got that talking to teachers wasn't something he was used to, it was out of his comfort zone, but he'd been the one who had insisted that he came with me.

"He's been removed now," Miss Carmichael replied, twisting her fingers together. "And I can assure you Frankie will not be put in the care of anyone other than yourself, your parents, or your sister." She glanced down at the list in front of her, obviously checking her facts.

"You need to add me to that." Sam's deep voice boomed.

Mrs. Rowntree looked at him quizzically, glanced at the list in Miss Carmichael's hand and then looked back up to me.

"This is..." I cleared my throat. "Mr. Cooper is Frankie's father, but we'd prefer if you didn't broadcast that," I said, glancing at Sam. "Especially to Frankie."

Initially I'd only introduced Sam as Mr. Cooper and not explained who he was, so it was no surprise when the headmistress tried to hide her shock, but I heard the slight gasp and saw how she reared back slightly, seeing as Sam had never been in the picture before.

"It's complicated," I explained as Mrs. Rowntree looked between me and Sam.

"Could you provide a photograph for the records, Mr. Cooper?" Miss Carmichael started to scribble on the list and then looked up at Sam.

Sam nodded curtly and reached around to the back pocket of his charcoal grey suit trousers and pulled out his wallet.

"I have a spare passport photograph in here I think."

After a couple of seconds, he pulled out the small picture and passed it to the clearly stressed young teacher. She took it from him with a slight shake in her hand and reached for the stapler on Mrs. Rowntree's desk, attaching it to her list.

"Thank you," she said quietly.

"Miss Carmichael, we don't blame you."

She looked up at me and her eyes were suddenly full of emotion. "I should have checked, especially as Frankie wasn't sure he should go with him."

Mrs. Rowntree gave a quiet groan, while Sam growled beside me.

"He didn't want to go with him?" he asked, leaning forward and slamming his mug down on the desk.

"Frankie was a little unsure, that's all." The headmistress looked at her employee and blinked slowly. "That's right isn't it Julia."

Miss Carmichael nodded vigorously and looked between me and Sam. Her neck was bright red and I could see a thin sheen of sweat on her top lip.

"He didn't refuse or anything like that, he just said he wasn't sure he should. Mr. Brent seemed genuine though, he told me and Frankie that Frankie's grandmother couldn't make it, so you'd sent him. I just thought Frankie was being cautious because he'd been expecting Mrs. West."

"And you didn't think that maybe it was because he didn't *actually* want to go with him?" Sam's nostrils flared as he shook his head in disbelief. "Did you not ask him *why* he didn't want to go with him?"

Miss Carmichael bit her lip and shook her head.

"Mr. Cooper," Mrs. Rowntree sighed. "We are where we are and have learned from it. We are going to change our process;

we're now taking photographs and the school secretary will contact the child's main guardian every term to ensure that the list hasn't changed. We are also considering issuing some sort of pass card too, but rest assured nothing of this nature will happen again."

"All great ideas, Mrs. Rowntree," Sam replied. "But the fact of the matter is, Frankie didn't want to go with Brent and you still let him take our son."

My heart tripped from its regular beat when Sam said the words 'our son', and it scared me how much I liked hearing it.

"I am so sorry, Mr. Cooper."

Miss Carmichael was almost in tears now and while she'd helped to create the scariest experience of my life, I couldn't help but feel sorry for her.

"I think we all could have done things differently," I said and, for Miss Carmichael's benefit, I copied Sam's comforting move from the car and put my hand on his thigh "I should have ensured I told you that Josh was off the list, but you should have listened to Frankie, and taken note of his hesitancy."

Mrs. Rowntree nodded and folded her hands in front of her on her desk.

"We apologise again, wholeheartedly. We can promise you nothing like this will happen again and hope you can both feel confident that Frankie is safe here."

I nodded. "Yes, we do."

Sam didn't answer, but nodded with a sharp exhale of breath.

When Mrs. Rowntree pushed back her chair, Sam's pushed to his feet and shoved his hands in his pockets. Anger was seeping from him, which in turn pissed me off. All of a sudden he was the concerned father. After eight years of nothing he now felt it was okay to go into my son's school, the one I chose, the one that had served him perfectly well so far, and tell everyone what they'd done wrong. I then remembered the look of absolute fear on his face the night before and I understood. He'd fallen in love with his son and the thought of losing him had been too much to bear. At least it proved that I'd been right to let him into Frankie's life – but whether that included me, well of that I wasn't so sure.

31

the present

It had been almost a week since Josh had taken Frankie, and he had been charged and was awaiting sentencing. Maisie was adamant she didn't want to go to court and find out what the bastard got. Initially I had wanted to but if I was honest, I'd probably have jumped into the fucking dock and punched him, so decided whenever his court date was, I'd be best staying away.

As for Frankie, well he seemed none the worse for what happened. Yes, he'd been worried when Josh picked him up and unsure whether he should go, but to all intents and purposes he'd gone on a play date and had some fun, his biggest concern being he'd upset his mum when he saw how upset she was. It amazed me how quickly kids bounced back and I had realised I had a lot to learn about parenting.

Over the week I'd see Frankie a couple of times, for a cinema visit and a trip to the Football Museum, but the kid was smart and at the cinema had actually said, "So what's the deal, Sam? How come you're doing things with me, are you wanting to take my mum out and daren't ask me if it's okay? 'Cause you don't need to spoil me, I'd say yes."

I had to admit it floored me and I wanted to confess every-

223

thing; that I was his dad *and* wanted a relationship with his mum, but I knew Maisie would have my balls if I did. Instead, I told him that I liked him and his mum and maybe in the future I'd like to take her on a date but for now was happy to be friends. He looked at me as though he didn't believe a fucking word, but didn't say anything, only nodding and then running off to the pick 'n' mix sweets.

I was now about to teach the swimming lesson and Frankie was already in the pool, seeing as I'd picked him up. We'd had a splash around, even though he'd wanted me to watch him do laps, but I wanted him to enjoy swimming too, so had insisted he wait for the lesson. He'd pouted but as soon as I splashed him, he soon decided he was happy to play.

"Okay guys," I called to the group. "Get yourself into the water and duck right under."

They all moaned a little, except for Frankie and a petite little girl called Sophia, but were soon dropping into the water and submerging themselves. Timothy, as usual with everything we did, struggled a little and bobbed around until he finally just pushed his face into the water.

"You okay?" I asked him, squatting down on the poolside.

Timothy gasped and nodded. "Yeah, I'm okay. It's a bit cold, Sam."

"I know buddy, which is why you need to get your shoulders under too."

Timothy took a deep breath and tried to push himself under, but he just floated to the top again. Thankfully the pool was heated, albeit a low temperature, so he'd get used to it soon enough.

"Right, everyone against the wall and you're going to show me a width of breast stroke."

A couple of the boys giggled and Frankie and the two girls in the group rolled their eyes. I smirked to myself thinking that there were some aspects where Frankie was nothing like me.

The kids had done some drills and I'd just called them to my side of the pool using back stroke when I saw Timothy starting to struggle. He'd been in the middle of the pack, I guessed he'd either been hit by a flying arm or had cramped up. There was no real danger of him drowning, but because the others were all kicking and splashing, I couldn't see him and my heart rate spiked. I blew two sharp whistles to indicate someone was in trouble and trying not to panic, looked amongst the kids who were in a cluster in the small section of pool we'd been using. After what can only have been a couple of seconds, I saw Timothy's hands thrashing against the water as he struggled to keep afloat. Spotting the flash of the red costume of Paula the lifeguard on duty, out of the corner of my eye, knowing Timothy was too far away to catch the life buoy I didn't hesitate any longer and dived in.

When I reached him, his limbs were lashing out and an arm smacked me right in the chest as he continued to panic. He was now getting tired and getting more anxious which was affecting his breathing, which in turn was intensifying his fear. Furiously treading water, somehow I managed to grab him under the arms and pull him against me. At first he fought with me, thrashing out with his arms and grabbing at my head, but once I got the crooks of my elbows under his arms pits he started to calm down.

"You're okay Timothy," I said, my mouth close to his ear. "I've got you. You're not going to drown."

He gasped in the air, his little chest heaving and tears mixing with the pool water on his face. As I swam backwards to the poolside, the poor kid began to sob, but thankfully let me pull him along without any further struggle.

When we got back to the side, all the other kids were standing along the edge, holding themselves tight and shivering. Sophie was comforting Molly, one of the younger girls, and Toby, the kid who always had a smart comment whenever Timothy struggled with anything, was crying quietly, his shoulders shaking as he swiped at his face.

As Paula and Kieran, another lifeguard, pulled Timothy out onto the side, my eyes searched for Frankie. He was standing right near the edge his body hunched over, hands between his knees and mouth open. My heart stalled as I looked at him and saw awe in his eyes and I had never felt so humble.

"These kids should have been sent to the changing room," I snapped as I pushed myself out of the water.

"They wouldn't go." Paula looked up at me as she wrapped Timothy in a huge towel. "They wanted to be sure Timothy was okay."

I looked around the pool to see the other groups that had been having lessons had all disappeared and my group were the only ones still there, their gasps and sniffles echoing around.

Kieran took over from Paula, checking Timothy's breathing and pulse rate and asking him questions.

"Come on kids," Paula said, ushering the group along. "Let's get you all into the changing rooms."

As they all started to file away, a loud screaming sounded around the pool. Everyone stopped to watch Timothy's mother racing towards us calling out his name. As she got nearer, a small hand slipped into mine and when I looked down I saw it was Frankie's.

At huge lump of emotion lodged in my throat as he stepped

closer to me and wrapped his other hand around my wrist. I didn't think I'd ever felt so tall and yet so small all at the same time.

"Oh my god, Timothy. Are you okay?" His mum threw herself at him, pushing Kieran out of the way. "I nipped out to get some bread from the shop on the corner. When I got back everyone was crowded around the café window, they were watching and Molly's mum said it was you. Oh my baby."

She pulled him into her arms, smothering him with kisses and wrapping the towel tighter around him.

"He's fine," Kieran said, putting a hand on her shoulder. "I've checked him out and there's no damage, he's just a little shocked and needs to be kept warm. Maybe a hot, sweet drink will help."

"Oh god, I can't stand the thought you might have drowned," Timothy's mother sobbed. "And I wasn't here."

"Honestly, he wasn't in danger of drowning," Paula added. "From what I saw he was panicking, but we got to him pretty quickly."

Timothy's mum looked up at Paula with tears in her eyes. "Who saved him?" she asked.

"Sa-." Paula started, but Frankie cut her off.

"My dad," he called out. "My dad saved Timothy."

32

MAISIE

the present

Sam had called me from the Leisure Centre to let me know what had happened with the poor little boy and of course what Frankie had said. I swear he was crying, or had been, because his voice was thick and full of emotion and he kept sniffing.

I couldn't help but wonder how Frankie knew, wondering if Josh had told him in a spate of temper on the day he'd taken him, but I would have thought Josh would have let that one slip at the police station. I supposed all the time Sam had spent with us must have made Frankie wonder why he was doing it, but I never for one minute expected him to guess the truth.

When we spoke, Sam and I agreed that we no longer had a choice and when they got back we'd sit Frankie down and talk to him. Which was why I was sitting on the arm of a chair and looking through the lounge window, waiting for Sam's car to appear. I didn't have to wait long, because within a couple of minutes the big, black Range Rover came along the road.

Sam pulled up onto the drive and in an almost synchronised movement, father and son stepped out of the car and with a similar gait to each other walked up the driveway to the door. I stood and turned, waiting for them to come in.

"Why is the front door unlocked?" Sam asked, barely in the lounge.

I rolled my eyes. "I knew you were on the way back."

Preferring to speak to Frankie than argue with Sam about whether my doors were locked or not, I looked past him to Frankie who was trailing in behind him.

"Hey, you okay?" I asked, going to him and pulling him against me. "I bet it was scary, wasn't it?"

Frankie nodded his head against my stomach. "Yeah, but Sam was amazing."

Sam drew in a breath and rubbed a hand down his face.

"Has he said anymore?" I mouthed silently.

Sam shook his head and nodded toward the sofa.

"Hey," I said, lifting Frankie's chin so he was looking up at me. "You think we'd better talk?"

His eyes darted to Sam and then back to me. "Yes please."

I moved to the sofa, taking Frankie's hand and pulling him with me. Sam took the chair opposite and cleared his throat.

"So what you said at the pool," he started. "What made you say it?"

"Is it not true?" Frankie asked, looking at me.

"No sweetheart, it's true." I grabbed his hand and gave it a quick squeeze. "How did you find out?"

Frankie shrugged. "I guessed."

"What helped you to guess?" Sam asked, leaning forward with his forearms on his knees.

Pulling his hand from mine, Frankie got up and stood in front of Sam. He didn't speak but lifted his hand and pointed a finger at Sam's eyes and then his own. As silence hung in the air Frankie's finger went to Sam's ears before moving to his. Father and son stared at each other and I felt as though my heart was going burst through my chest, it was beating so hard. Frankie was so young yet stood himself as tall as he could while pointing out all his like-nesses to Sam with a shaky finge,r and it was evident they shared something else - vulnerability; Sam was scared of failing while Frankie was scared of rejection and was plainly worried that Sam might push him away, despite how much he looked like him. Finally, very slowly Frankie pointed at Sam's lips and then touched his own as I let out a ragged breath. How I wished things could have been different and that Sam had had more faith in himself so they could have shared the joy of being father and son for the last eight years.

"We look the same," Frankie stated, looking over his shoulder at me. "We like the same music and we're both brilliant swimmers."

Mine and Sam's eyes met over the top of ours son's dark head and we both smiled widely, Sam shaking his head at the same time. That was another thing; my son had his father's confidence too.

"And how do you feel about it?" Sam asked, reaching forward and taking Frankie's hand.

Frankie's attention went back to Sam and he shrugged. "I don't know, how do you feel about it?"

Sam looked to me.

"I know I always told you that your Dad went away and didn't know about you." I wondered whether my lie would hold up now, or whether we should come clean with Frankie. I didn't want him to feel animosity toward Sam, purely for his sake because I knew he was at a point in his life when he needed his father. I only hoped Sam held up his end of the bargain.

"That's not true though, is it?" My little brainbox replied, still looking at Sam.

I held my breath, watching them both carefully, wondering whether this was to be the shortest lived reunion ever.

Sam blinked slowly and shook his head. "No Frankie it isn't. I treated your mum badly and told her I wasn't ready to be a dad, but I want you to know that it wasn't you specifically I didn't want, I didn't want any child."

Frankie tilted his head and studied Sam thoughtfully, and I took it as a good sign that he left his hand in his. Finally, he took a deep breath and took a step forward.

"Why did you change your mind? Is it because you want to take Mummy on a date?"

I gasped and opened my mouth to deny anything of the sort, but Sam flashed me a look that begged me to let him speak.

"No. I changed my mind because I realised I'd been wrong all those years ago. I realised what an idiot I'd been because you are *the best* little boy I have ever known. You're funny, clever, and brave, and you have great taste in music."

Sam gave a quiet laugh, but Frankie didn't respond, remaining impassive as he watched Sam.

"Why were you an idiot?"

"Frankie, that's rude to call Sam an idiot," I admonished.

Frankie turned to me and shrugged. "He said it first."

"Frankie's right," Sam said. "I was an idiot and it was because of something that happened to me." When Frankie opened his mouth, probably to ask what had happened to him, Sam held his hand up and continued.

"I'm not going to tell you what that was, not yet, maybe when you're older, but it made me think stupid things and act stupidly. Spending time with you though, has shown me how much I've missed and I really regret that."

"If you're going to be my dad does that mean you're going to live here with us?"

I sagged back in my chair, desperately not wanting Frankie to think that we were suddenly going to become a family. I knew after the night we'd had together I was falling for Sam all over again, but I had to protect my heart in order to protect my son's, which was why Sam and I couldn't happen – not unless I trusted that he truly wanted us for life.

"No buddy," Sam said with a little smirk on his lips. "Not all mum and dad's live together."

"But you like Mummy, I know you do. You told me you wanted to take her out on a date one day and I said you could."

"What?" I asked shocked. "And who said it's up to you?"

Frankie shrugged one shoulder. "I just thought as the man of the house, I should give him permission."

I couldn't help but laugh and knew exactly why Samuel Cooper had fallen in love with his son; how could he not.

"The point is," Sam said trying to hide a grin, "it's not enough to like someone. You need to love them to live together."

"So you don't love me? Is that why you won't live here?"

The colour drained instantly from Sam's face and he looked as though he'd been punched in his stomach.

"Of course I do," he replied vehemently, pulling Frankie to him. "I am so sorry that I haven't been in your life, but I'm here now and I love you, don't ever forget that."

Sam's arm moved tentatively toward Frankie and he hesitated for a few seconds before pulling him into a hug. Clutching him to his chest, his arms wrapped tightly around his son's small body, I watched with tears stinging my eyes as Frankie hugged him back. As he laid his head on Sam's shoulder, Sam buried his nose in his hair and breathed him in and closed his eyes as he relished every moment.

Their hug lasted a couple of minutes and I almost wanted to tiptoe from the room, feeling like an intruder on their moment, but I couldn't drag myself away. The scene in front of me was what I'd wanted for my son from the moment he'd let out his first cry. There'd been a time when I thought Josh might have provided him with the fatherly security he needed, but I'd been so wrong on that one. I just hoped I wasn't wrong this time.

Frankie was the first to pull away and I had to smile when Sam seemed a little reluctant to let him go – oh how things had changed in a few short weeks.

"Do I get to meet my other Nanna and Grandad now?" he asked.

"If you want to." Sam's voice was a little tight.

"You don't want him to?" I asked, hoping Sam wasn't already about to let him down.

"God, yeah. I just know my mum is going to freak out and go crazy with grandma hugs and kisses. I'm not sure Frankie will be up to it."

Frankie grimaced and then shrugged. "A man has to do what a man has to do," he announced.

Sam and I started to laugh, earning a look of despair from our son.

"What do I call you?"

His sudden question quietened us both as we both stared at him. Sam swallowed deeply and rubbed the back of his neck.

"What do want to call me?" he asked.

Frankie let out a frustrated sigh. "Dad, of course."

Sam's gaze swiveled to meet mine as I whimpered.

"Are *you* okay with that?"

I nodded biting my bottom lip, desperately trying not to sob with the emotion of it all.

Sam looked back to Frankie and gave him the warmest smile I'd ever seen. There was no doubting it was full of love and pride.

"I'd love that," he said.

Frankie nodded and said breezily. "Okay. Can we go for burgers then Dad, I'm starving?"

I would never want the boy in front of me to change, he was loving and funny and he faced everything with gusto and when I looked at the beaming smile on Sam's face, I knew he felt that way too and I was hopeful for the future the two of them would have together.

33

the present

Most people have a time in their life when they realise that it's pretty much perfect and nothing else at that moment could top it. Yes, there may have been periods where they had more money, or a better job, but something in the background was causing a blot on their happiness, but there will be a week, a month, a year or even a day where every single planet aligns to ensure they have everything that makes them happier and more content than they've ever been, and I was in that moment. Driving onto my parents' driveway with my son sitting next to me and the woman I was falling deeper and deeper for in the back seat, I wasn't sure I would ever feel the same level of bliss again.

I knew it had to be an about turn of the most mammoth proportions, but I was at peace with it and how right the change in my circumstances felt. I wasn't sure getting to know Frankie before now would have had the same affect, and I would never know, but I was grateful for the here and now and determined to make it work.

"You okay?" I asked Frankie, rubbing a hand over his head.

He nodded, barely looking at me and clutching the bunch of flowers he'd insisted on bringing for my mum.

"You know they're really looking forward to meeting you?"

He nodded again and I was pretty sure one of the stems had broken when his knuckles went white.

Maisie leaned between the two seats and placed a comforting hand on his shoulder. "Sweetheart it's going to be fine. They're probably as nervous as you are."

"Really?" his tiny voice asked.

Maisie nodded and then it was my turn to put a comforting hand on her, placing my large one over the top of her small one. I knew she was feeling just as anxious as Frankie and had said she'd stay at home, but I'd insisted. If I was to persuade her that I wanted her in my life and that I was serious about being a good dad to Frankie, she needed to be involved and see for herself how much I had changed.

Her big brown eyes landed on mind and she gave me a nervous smile before turning back to Frankie. "Yes, really. Me and Sam..." she quickly glanced at me and then corrected herself, "your dad, will be there so there's really nothing to worry about."

Sensing if I didn't get them out of the car soon, I might struggle, I quickly opened the door. "Okay then," I said brightly. "Let's go and eat some of your grandma's apple pie."

"We don't have to eat firsts first?" Frankie asked, eyes wide and suddenly sounding more than eager to get inside and meet his new family.

"No," Maisie responded quickly. "Lunch first."

Frankie rolled his eyes at me as if to say 'she's the no fun parent' and I couldn't help but chuckle.

"Come on," I said, scruffing his hair. "Let's get those flowers to your grandma before you strangle the life out of them. Oh and don't forget, you can ask Elijah all about *Only Fools & Horses*."

We'd had the chat about what he was going to call everyone and Frankie had been adamant that my mum and dad were going to be Grandma and Grandpa, as he already had a Nanna and a Grandad. I had to admit it had made me feel a little emotional that he wanted to acknowledge them as his grandparents and I knew my mum and dad would probably burst with fucking pride when he did. They obviously knew we were visiting, but I hadn't mentioned Frankie's decision on their names, so I couldn't wait to see the look on their faces. I'd also discovered his love of the comedy that my brother was obsessed with; more proof that Frankie truly was a Cooper.

As we approached the house, the front door was swung open and Mum and Dad came barrelling out like two eager puppies let outside for the first time.

"Hey Mum," I said, leaning in to kiss her cheek.

"Oh Sam," she whispered. "He's adorable."

Pushing me to one side, she moved to stand in front of Frankie, a hand going to her mouth as he thrust out the flowers to her.

"These are for you, Grandma." His voice was a little shaky, but I could see he was trying to act confident.

"Oh my goodness." Mum took the flowers and bent down to pull Frankie into a tight hug. She held him for what was probably too long and I was worried she'd cut off his air supply.

"Mum." I leaned down and whispered into her ear. "Let him breathe."

"I'm so sorry," she said, letting him go. "I'm just so excited to meet you."

Frankie gave her a huge toothy smile and then looked up at my dad. "Hi Grandpa."

Dad, who always held it together, pulled in a sharp, almost inaudible gasp. "Hi Frankie," he replied, and held a hand out to my son. Frankie looked at it, but moved away from Mum and wrapped his arms around dad's waist and hugged him.

Everybody felt the emotion that was hanging in the air and we all stood silently watching as my parents pulled their grandson into a three-way hug.

I felt for Maisie's hand and linked my fingers with hers, rubbing my thumb along her wrist. Her brown eyes softened as they found mine and my heart fucking ached in my chest for what I wanted, what I could have had for so damn long. I reached up and brushed her hair from her face, my fingers lingering on her skin.

"Don't say anything," she said softly. "It doesn't matter anymore."

My shoulders dropped as regret once more weighed them down. "They're so happy to have him here."

"I know." She glanced over at my mum and dad and I could see remorse in her own expression.

"Hey, this is all on me."

"Should I have pushed you more?" she asked.

"It wouldn't have made any difference, I was a prick."

Maisie laughed softly but didn't disagree, but she didn't need to say anything, I knew exactly what I'd been.

As we watched the scene in front of us, Elijah and Amy appeared in the doorway and smiled at us both. Elijah came over and leaned in to kiss Maisie's cheek.

"Nice to see you again, Maisie."

"You too. It's all a bit surreal, but I think Frankie is enjoying the attention." She looked over at my parents and grinned.

"He looks just like you," Eli said, nudging me. "Fucking hell, one of you is bad enough."

"You Cooper boys certainly know how to produce beautiful children." Amy had joined us with Bella in her arms. "Hi Maisie, it's been a long time."

Maisie nodded and went to move closer to Amy, but I kept a firm grip on her hand.

"It has. Lovely to see you and who is this little beauty?" she asked, using her free hand to tickle Bella under the chin.

"This is Bella. Say hello, Bella."

Bella leaned forward and squeezing Maisie's face between her tiny hands, kissed her smack on the lips. We all started to laugh and Bella tilted her head to one side, enjoying the attention.

"I Bella," she said. "You come play with my Barbie with me?"

"Well of course I will," Maisie responded. "And which Barbie do you have?"

"Which doesn't she have?" Elijah groaned.

"Dadda no be naughty," my cute, two year old niece shouted, glaring at Elijah.

Elijah like the sap he was for his little princess, simply laughed and rolled his eyes. "I'm so totally whipped," he muttered. "I have no damn balls left."

We all laughed, except for Bella who had no clue what was so funny.

"Come on in, all of you," Mum said above our laughter, finally letting go of Frankie. "Lunch is almost ready."

As everyone filed in, I tugged on Maisie's hand.

"You okay?"

She nodded. "Yes, I'm so happy for him."

Then she smiled at me and all I wanted to do was apologise once again.

Finally, with lunch finished and Frankie having polished off two helpings of apple pie, I was sitting on the patio with my dad and Elijah, watching as Bella and Frankie chased each other around the garden.

"He's so like you were as a kid," Dad said, turning to me with a wistful look in his eyes. "He even walks like you."

"I know," Elijah added. "How the hell people haven't noticed is beyond me."

I shrugged. "We've never been seen together until recently. It wasn't as though Maisie and I were a thing for long and people we know would put two and two together if they saw her with him."

Dad stared out over at his grandchildren and I knew he was thinking about all the time that had been wasted, something else I felt guilty about. I'd never considered how everything had affected my parents, yet it obviously had because they'd both spent most of lunch staring at Frankie and getting emotional.

Suddenly Bella screamed making Elijah shoot up from his chair, but the air was quickly filled with laughter.

"She okay, buddy?" I called to Frankie.

He nodded. "Yeah, a ladybird landed on her arm."

"It tickle," Bella shouted, holding her arm out in front of her.

"Count the spots," Frankie said, crouching down to Bella's height. "Then you'll know how old she is."

As Frankie helped Bella to count the spots, Elijah bent to pick up his beer bottle. "I'd better take her to the toilet," he sighed. "She forgets when she's having fun that she needs to go."

Dad chuckled. "I seem to remember you being like that, whereas Sam, he went every five minutes. He was obsessed with it."

"I remember that," I replied, grinning with my eyes still on Frankie and Bella. "In the end Mum kept me in just my undies when we were at home, because I kept complaining about having to pull my trousers down all the time."

"Oh yes." Dad smiled. "You decided to call yourself Tarzan and wouldn't answer to anything else for about a week."

"God, you always were a dick."

Elijah jumped out of the way as I threw a fist out to punch him in the leg.

"Pussy," I grumbled but he just winked at me.

"Bella, come on toilet time." Elijah's voice boomed across the garden to the kids who were now near the fence at the bottom, studying something in the flower bed.

Bella ignored him, but when Frankie said something in her ear, she turned and ran back up the garden, with my boy chasing after her. When Bella ran into Elijah's waiting arms, Frankie ran to me and flung himself onto my knee and I'd swear my fucking heart swelled to twice its normal size.

"Dad can I stay with Aunty Amy and Uncle Elijah one night?" he asked. "Uncle Elijah said I could watch his DVDs of *Only Fools*."

My eyes immediately went to my brother and watched as he stopped walking and stared down at Frankie. Elijah blew out a shaky breath and smiled at him.

"Anytime you want to Frankie," he replied and rubbed a loving hand over Frankie's hair.

"You need to ask your mum first," I added, wrapping my arms around him wishing for the time when I didn't need to say that. When I could confidently tell him what he could or couldn't do. When I could act like his dad without second guessing myself.

"I'll ask her now," Frankie cried enthusiastically.

I laughed and let him go, expecting him to immediately run to Maisie, but he planted a kiss on my cheek and squeezed me tightly. "See you later."

He jumped down and ran into the house, shouting for his mum with each step.

"Woah," Elijah said. "I never expected that, to be called Uncle Elijah straight away. He didn't really call me anything at lunch."

He stared after Frankie, his smile wide and gleaming.

"He's certainly settled in well," Dad said proudly. "You've done a good thing son."

"What abandoning my son for eight years."

Bella squirmed in Elijah's arms. "Down Dadda, down."

"Nope, toilet time." As Elijah passed me he put a hand on my shoulder. "Don't beat yourself up too much bro. You fixed it, that's the main thing."

As soon as the patio door closed behind Elijah and Bella, Dad leaned forward and laid his hand where Elijah's had been.

"He's right, you've fixed it now so stop thinking about what you should have done. The past can't be changed, so don't waste your energy on it."

"I let him down, Dad. I let them both down. Fuck, I let all of you down."

Dad ran a hand over his short cropped hair that was mostly the exact same colour as mine and Elijah's, and his kind eyes glowed with emotion.

"I'm not going to lie and say you did the right thing," he replied. "And I'll admit, me and your mum were hurt that we'd missed out on our grandson, but you've got the time now to make it up to him. To him *and* Maisie, because I'm guessing by the way you look at her that she means something to you as well."

As he studied me, I shifted in my seat wondering whether I should say the words and possibly build him up for more disappointment. He and Mum seemed to like her, but what if I cocked things up or she really didn't want me in that way, I'd be letting them down again.

"Sam, son, it's how you feel, not us," he said.

I should never have been shocked by his ability to know what I was thinking, but I always was.

"I really care about her Dad, but I was such a prick when

Frankie was born, I'm not sure I deserve her even considering having a relationship with me, never mind agreeing to one."

"So you have asked her?"

I nodded. "I've told her that I want to, but she doesn't trust me and I don't blame her."

"She knows deep down you're a good man, son, she probably just doesn't want to believe it at the moment."

"What do I do?"

Dad smiled and sat back in his chair. "You show her and prove to her that you're who you say you are. That you want to be there for Frankie and for her. You do know though, don't you, that you won't get more than one shot at this? You stuff up and that'll be it."

"I do." I nodded. "Maisie said as much."

"That's because she's a good mum," he replied with a smile. "I couldn't ask for anyone better for my grandson, or my son for that matter."

"Except for Amy maybe." I laughed because we all knew of everyone, she was my dad's favourite.

He raised a brow. "She wasn't always in my good books, you know that. The main thing is she realised she was wrong and that Elijah loved her, and I'm sure Maisie will too."

"Love," I scoffed. "I'm not sure she'd say that."

"Why not, you love her don't you?"

My heart beat thundered in my ears as I thought about what he'd said. Love was a strong word and a powerful feeling and I wasn't sure I'd ever truly felt it. Looking back Ali had actually been an infatuation. I loved my family and Frankie, but was I *in* love with Maisie – I wasn't sure I was worthy of feeling such an emotion about her.

"I...um...I don't know about that."

He waved a dismissive hand at me. "Of course you do you big idiot. Your head just needs time to catch up with your heart."

"Shit, Dad, when did you get so profound?" I asked around a nervous laugh.

"When I became a father. The same will happen to you too."

I looked at him carefully, noticing the wrinkles at his eyes and the greying hair at his temples and it struck me how I barely ever told him I loved him. He was a quiet man who stood by my mum whatever crusade she was on. He'd provided for us all our lives, never once complaining that he was tired or that we were a burden to him and when we'd grown into men he'd always shown us respect, and I had never known him to ask for anything from any of us in return.

"I love you Dad." I got up out of my chair and went to him, leaned down and kissed the top of his head. "Thank you for everything and if I'm half the father you are, I'll be doing a great job."

He looked up at me with emotion swimming in his eyes and smiled. "I think you're already doing that son. That boy already adores you and that's not because you're his dad, but because you're a great man."

Dad stood, kissed my forehead and then left me to my own thoughts and because of him, I was more determined than ever that I was going to do everything I could to make a family as great as the one that James Cooper had.

34

the present

"Do your parents know about Sam?" Yvetta, Sam's mum asked as we sat at the dining room table with Amy, the three of us drinking wine.

"Yes, they do. They were a little cautious about him at first, but the fact that Frankie never stops talking about him has gone a long way to making them feel better about it."

"Have they met him yet?" Amy paused from topping my wine up, waiting for my answer.

"They have, but not exactly in a nice relaxed situation. It was kind of a fraught situation with my ex."

Yvetta frowned at me, but I waved her away as Sam and I had agreed today wasn't the right time to mention Josh taking Frankie. That could wait for another day.

"It was nothing, but Sam still has to meet my sister and I think Dad and Mum would like a chance to talk to him properly, so I'm sure we'll be going to their house in the near future."

"So he still has to enter the Lion's den, so to speak."

Yvetta joked, but I could see the worry lines etching her face. Sam was her son, so I totally understood her concern.

"They'll be fine," I replied.

247

"I wouldn't blame them if they weren't. He's my son and I love him, but he was wrong in what he did to you and Frankie. They've every right to be angry with him."

"He's changed, Yvetta," Amy said, moving to fill up her mother-in-law's glass. "It's taken a while admittedly, but he's realised he did wrong."

"It's just not like him, Amy. He's normally so responsible." Yvetta sighed.

"The main thing is, he's in Frankie's life now, isn't that right Maisie?"

Amy gave me a sideways glance and I wondered if she knew about Sam's swimming coach and what had happened.

"Yes," I replied. "As long as he does right by Frankie that's all I can ask of him. He never lied to me when we were younger, I knew he didn't want to be a dad, but he always provided for him."

"He did?"

Yvetta's face broke into a smile, glad that her son had redeemed himself in some way at least.

"Yes, without fail, and when my ex-partner decided he didn't want the money and that he could provide for Frankie, Sam carried on putting the money into an account for him. He actually gave me a pretty big check last week."

Yvetta's eyes widened. "Really?"

"Yes, huge in fact."

She raised her glass to me and smiled. "And nothing that you don't deserve. You've done a brilliant job with my grandson, Maisie. He's a wonderful boy and I can't thank you enough for giving my son another chance."

The way she looked at me, with emotion in her eyes, I knew she was thinking things that weren't actually happening and I didn't want her to get her hopes up.

"No, Yvetta, this is all about Frankie and Sam. I'm just happy

Frankie finally has his dad around."

Yvetta gave me a knowing smile which made me frown.

"Has Sam said something?"

Amy spluttered and almost spat out her wine. "As if he needs to say anything," she said, wiping the wetness from her chin. "You've only got to see the way he looks at you to know he cares about you – a lot."

I shook my head. "No, it's not like that. It really isn't."

"I think Amy is right," Yvetta sighed. "I think he most definitely has feelings for you, and they're probably deeper than you think."

My stomach flipped at the thought of me and Sam, and of us becoming more than two people who'd had sex a couple of times. Of course I liked him, he was sexy, good looking, had an amazing body, and his tattoos just added to the plethora of good things I could say about him, but despite the fact that I'd accepted him not wanting to be involved in Frankie's life, my heart still hurt on behalf of my baby boy. Frankie had my dad, but he'd craved a father figure and unfortunately Josh hadn't been the man to give that to him. I had to hope Sam stepped up now and gave Frankie everything he needed, but as for me, well I had to trust him with Frankie's heart before I could trust him with mine.

"We're just friends, Yvetta."

Amy snorted and Yvetta slapped at her arm.

"Stop teasing her and stop snorting, you sound like a pig."

"Sorry," Amy laughed. "But if she thinks they're just friends then I'm standing for Prime Minister in the next General Election."

"Well you couldn't do much worse love." Yvetta grinned and then took my hand and squeezed it. "You take things at your pace, sweetheart, but remember this conversation when you realise you and Sam are meant to be together."

I shook my head wondering how on earth she'd come to that conclusion after just one meeting – but then I noticed it was our second bottle of wine and realised that alcohol probably had a lot to do with it.

We continued chatting for a few more minutes until Yvetta told us she needed to make a call about a march she was due to go on in a few days, leaving Amy and I at the table. As soon as she'd disappeared from the room, Amy pulled her chair closer to mine.

"So," she whispered. "You can tell me now what's really going on with you and Sam."

"Nothing," I replied, shaking my head. "Honestly."

"Ooh you little liar. I know for a fact that something has happened."

"How? Has he said something?" I flopped back in my chair, throwing a glance toward the patio on the other side of the doors, where Sam, his dad, and Elijah were sitting.

Amy began to laugh. "No, but you just have."

"No I didn't." I could tell my face was red because of the heat blazing from my cheeks.

"Oh you did," she said swigging back some more wine. "You're a rubbish liar."

I opened my mouth to deny it, but her grin told me she wouldn't believe me if I did.

"We had sex," I whispered. "Twice."

Amy slapped the table. "I knew it. He's been acting strange all week."

"Strange? In what way?"

"Oh you know, like a man who had great sex and wants more but isn't getting any; all mean and moody. It was great I presume?" she asked, her brows arching.

For a few seconds I thought about abstaining from answering, but the thing was I actually wanted to talk about it. I didn't really have anyone to discuss the mind blowing sex with. My sister was too caught up in her own life to have time to listen to me, and Angie and I didn't really have that sort of relationship – it was purely employer and employee. As for my mum, well that conversation definitely wasn't happening.

"It was awesome," I rushed out. "*He* was awesome."

Heat flooded my veins as I thought back to that night and how Sam had almost made me see stars with the orgasms that he'd given me. The first time had been hard and fast, making me scream, but the second time when I'd woken up sleepy and horny, it had been soft, slow and so, so good with me on top. I'd taken it for what it was though; sex between two people who just wanted comfort from each other, but it had still been better than I'd ever had before, including my night with Sam all those years before.

"If it runs in the family then I'm pretty sure I know how good it was," Amy giggled. "And not that I really want to discuss my brother-in-law's prowess in too much depth, but is it something you'd want to repeat?"

I dropped my head to the table and groaned.

"Well?"

I squinted up at her. "Yes, but I'm scared," I replied, sitting back upright.

"What of? He didn't hurt you, did he?"

"God, no." I huffed out a breath. "I'm just scared that if I let myself trust him and start something with him, we won't work and then I'll have to tell Frankie. Can you imagine how he'd feel, thinking he was finally getting a mum and a dad who were actually together, and then being told it's back to being just me and him, maybe with Sam at weekends; if he'd even stick around."

Amy's eyes narrowed. "He wouldn't do that to Frankie, not again. We can all see how hard he's trying and how much he wants to be Frankie's dad."

"I know you believe that, Amy, and you're right, he is trying, but you have to see it from my point of view. He hasn't always wanted to be Frankie's dad, don't forget."

Amy let out a long sigh, pushed her glass away and placed her palms face down on the table. She closed her eyes for a few seconds and when she opened them I saw pain and regret in them.

"You know about me and Elijah, what happened all those years ago?"

I nodded.

"And I'm guessing you know that I'd lost a baby a few months before."

Again I nodded.

"Well you know that when I left, Sam had to deal with all that pain that Elijah was feeling. Elijah told me that Sam was the one who held him together, the one who made sure he didn't go under and drown in the grief of losing not only the baby but me too. Then you told him you were pregnant."

"Yes, I understand all that but-."

"Yeah, I know you do and I'm guessing you also know what he went through with that sick woman who was his swimming coach." She glanced at the door and then leaned closer. "You know what she put him through, making him believe he was going to be a dad. Even though it had happened years before, I don't think he ever dealt with it because he never told anyone about it. He only told Eli a couple of weeks ago, so all of that was still inside him when you told him about Frankie. He had seen what losing a child had done to his brother and how our split broke him even more, so I just think it was all too much for Sam. I'm not making excuses for him Maisie, but I do think you need to take it all into consideration."

She was right, Sam had been through a lot, but being a single parent hadn't exactly been plain sailing. To experience it all must have been hard for him though and I wasn't totally heartless.

"I do feel for him," I whispered. "I just need to be sure for Frankie's sake."

Amy nodded and squeezed my hand. "I know."

"Mum, Mum."

Frankie suddenly came charging through the patio doors, shouting excitedly.

"Hey, where's the fire?" I asked, grinning at the sight of his sweaty, happy face.

"Can I stay over at Uncle Elijah's and Auntie Amy's one night please? Uncle Elijah said I could. He's got all the *Only Fools & Horses* DVDs. Dad said I had to ask you," he said breathlessly.

He looked so happy and it was all to do with having a dad and an uncle who he could look up to. He loved my dad, but he wasn't cool like Sam and Elijah and he certainly didn't like Northern Soul music or *Only Fools & Horses*. Plus, there was the small matter of his cute little cousin who he had instantly fallen in love with.

"As long as it's okay with Auntie Amy too."

I looked at Amy who was gazing at Frankie lovingly.

"Of course you can."

"Aces," Frankie cried. "That's what Uncle Elijah said." He flung his arms around me and kissed my cheek. "I'm so glad we're in this family, Mum."

"You are?" I asked, a huge lump in my throat making it almost impossible to speak.

"Yeah. It's cool."

I had no words that would be enough to express how happy I was for my baby boy. He had what he'd always wanted and even though it was probably stupid to do so, I couldn't help but hope for more.

35

the present

"Right," I said crouching down in front of Frankie. "You know the plan?"

"Yes, Dad," he sighed and rolled his eyes. "I tell Mum that I want you both to take me on a picnic, but when it's time to go, Uncle Elijah will ring you and ask if I can go and play with Bella. I say I want to go and you'll say you'll drop me off on the way to the picnic as it will be a shame to waste the food that you bought. Food you bought because you didn't want Mum to have to spend time doing it."

I straightened up and ruffled his hair. "Okay, you cheeky little devil."

I glanced over his shoulder to see Maisie's car pull up on the driveway, back from having to show someone around a house that was for sale. "Right, she's here. Let's do this."

I held my hand up to high five Frankie, but once more got the eye roll and no high five. Obviously I was not the cool dad I seemed to think I was.

"Hi Mummy," Frankie cried as Maisie walked through the door. He ran to her and wrapped his arms around her waist. "Can we go on a picnic this afternoon? Me and Daddy went to the

255

supermarket and bought some food so you don't have to do anything."

God – this kid was good, rolling out the 'mummy' and 'daddy' card, sounding all sweet when he wanted something.

"Is that okay?" I asked. "He didn't stop going on about it for an hour, so I kind of said we would and then thought you wouldn't mind if you didn't have to do anything, hence the trip to the supermarket."

"And hello to both of you too," Maisie said with a grin.

"Sorry." It was my turn to roll my eyes. "Hi, Maisie."

She laughed and turned to Frankie. "Okay, so tell me about this picnic."

"We're going to go to a lake and Daddy has made sandwiches and bought strawberries and cheese cake and he got you some of that pink wine you like."

"You have?" Maisie asked, tilting her head to one side.

I nodded. "Yep. I saw the bottle that's almost finished in the fridge. I got picnic eggs too."

I was pretty proud of myself having rifled through the fridge and some wrappers in the kitchen waste bin. Frankie had given me some tips too on what she did and didn't like, hence the absence of sausage rolls; apparently she hated them.

"And what about you?" Maisie asked him, holding his chin up with a thumb and forefinger. "What did your dad get for you? Let me guess, chocolate rolls, chocolate biscuits, and cheese triangles."

I looked at Frankie, wondering whether he'd give the game away, but like a true Cooper he kept his cool.

"Only cheese triangles, oh and strawberry milk, because I had a piece of chocolate cake in the supermarket café and he said I'd had enough chocolate for one day."

Maisie's amused gaze turned to me. "Really?"

"Yeah," I replied, trying to seem nonchalant about it. "It was a huge piece."

I almost pumped the fucking air when she looked at me with pride. I just hoped she never found out I'd let him have two pieces and a hot chocolate.

"You're getting quite good at this daddy thing," she whispered as she moved past me to the sofa where she flopped down and kicked off her shoes.

As she sank back into the cushions, I couldn't help but remember her sitting on the edge of the seat with her legs open for me. She'd been as desperate for me as I was for her and her moans when she came were the sexiest sound I'd ever heard. Thinking about being inside her that night made my dick jerk and my jeans started to feel a little tight.

"I'll get you a cuppa," I said clearing my throat and sneakily readjusting myself. "We'll go in about half an hour. You okay with that?"

She looked at Frankie and smiled. "Yes, no problem. Looking forward to it."

As I left the lounge, Frankie gave me a secretive smile and all I had to do then was text my brother when it was time for his call.

"We could have postponed until Frankie could come," Maisie said glancing across at me.

"Seems as shame to waste the food." I looked back to the road, not wanting her to see the lies in my eyes. She was pretty astute and a mother of an eight year old, so I was pretty sure she could spot bullshit when she needed to. I was feeling pretty lucky that we'd got away with it so far, although Elijah had pulled a blinder calling me via my hands free in the car. Maisie had heard every word of his convincing pleading for Frankie to go over there; even Bella had come on the line shouting for Frankie. I had to admit though the Cooper's had been a great team, my son included.

"I guess so."

She fidgeted in her seat and twisted her hands in front of her.

"You okay?" I asked, glancing at her.

"Hmm fine."

She didn't sound fine, her tone was unsure and I worried whether I'd totally cocked up. Maybe she wasn't ready for us to spend time alone.

"I can take you back home, or we can go back to Elijah's if you like."

There was no fucking way I wanted to do either of those things, but I certainly didn't want her to feel uncomfortable.

I held my breath, my eyes pinned to the road, as I waited for her to answer. When she did I let out a quiet breath of relief.

"No, it'll be nice to be able to relax a little."

"You sure?"

"Yes," she replied, sounding much more positive. "The last couple of weeks have been a bit manic with one thing after another."

As we pulled up at a red traffic light, I took the opportunity to look at her. She'd relaxed back into the seat a little more, but her fingers were still twisted around each other.

"I know it's all been a bit much," I said. "But, we're getting into a routine and Frankie seems to have adjusted pretty well to it all."

Big brown eyes stared out from under thick lashes and studied me. "I'm scared, Sam."

Her words hit me hard and I jumped in my seat when the car behind beeped its horn – the lights had turned to green. I moved off and then immediately pulled up on the side of the road.

"*I* scare you?"

She closed her eyes and nodded. "Yes," she breathed out.

"Maisie, look at me," I pleaded. "And tell me why."

Her eyes opened slowly and she looked up at me. "Being alone with you scares me," she admitted.

I frowned and turned in my seat. "Maisie we've been alone with each other plenty of times. We had sex."

Colour spread up her neck and her fingers started fidgeting again.

"You don't want me to remind you that we had sex?" I asked.

"No, it's not that, it's...I don't know."

She placed a palm against her throat and as she swallowed, all I could think of was her swallowing my cum after giving me a blow job. Okay, it wasn't the most appropriate moment, but it was getting that I was becoming more and more obsessed with her and the thought of us having a relationship; not to mention the idea of taking that perfect pussy of hers again.

"Then what is it, Maisie?"

I leaned closer and took the hand that was placed on her throat and pulled her to me so that we were inches apart.

"You know what I want, I haven't hidden it from you. You have absolutely nothing to be scared of because I know exactly what's at stake if I cock anything up. I know I have this one chance with Frankie and maybe I have no chance with you, but I need you to know I'm willing to work so fucking hard to make you under-stand how much I want it *all* – I want to be a damn good dad to Frankie, the best I can be, but I want you too. I don't want you just to make it easier for me to be Frankie's father, I want you because I care about *you*. You're amazing. You're strong and brave, you're a brilliant mother and you don't *need* anyone. Everything about you makes me feel like an inadequate dick, that I don't deserve someone like you, but you also make me want to change. I *want* to deserve you because I fucking want you so badly I feel like I'm turning into an addict."

Maisie's mouth dropped open in shock and my own almost mimicked hers, because I hadn't realised that was how I was feeling, but I was. I knew she was all the things I'd said, but I hadn't realised how fucking much I loved those things; not until the words were spewing from my mouth and my heart was beating hard in agreement. I really wanted her and if I was truthful it was her beauty that had started the desire, the sex that had created the need and the way her body reacted to mine that had built the want; all of that plus her strength and determination had got me hooked to the point where the necessity for a daily fix had crept up on me.

"And if you change your mind?" she asked, her voice tiny and quiet. "What then?"

"I can't tell you the future Maisie, because I don't have a crystal ball. I have no way of knowing what might happen between us, but what I do know is at this moment I know I want us and I want the opportunity to make us into something that *could* last a lifetime. I'm not going to promise you things that neither of us can be sure of, all I can promise you is I'll do my fucking best to be the best partner that I can be. Me being a good dad isn't dependent on that, so if we don't work out then we find a way to make the situation work. If that means Frankie has two parents that love him but aren't together, then that's what will happen. Plenty of families in the same situation make it work. If it does go that way then our son will cope because he's an amazing, clever kid who is so much like his mum there's no chance he won't be able to deal."

Pulling her even closer to me, I dropped a soft kiss on her lips, breathing her in at the same time and relishing in the smell of the delicate, fresh perfume that she always wore.

"So, do you want me to take you back?" I asked, my eyes begging her to say no.

She watched me carefully and then after a few seconds, hesitantly shook her head.

"No," she whispered. "Let's go and have a picnic."

I kissed her once more and then started the engine and drove away.

36

the present

The afternoon sun cast long shadows over the ground, and created sparkles of light which skimmed across the lake. The trees around the edge reflected back into the water as a few ducks swam along, diving intermittently for food. It was beautiful, like a scene from a nature book, and I couldn't help but pull out my phone and snap a picture.

"This place is gorgeous," I called over my shoulder to Sam. "I had no idea it was even here."

"I only know about it because a guy I know works for the RSPB and often releases ducks here if they've been injured and taken into the rescue centre where he's based. You're not even allowed to fish here and you can't get all the way around, so no one comes here with dogs or to go walking."

I looked around the space and could see that to the right was a picnic table and a small grassy bank, but beyond that were dense trees and bushes. The other side was pretty much the same, except there was no picnic table but a slightly overgrown forest path.

"I wonder where that leads to."

Sam shrugged. "No idea, but we can check it out after lunch."

I looked down at the rolled blanket under his arm and the cool box and large shopping bag that he'd carried from the car where we parked in a layby about a quarter of a mile down the road. That was how secluded the place was, you couldn't even park close by.

"I could have carried some of that." I held out a hand to take one of the bags, but Sam shook his head.

"Nope, you're relaxing today and I can manage, they're not heavy."

I followed him to the grassy bank and waited while he put the bags down and spread out the blanket.

"I'm not sure how clean that table is," Sam said as he took out all the food. "And it looks like it might collapse under the weight of a sandwich."

I had to agree, it was a bit rickety and covered in all kinds of mess and green moss.

"No, you're right. I think we're better sticking to a blanket that we know where it's been. You do know, don't you?"

Sam grinned at me. "Yes, I only bought it this morning, so it's perfectly clean."

"It's not one you have in the back of your car then, you know, just in case you break down when you're giving a girlfriend a lift home."

I was smiling because it was a joke, but Sam's expression was dead-pan.

"No, Maisie, that's not my style and even if it was there'd be no way I'd use a blanket I'd had a quick, meaningless fuck on for you."

"What for a picnic or a quick, meaningless fuck?" I asked, the words out of my mouth before I even had chance to tell myself to shut up.

"There's nothing quick and meaningless about how I feel about you," he replied, reaching up to brush my hair over my shoulder. "I thought we'd already established that."

His fingers lingered on the sensitive skin on my neck, and as quickly as I drew in a lustful breath, he'd turned away and gone back to arranging the food. I watched him carefully, drinking in his taught muscles and handsome profile, quenching my thirst on the beauty of him. He was a gorgeous man, of that there was no doubt, but I'd had a relationship without the desire, with a man who I loved because he was supportive, and I'd had tried being with Sam simply for the incredible sex, but neither had satisfied me. I wanted the desire *and* the mind blowing sex, but I wanted someone to be a partner too, like Josh had been in the first couple of years before he changed. I wanted someone who would help me with life, to help me make decisions. I didn't want to be strong *all* the time, I needed someone to share things with. I wanted it all and I was sure I wanted it with Sam, which scared the shit out of me still, despite his words in the car earlier.

"Okay, take a seat." Sam waved a hand toward the blanket. "Let's eat."

"Okay next question," Sam said as we lay back on the blanket, looking up at the clear sky. "How old was he when he first asked about his dad?"

Sam wanted to know more about Frankie and the years he'd missed and I'd been answering his questions for almost an hour. He'd asked all sorts of things, wanting to know Frankie's first words, his favourite food and even what he'd worn on his first day at school. While I'd answered, I'd tried to make a mental note of all he asked, thinking I'd put a photograph album together of as many of those occasions as I could.

"He was just five," I replied. "The kids at school had been talking about their dads and he came home that night and asked me. Josh had moved in, but Frankie knew he wasn't his dad, so he asked where his was."

I remembered that night clearly, and being unsure what to say, I'd looked at Josh who was staring at me intently, but I knew that I didn't want to lie and tell Frankie that he was his dad. I often wondered whether Josh held that against me, and whether that was why he'd never bonded with Frankie, but it was something I would never know and didn't actually care about any longer.

"What exactly did you say?" Sam asked, his voice unsure. "I know it was something about me leaving before I knew about him."

"Exactly that. That you left before you knew about him and that I couldn't find you to tell you.

Sam let out an unsteady breath and I felt for his hand on the blanket next to mine.

"He accepted it Sam," I replied, turning my head to face him.

"And then he finds out I was just a fucking shit who didn't give a damn."

"Sam, he doesn't care."

He looked back up to the sky. "I'm glad he knows the truth Maisie, but I don't want him to hate me for it."

"The fact that he hasn't questioned either of us about it since we told him should tell you something, shouldn't it?"

Sam shrugged and turned his gaze back to me.

"That he doesn't care," I answered. "I know him and if he was really upset about it, he'd have asked me a load of questions and would have been wary around you, but he isn't; he loves you already. He idolised you when he thought you were only his swimming coach and the man who protected us from Josh, but it's gone to a whole new level now you're his dad."

"You think so?"

"Yes, now what's your next question?"

Sam leaned up on one elbow and looked down on me, deliberating what his next question would be. As his eyes grazed down my face and then my body, all my senses started to tingle. His breathing was steady as he took in my hands resting on my stomach and down my bare legs to my pink painted toes.

Slowly Sam's eyes travelled back up and when they rested on my face he took his bottom lip into his mouth and sucked on it as he perused me. The want in his gaze sent adrenalin rushing around my body, heating my skin and turning my nipples hard.

I wondered how we'd gone from me answering questions about Frankie, to him making me wet just by looking at me.

"Sam?"

"Okay my next question," he said, lowering his face to mine. "Can I kiss you?"

I blinked rapidly, stupidly thinking I had a choice and that I could tell him no, but my body was arguing with my stupid brain. It was telling it that I was an idiot if I didn't give this man a chance, that all he wanted was to prove himself and that I should give him that opportunity.

"If this goes wrong," I whispered with Sam's lips merely inches from mine.

"We deal with it, like adults, but I'll swear I'll do everything in my power to make this work."

I shook my head and almost cried out as he ran a gentle finger down the side of my face.

"No, if you have to try too hard then it's not working."

Sam nodded once and then lowered his head, taking my lips in a soft yet insistent kiss. His tongue pushed for me to open up my mouth and as soon as I did, the ecstasy began.

Slow, languid strokes and gentle nips coupled with his teeth dragging slowly across by bottom lip stoked up the fire starting in the pit of my stomach. A hand threaded through my hair and a

267

knee pushing my legs open fanned the flames until my whole body was heated with need and want and lust.

I reached up and grabbed Sam's shoulders, pulling him down on top of me and loving how heavy he felt. My heart may have been timid and nervous, but my body was screaming for him to be all the things I wanted him to be and do all the things I needed him to do.

His large hand moved up my side pushing my dress up to my waist, before continuing upwards and cupping the side of my breast. His thumb skimmed my already hard nipple while his other hand cupped my face gently.

Desperate for more than just his hard cock pushing against me through his jeans, I let out a frustrated moan and moved my hands down to his waistband and grabbed at his button. Sam gave a throaty 'no' and started to move down my body. He kissed along the swell of my chest, down my body and over my stomach, all the time pushing my dress further up.

"Take it off, Maisie," he groaned as he reached the waistband of my knickers and reverently kissed the stretch marks that I'd tried to hide from him once before.

I lifted my shoulders and dragged my cotton dress over my head, leaving my hair messed over my face. As I threw it to one side, Sam looked up at me, his chin resting on my stomach and his eyes hooded.

"How the fuck did I not know you had no bra on?"

I smiled coyly, glad for the hidden support within the dress when I saw the pure, heated desire in Sam's eyes.

His mouth moved away from my stomach and he instantly took my nipple into his mouth sucking, licking, and biting, making me cry out with the pleasure. As he continued to elicit mewls of yearning from me, his hands moved down to my knickers, pulling them to one side and running a finger over my centre coating it with my wetness.

"Oh my god," I gasped, as his knuckle grazed my clit.

Sam didn't speak but continued to administer kisses to my almost naked body, adding an extra finger inside my knickers as he pumped them in and out of me, intermitting it with circling the tiny bud of nerves which sent me spiraling.

I was about to cry out that I was almost there, when Sam hooked his fingers into the sides of my knickers, pulled them down and then dragged them over my feet and threw them to one side. "I need to taste you," he said as he pulled away and moved his hands down my legs until they were wrapped around my ankles. Slowly he pushed my legs apart, encouraging me to put my feet flat on the ground.

I drew in a deep breath and held it, looking up at Sam and begging him with my eyes to do it. I needed it and him so badly.

With a deep groan his hands went up to my inner thighs and gripped them, his fingertips pushing into my soft skin. I let out the breath and as I did, Sam dropped his head and with one long lick, pulled his tongue through my wetness causing me to scream out with the pleasure that engulfed me. He suckled on me and fucked me with his tongue, his stubble adding extra friction that made me buck my hips wildly.

In and out and sucking, in and out and sucking. Repeating it until I couldn't hold back the wall of noise that escaped from my mouth that was already parted on a gasp.

"Sam."

My voice echoed around the stillness of the lake, disappearing into the air as I came and came and came. Every part of my body shook as Sam continued with his rhythmic pattern, not stopping until he was sure he had drained me of every last pulse of my orgasm.

"Oh shit," I gasped, my chest heaving.

Sam dropped a kiss to the inside of my knee, his touch on my sensitive skin made me quiver.

"No, oh god no more."

Sam chuckled and smoothed his hand down my leg before reaching over to one of the bags.

"I've got wet wipes," he said, clearing his throat. "But I didn't bring them because I thought we'd be...anyway hope they're okay."

I lifted up onto both of my elbows and still breathing hard, grinned at him.

"They're fine...thank you...but...what about you?"

Sam arched a brow. "What about me?"

"Well you haven't...you know."

He let out a laugh and shook his head. "I haven't, you're right, but I wanted this to be about you today. I wanted you to relax and me to relax you."

He wiggled his eyebrows and reached for my dress.

"Here you go." As he passed it to me, he stooped to kiss my cheek. "You look beautiful when you've just come."

He watched me for a few seconds until I smiled and then moved away. As I dressed and cleaned up I could see from the corner of my eye that he was tidying things into the bags and I was pretty sure I saw him wipe his face too, which made mine flame with embarrassment. Once I was finished, I turned back to see Sam straightening out the blanket.

"We're not going?" I asked.

"Do you want to?" He paused, a hand on one corner of the blanket.

"God no, I just thought you were packing up."

A beautiful smile broke out on his face and I could only bask in the warmth it brought.

"No, just making it more comfortable." He dropped down onto

the ground and patted the spot next to him on the blanket.

I did as asked and once I was sitting, he pulled me into his arms and dropped us back to looking up at the sky again.

"You okay?" he asked softly as he rubbed a hand up and down my bare arm.

Snuggling closer to him, I nodded. "Hmm, I'm very good, thank you."

He kissed the top of my head and wrapped his other arm around me. "The sun is going to go behind the trees in a minute, you might start to feel cold."

"I've got my jacket," I replied with a yawn, my orgasm having taking a lot out of me.

"I think this is better."

Sam's chest was comfy and his arms around me made me feel warm and cosy and before I knew it my eyes were getting heavier and heavier. Just as I was about to fall into that wonderful place between relaxation and sleep, Sam's chest started to move up and down as he started to laugh.

"What?" I asked, lifting my head on another yawn.

"You," he replied, smoothing my messy hair back from my face. "Every time I give you an orgasm you fall asleep on me. I don't know whether to be offended or feel like a King because I'm so damn good."

I started to giggle. "I'm sorry, but it really isn't anything to be offended by."

"You sure?" he asked, looking down at me.

"Yep. It's a great skill you have there."

"That's good."

As we lay in silence a thought suddenly struck me.

"How come none of the food Frankie wanted was in the bag?" I asked, suddenly awake. "There were no cheese triangles or straw-berry milk in either of those bags."

I sat up and poked Sam in his hard chest.

"Frankie was never coming with us, was he?"

Sam grimaced and scratched his head.

"Sam, was he?"

"Nope," he groaned. "It was our little plan for me to get you on a date."

"You could have just asked me?" I rolled my eyes. "What sort of example is that to show your son?"

Because I was grinning, Sam did too and started to laugh. Soon I was joining in with him and it felt good, both of us laughing and smiling and enjoying being together.

"So what next?" Sam asked.

"About what?"

"Us. What happens now?" He placed a hand on my cheek. "Are we doing this?"

"This being?"

He picked up my hand and playfully nibbled on my fingers. "You want me to beg, Maisie?"

I shook my head.

"Are we doing this being a couple thing?" he reiterated. "I want to and I think you want to, but I'm happy to keep if from Frankie for a little while, if that's what you'd prefer."

"You wouldn't mind? I just want us to be sure first. Maybe have a date without sex," I ground out, feeling a little embarrassed.

Thankfully, Sam nodded. "I agree. Let's do that, although I swear I didn't plan on that happening today, I just looked down on you and you looked so fucking adorable and beautiful and sexy and I couldn't resist it."

I leaned forward and kissed the corner of Sam's mouth, wrapping my arms around his neck as I pressed against him. I wanted to move forward and I wanted more with Sam, so I was going to be brave and trust that he wouldn't hurt either me or Frankie.

"I think we better go," Sam said on a chuckle as I snuggled closer. "I might just have you on your back again if you keep pushing those tits against me."

"Sam," I admonished, pushing back and slapping at his chest.

"Sorry, but it's the truth." He jumped to his feet and held out his hand for me. "Besides, I'd like to spend a bit of time with Frankie before I have to go to the Leisure Centre at six."

"You're going to the Leisure Centre, on a Saturday night?" I asked, feeling deflated as he pulled me up.

Sam curled his top lip. "Yeah, you know Timothy the kid that got into trouble at the pool?"

I nodded.

"Well his younger brother can't swim and the family are going on holiday next week, so his parents asked me if I could give him some intensive lessons before they go. I couldn't really say no."

"How's he getting on?" I asked, picking up the blanket.

"Okay. This will be his fourth one, I've been taking an hour or two out of work and doing them straight after he finishes school all week."

"You never said."

As I looked at him, Sam blushed, something I had never expected from him; he was usually so confident.

"Well, you know teaching kids to swim isn't my favourite pastime."

I started to laugh. "Only because I gave you shit about it."

"Yeah, you did, but it worked out okay in the end."

He winked at me and a whole host of butterflies swarmed in my stomach. "Yes, I suppose it did."

With that Sam pulled me to him and kissed me again and I was sure if my phone hadn't started ringing, I'd have gladly laid down on the blanket for him all over again.

37

MAISIE

the present

"I can't believe they've let the fucker out on bail," Sam hissed as Frankie shot upstairs to go to the toilet.

The phone call had been my solicitor telling me that Josh had his court date, but had been given bail. It was something he'd warned me about, but as I had a restraining order against him, I knew Josh would be an idiot to come anywhere near me or Frankie.

"We knew it might happen," I said, taking an opportunity to curl up on my toes to kiss him.

He kissed me back but his face was heavy with a thunderous glare. "If he comes near you and Frankie, I'll fucking kill him."

"He won't. He'd be stupid to."

"And?"

"He's not that much of an idiot, Sam. He knows he's already in a lot of trouble, I don't think he'd give himself anymore."

"Well whatever, there's no way I'm going to the pool now. I'm staying here. I'll sleep on the sofa, I don't mind."

I rolled my eyes. "You're not letting that little boy down. Plus, aren't you supposed to be going out with Elijah and your mates tonight? I heard you organizing it earlier with Elijah when we dropped Frankie off."

"That definitely isn't happening." He started to pull his phone out of his pocket. "I'll do the swimming lesson, but I'll be back here by eight at the latest."

As much as I wanted him to come back, I also didn't want to stop him having a life, or more to the point, start rushing things. Okay we had a child together, but that didn't mean we should fall into him staying over or being here all the time.

I put my hand on his phone and pushed it down. "No, Sam. Go out tonight. We'll be fine and if I hear even the slightest noise I'll call you and the police straight away. There's new locks on the door, and on the side gate, so he can't get into the back garden, so I swear to you we will be okay. Plus, I'm pretty tired after a really intense orgasm some guy gave me down at the lake, so I'm going to go to bed early."

That brought a grin to his face and he kissed me hard, pulling away as soon as we heard Frankie clattering down the stairs.

"Hey, Dad," he cried. "Will you play *Fifa* with me?"

Sam looked at me and when I nodded, he turned back to Frankie. "Yep, come on then, let me show you how good I am."

With a quick squeeze of my bum he left me staring after him and hoping that we got it right this time, because it wasn't just Frankie's heart that was invested.

I was slightly disappointed in the fact that Sam hadn't called me or Frankie before his night out, but figured he was busy with the swimming lesson and then getting ready.

I still went to bed feeling a little disgruntled though, particularly after what we'd done at the lake. Grumpily I'd stomped up the stairs, checked in on Frankie and then slipped into bed and immediately chastised myself for being such a girl. I'd managed to get on with my life when he'd abandoned me after getting me pregnant, so I was damn sure I could survive one night without a text message.

When my phone started to ring, pulling me from a deep sleep, my heart jumped because my first thought was it was Sam. He was probably home and had drunk dialled me. When I picked up my phone though it said it was Amy calling.

"H-hello," I stammered, my heart pounding in my chest.

"Maisie, I'm so sorry to call you this late, but I thought you should know-."

"Oh my God, is it Sam?" I cried over the top of her, knowing there would be only one reason why she'd call me at one in the morning.

Amy drew in a breath on the other end of the phone. "He didn't turn up to go out with Elijah and their friends, so they just thought he was running late, but when he still wasn't there after a couple of hours and they couldn't get hold of him, Elijah was worried. He was going to get a taxi over to Sam's apartment, but got a call from his mum and dad saying a local patrol car had seen the lights on in the leisure centre and the door was open so went to investigate. They found Sam in the changing rooms."

With each word my skin got colder and colder as fear crept over me. "Is he...?"

"He's in intensive care at the moment," Amy continued, her voice breaking. "He hit his head and has only drifted in and out of consciousness."

Tears crawled down my cheeks and my stomach turned over and over as I thought about Sam being hurt and us possibly losing him before we'd even had a chance of a future together – as a family.

"Can I see him, can we..."

I let out a painful sob unable to speak any further.

"Y-yes." Amy stuttered, evidently in as much pain as I was. "Elijah and his parents are with him, but of course. That's why I called you, Yvetta thought you might want to go."

"I'll be there in twenty minutes," I rushed out breathily as I scrambled out of bed. Then a thought struck me. "Frankie," I gasped. "What do I do about him? My parents are away and my sister will probably only just be on her way home from some club, I have no one to have him."

"Why don't you drop him here?" Amy offered.

"Are you sure?"

"Positive. I can't go because of Bella, so it's fine."

"Oh god, what am I going to tell him, Amy? He'll be devastated."

The line was silent for a few seconds and then Amy said. "How about Sam's car's broken down, so you're going to pick him up. That'll do for now."

Giving Amy my thanks, we quickly finished the call and I rushed to get dressed and then giving Frankie the cover story Amy and I had agreed on, got him wrapped up warm and into the car, trying to keep my tears at bay as I drove through the almost empty streets hoping that Sam was going to be okay.

38

the present

I had been at the hospital for hours, my back was aching, my eyes were sore and my head was thumping due to the dry heat and the constant worry. There was no way I was leaving though, not until I had some good news for Frankie – not that he knew that anything was wrong. By the time I'd laid him into the spare bed at Amy and Elijah's house, he was already fast asleep.

Every time the door to the waiting room had swung open, I'd hoped that it was someone with some news, but the hours had stretched on and on and before we knew it the sun was coming up. I'd told myself that I was waiting for Frankie's sake, but I couldn't stand the thought of not being there if Sam woke or...shit, I hadn't wanted to think about the alternative.

All our nerves were on edge; mine, Elijah's, and Mr. & Mrs. Cooper's, but I had an extra worry throwing itself around my brain. I couldn't help but think about Josh being out on bail and wondering whether he'd had any part in Sam's accident. For a long time Sam's parents and Elijah were too pre-occupied for me to bother them with it, so when the policeman who'd found Sam popped in to check on him, I'd mentioned it to him. He'd radioed it in and stayed for quite a while until he got a reply, but he heard

279

back that Josh's dad had vouched for him being in the house all night. I wasn't so sure he was telling the truth, but the police seemed satisfied. Apart from which, the policeman said nothing looked particularly suspicious when he found Sam.

Having to accept what they were saying, I'd tried to get comfy as I'd continued waiting, hoping that I hadn't risked Sam's life by getting him involved in mine.

Giving up the idea of trying to get any sleep, I alternated between pacing the floor, watching through the first floor window, and sitting and staring at the wall. While I was flicking mindlessly through a magazine, Elijah came into the waiting room, rubbing at his eyes.

"You okay?" he asked with a tired sigh, flopping down onto the chair next to mine.

"I'm fine. Any change?"

He shook his head. "Nope. He's back from his scan, but he's still dead to -." He clamped his mouth shut and inhaled deeply. "What a dick."

"It's just a phrase," I replied, placing a comforting hand on his bicep. "He'd laugh if he knew what you'd said."

Elijah looked up at me and smiled. "Yeah, yeah he would."

"When will the results be back?"

He shrugged. "They didn't say, but the doctor is hoping it's not a clot, but just swelling, but he's worried that he can't seem to keep consciousness."

"If it's a clot?" I asked, a cold fear sweeping over me.

"They'll need to operate." He averted his eyes, looking through the window to grey light outside.

"What the hell could have happened, Elijah?"

I chewed on my bottom lip, wondering whether I should mention Josh.

"The copper thinks he just slipped and that maybe it was on a wet floor. There was a mop and bucket nearby and he only had one slider on, the other was near his body. Who wears those fucking stupid things anyway?"

As Elijah turned to me, I saw the utter torment in his eyes as he thought about what might happen to his brother.

"He's always been there for me, you know," he said, running a hand through his hair. "When Amy left, Sam was the one who held me together and when Amy came back, well Sam was the one who made me see I had to get her back."

"He told me all about it," I replied. "How you were with someone else, but he made you see sense."

Elijah rumbled a low laugh. "Yeah, you could say that. I just wish he'd told me about that fucking sick bitch who was his swimming coach when it happened." His head shot up and he looked at me with wide eyes. "Amy said you knew, you do know don't you?"

"Yeah," I said, nudging Elijah with my shoulder. "He told me. I think he thought it might explain why he'd wanted nothing to do with Frankie when he was born."

"And did it?"

"A little, but like I told Sam, he couldn't use that as an excuse. I would have hoped he'd realise that what *she* did was wrong but I wasn't the same type of person as her."

"It must have still been pretty fresh for him at that time I guess."

Elijah leaned forward, rested his forearms on his knees and stared down at the floor.

"Even so, thank you, Maisie," he said without looking up. "You allowing Sam to be a dad to Frankie and letting him come into our family has been the best thing to happen to Sam."

Elijah finally looked up at me and the tears in his eyes caused my throat to tingle with emotion.

"He's going to be okay," I said softly, not sure I believed it.

As Elijah nodded and gave me a weak smile, the door to the waiting room swung open and before I knew what was happening, Frankie was throwing himself at me. As he landed on me, I heard Amy.

"I'm so sorry," she said, her voice cracking. "He heard me on the phone to Eli earlier. I thought he was still asleep, but he'd gotten up to go to the toilet and since then he's been really upset, so as soon as I thought they were awake I dropped Bella off with my mum and dad and brought him here. I didn't know what else to do, I couldn't console him."

Elijah grabbed Amy's hand and pulled her to him, resting his head against her stomach and as he looked down at the floor she bent forward and kissed the top of his head.

"It's fine, Amy," I replied as I pulled Frankie closer to me."

"Where is he Mummy, I want to see him," Frankie cried, verging on becoming hysterical.

"He's being looked after by the doctor baby, so I'm not sure you'll be allowed."

"Please Mummy, please," he begged, shaking my shoulders with his little hands. "I want to see Daddy. I want to see him."

There was movement beside me and Elijah appeared, placing his hand on Frankie's shoulder.

"He's sleeping buddy, but if you want me to I'll go and ask if you can go in there."

Frankie's chest heaved as he nodded and tears dripped from the end of his wobbling chin. I looked up at Elijah, hoping he saw the thanks in my eyes.

"Hey, come on," I soothed, rocking him gently. "Uncle Elijah is going to ask, so try and stop crying, okay."

Frankie nodded again, but the tears and hiccupping sobs continued.

"I'm so sorry," Amy mouthed as I glanced at her.

"It's fine, I'd have had to tell him at some point."

We waited, the silence of the stark waiting room only broken by Frankie's sniffles. Finally, Elijah came back with his dad following. As soon as James Cooper walked through the door, his eyes immediately went to Frankie still shaking in my arms. He paused, visibly flinching and then taking a deep breath and pulling back his shoulders came over to us. As he reached Amy he cupped her cheek gently and gave her a soft smile. Once she smiled back, he continued to me and Frankie.

"Hey Frankie," he whispered, leaning down to his level. "You okay?"

Frankie looked up at him with tear filled eyes and shook his head. "Can I see Daddy?" he asked.

James looked over to Elijah who rubbed a hand over his head and then back to his grandson. His eyes searched Frankie's features and I saw his Adam's apple bob sharply.

"Yes, come on." He held his hand out to Frankie, who placed his tiny one in it instantly.

"Dad-."

He didn't look at Elijah, keeping his eyes on Frankie.

"No, Eli. He needs to see him. Come on, let's go and see your dad. You should come too, Maisie."

I nodded and pushed up from the hard chair and followed him toward the door.

"Amy," I said, turning just before we left. "Do you want to go in before me?"

She shook her head and chewed on her bottom lip, grabbing hold of Elijah's hand. "I'll go later."

Taking a deep breath, I followed James and Frankie, hoping I would hold it together.

As we reached the small private room that Sam was in, James let go of Frankie's hand and went over to the nurse who was writing on the chart at the end of Sam's bed. Yvetta looked up and her face broke into a smile as she spotted us. She held out her arms and without hesitation, Frankie ran into them leaving me standing in the doorway, my eyes drawn to Sam's body lying motionless in the bed.

His face was as white as the sheets that were pulled up to his chest, but he looked peaceful as his chest slowly moved up and down. He wasn't hooked up to any machines to help him breathe, which had to be a good sign, and the heart monitor next to his bed beeped rhythmically; I would have thought he was simply sleeping if I didn't know any better.

"Maisie," Yvetta's soft voice floated into my ears.

I looked over to see her beckoning me over, holding out her hand, not unlike James had done to Frankie. Her other arm was wound tightly around my son, who was turned toward the bed, watching Sam carefully.

"Five minutes, that's all," the nurse said a little sternly to James, who rolled his eyes.

When the door clicked shut, Frankie looked up at James who had moved to the other side of Sam's bed.

"Why won't he wake up Grandpa?"

James looked down at Sam and then back to Frankie. "He needs to sleep to get better." His eyes were soft and his voice gentle and I knew he was going to be an amazing grandfather, just as he was evidently an amazing dad.

"But I want him to wake up now," Frankie said, pulling away from Yvetta. "I start practicing lines for my school play next week. I'm Grandpa Joe and I want him to help me to learn them."

"Maybe Grandpa and I can help you," Yvetta said, her voice breaking.

Frankie didn't look at her, but stared down at Sam and shook his head vigorously.

"No, I want Daddy." He laid a tiny hand on Sam's cheek and leaned down to his ear. "Please wake up Daddy. Please. "

His plea was heart rending and all three of us gasped in unison. I moved quickly to take Frankie into my arms, but he shrugged me off and cupped Sam's face with both of his hands.

"No," he cried. "I want to stay with my dad. I want my dad to wake up."

"Frankie." Yvetta's call of his name was hiccupped out in a sob as she clutched a hand to her chest.

"Daddy please." Frankie continued to sob. "Please wake up, Daddy, please."

I couldn't stand the torment that my baby was going through and wished I hadn't thought it was a good idea for him to come in and see Sam. It was too much for his little heart to endure.

"We haven't finished our puzzle," Frankie cried as James managed to pull him away from the bedside. "He needs to help me finish it."

The last words were said through tears and sobs to his grandfather, as James enveloped him in his arms and hugged him tightly.

"I'm so sorry, Maisie," James said, his own eyes full of tears. "I thought it would help him."

"Baby, please don't cry." I swiped under my nose with the back of my hand as I reached for Frankie.

He turned in James' embrace and almost threw himself at me, wrapping tiny arms around my waist. We stood locked together for a few minutes, until his crying subsided and all that he had left to offer were sniffles.

"Let me take him," Yvetta offered. "You stay here with James."

I looked over at the bed and then down at Frankie. "I don't know, I think maybe I should take him home."

His grip around me tightened. "No, I want to stay." He looked up at me, his eyes, so like Sam's, pleading with me.

"Shall we go and see if we can get you some breakfast?" Yvetta asked, bending down to his level. "Maybe Uncle Elijah and Auntie Amy will come too."

Frankie nodded and letting go of me, took his grandma's hand. "You'll come and get me if Daddy wakes up?" he asked me.

"Of course I will."

He looked back up at Yvetta. "I *am* hungry."

"Good boy." She gave him a warm smile and led him from the room.

Once they'd gone, James let out a breath. "Oh my God, I'm so sorry Maisie. That was just heart breaking."

I hugged him. "James, it's fine. He wanted to come and nothing would have stopped him. I thought it would help too." My eyes went to the bed. "*Is* he going to be okay?"

"The doctor thinks so. He'll know more when he gets the scan results back, but all his vitals are fine, he just doesn't seem to want to stay awake."

"I hope he does soon," I whispered. "I ..."

My words tailed off, not knowing what to say or whether I had the right to say it.

"I know," James said, placing a hand on my shoulder. "You love him."

I opened my mouth to protest his words, but I didn't, there was no point because he was right, I did love him and the thought of losing him already was making my heart break open into a huge yawning chasm which I wasn't sure would ever mend.

39

the present

"Will someone tell those fucking men to stop drilling," I groaned with a grimace. "They're giving me headache."

"Sam," Mum's voice cried. "You're awake."

I slowly opened one eye and turned my head toward her voice, wincing with the pain. "You look like shit, Mum."

She laughed through tears and reached for my hand. "Because I've been here all night and all day, waiting for you to wake up and I think you'll find that drilling is in your head, love."

"You could be right. I could do with a drink."

My throat felt like sandpaper and my lips dry.

"Here you go son." Dad appeared, holding a cup with a straw in it. "Just little sips while you're lying down. Yvetta love, call for the nurse."

As I drank, Mum's chair scraped on the floor and I then heard the door open and close.

"You had us bloody worried there," Dad said, pulling the straw from my mouth. "Do you remember what happened?"

I groaned and reached to the back of my head, feeling thick wadding. "Yeah, I mopped the floor and I slipped, after that I can vaguely remember lights above my head and someone asking me questions, but not much else." Then something occurred to me. "Did I dream it or have you and Mum been on a cruise."

Dad laughed. "No, you definitely dreamt it. Imagine me getting your mother on a cruise."

"Well when I come to think of it, no. Unless it was to sail out and stop the tuna fisherman killing dolphins."

I moaned as the pain in my head intensified.

"Okay," a voice I didn't recognise said. "If you give us a few minutes, thedoctor would like to examine Sam."

Dad gave my shoulder a pat and moved away, leaving me with a nurse and a doctor, who prodded and poked me, asked me a load of questions about feeling nauseous or dizzy and took my blood pressure and temperature. Finally, he gave me a smile and hung his stethoscope back around his neck.

"Everything seems fine, Mr. Cooper. Your scan came back clear of any haematomas, but it appears you've had a severe concussion. It must have been a heavy bang of the head."

"I did have quite a way to fall, doc," I replied, closing my eyes against the pain.

"Quite." He gave me a placating smile. "We'll keep you in another night, just to keep you under observation on a normal ward, but I think you'll be okay to go home tomorrow. Kerry, if you could give Mr. Cooper some pain relief. The usual dosage."

"Yes, Dr. Shelton."

"Thanks, I could do with it."

"Okay, I'll be off and don't let the family stay too long."

When he'd gone, the nurse helped me to sit up a little more and straightened my blankets.

"I'll get that pain relief and send your family in. Your little boy is desperate to see you."

"Frankie's here?"

"Yes, he's been here since very early this morning, him, your partner, your brother, his wife, and your parents." She grinned. "You have quite a fan club out there."

Emotion grew within in me at the thought of them all being there and I was suddenly desperate to see my son, thinking about what if I hadn't just got a concussion, what if I'd hit my head harder than I had, what if I...? A huge lump formed in the back of my throat at the possibility that I might never have seen those I loved again and it took everything in me not to sob like a fucking baby.

Within seconds of the nurse disappearing from the room, the door swung open and everyone piled in, with Frankie at the front.

"Daddy, you're awake."

The volume of his voice made me wince and just as he was about to launch himself at me, Elijah caught hold of him and snagged him around the waist.

"Hold on, little man. Dad is still feeling a little fragile, so just be careful."

"It's fine," I croaked and held my arms out. "Come here."

As soon as Eli let Frankie go, he practically jumped onto the bed and flung his arms around me, snuggling his cheek against my chest.

"You wouldn't wake up. I tried to make you, but you wouldn't."

His excited voice trembled a little and his grip on me grew tighter. I felt like shit, but there was no way I was going to forgo cuddles with him simply because I had a pain in my fucking head.

"I'm sorry, buddy," I said, breathing him in. "I didn't mean to scare you."

"You scared us all," Mum said, emotion in her voice.

"If that isn't a lesson to stop wearing those freaking ridiculous *slider* shoes, I don't know what is." Eli's tone was derisory and I couldn't help giving him the finger behind Frankie's back.

Before I saw her, I felt Maisie at my other side. I could smell the faint aroma of her perfume and my heart beat sped up – thank fuck the doc had taken me off the heart monitor.

"Hey," I said softly, turning my head to look at her.

She took hold of my hand and gave me a beautiful, tearful smile. "Hey."

"You been here all day too?" I asked, still holding onto my boy.

"She was here all night," Dad chipped in.

Maisie blushed slightly and shrugged. "I wanted to be sure you were okay."

"Yeah?"

She nodded. "And you're sure you fell?" she asked, concern crossing her tired features.

"Yeah why?"

As I saw concern change to fear, I guessed what she was worried about.

"Seriously, Maisie, I fell. I'd let Dave go and said I'd close up and had just mopped the floor and slipped on it. I swear."

"Firstly," Elijah said, "what the hell are they thinking letting you have responsibility of closing up the leisure centre and secondly, what do you mean, Maisie? His feet are too big and he tripped over his stupid shoes, what else would it be?"

I turned back to my brother and rolled my eyes. "I'm fu-flipping responsible. I'm thirty-three and own a business, so it'd be a little bit crap if I couldn't close up the place wouldn't it?"

"Yeah but you obviously can't," Amy muttered. "I mean, you fell on the wet floor and knocked yourself out."

Elijah laughed and high-fived her, which earned them a flip of the finger each. Mum sighed and pushed her way to the side of the bed, laying a hand on Frankie's back as he continued to hug me and look up at me with his big soulful eyes.

"Come on Frankie," she said softly. "Let's go and give Mummy and Daddy a few minutes together, hey?"

"Mum," Elijah said. "I'm not sure he'll be allowed to do that just yet, if he's even up to it."

Amy back-handed him against his chest. "Just get out."

Eli laughed and blew me a kiss. "See you later bro. Come on Frankie, you come with me and Auntie Amy, we'll go and get Bella from her other nanna and grandad and then go for a burger, how does that sound?"

Frankie's head shot up and he looked up at me warily. "You'll be okay now, won't you?"

I ruffled his hair and nodded. "Yes, I'll be fine."

"You'll see Daddy soon," Maisie said. "He's going to come and stay with us until he's better."

My head almost swiveled off my neck, causing my pain to spike, but I swallowed back the groan.

"I am?"

She nodded and gave me a shy smile. "Yes, you are."

I was too busy watching her to notice everyone leave, even Frankie being taken from my arms didn't register. It was only when Maisie's gaze went toward the door that I realised we were alone and that my hand was still in hers.

"You sure you want to have me as a patient?" I asked, pulling her closer.

"Yes, I'm sure. I hate the thought you were lying there all that time."

"I'm not going to fall again. I'm not some doddery old bloke, I'll be okay."

She shook her head and took a deep breath as though steeling herself.

"I want you near us," she whispered. "I was so scared."

Tears formed in her eyes and if the pain hadn't been raging in

291

my head, I would have pulled her down and kissed her. I needed painkillers though and it was getting harder to concentrate on anything else, even the beautiful woman who I was falling for, standing in front of me.

"It wasn't Josh, you're sure?" she asked, her question hurried. "I know you need to get some rest, so I just need to know."

"No, babe. I would have said. You really thought he might have clocked me one over the head."

"Yeah," she groaned through a quiet laugh. "I suppose it was a little dramatic, but I got the police to check where he'd been all night."

Squeezing her hand, I lifted it to my lips and kissed it. "I promise you, I slipped. Now go home and get some sleep, okay?"

I was shattered and couldn't wait for the nurse to come back with my meds. I knew I'd been unconscious, but I was desperate to close my eyes again and get some sleep.

"Okay, and you make sure you rest too." Maisie leaned down, her soft lips landing on mine. "We'll be back later tonight."

My eyes drifted against sleep and discomfort and I nodded, loosening my grip on her hand. She gave me one last kiss to my forehead and then she was gone, her space next to my bed filled by Kerry the nurse who gave me what I needed to reach a few hours of painless oblivion.

40

Sam had been home, or at least in my home, for three days having received the all clear. After a couple of days of observation, the doctors were confident it *had* been a severe concussion and he shouldn't have any lasting effects of it.

Needless to say, I was still worried and insisted that he stay with us, particularly as he was tired and still had to take pain relief for his headache. He'd also had a few stitches in the back of his head, and I wanted to be sure they were looked after properly. Who the hell was I kidding? I wanted him close by because seeing him in the hospital bed, looking so pale, had scared the life out of me and I needed to know he was alright. Which was why I was taking a few days off work to look after him.

Obviously, I couldn't let him sleep on the sofa, so he'd had my bed and I'd started with a camp bed in Frankie's room, but when I found Frankie camped out on the floor next to Sam the following morning, I put the camp bed in there for him and *I* took Frankie's bed. Sam had tried to argue that we should swap, but his six feet plus frame would never fit the bed and I didn't like the idea of him sleeping with his feet hanging off the end, so, I'd spent my nights tossing and turning in a small blue wooden bed thinking about crawling into a huge King size with Sam and cuddling against his hard, warm chest.

"Hey," a voice said behind me. "What you doing?"

I looked up from where I was kneeling on the floor, surrounded by boxes and packing tape. "I thought you were still asleep."

Sam gave me a lazy smile and scratched at his chest. "Been awake about twenty minutes. That bed of yours is so comfy."

Yeah I know, I thought as I surreptitiously rubbed at a sore spot in the small of my back.

"You want some breakfast?"

"I can get it, you look busy." He crouched down next to me and picked up a paperback on the SAS and studied the back of it before throwing it back onto the floor. "His stuff?" he asked.

"Yeah," I sighed, surveying the clothes, books and general stuff that was piled over the carpet of my lounge. "I just want it out of here and I don't want him here to collect it, so boxing it up and getting it sent to him seems the best idea."

"Yeah well," he said gruffly. "Let's hope he has no need for it soon."

I wasn't totally convinced Josh would get a prison sentence, but I didn't really care if he didn't, as long as we never had to see him again. His court date was in three weeks' time and we were still hoping he pleaded guilty to avoid me having to give evidence.

"Anyway," I said, grinning at Sam. "What've you been doing if you woke up twenty minutes ago?"

His eyes softened and he gave me a wistful smile. "I dropped my phone and was looking for it under the bed and found Frankie's baby book."

"So you've been reading it?"

I cupped his cheek with my hand and gently stroked his stubble with my thumb. His eyes looked sad and full of regret.

"You know you can't keep doing this Sam," I whispered. "You have to move forward. I am, so you have to too."

"I know but-."

"No." I shook my head. "There is no but. If you keep holding on to this regret you will never be the father that Frankie needs. You'll treat him with kid gloves, walk on egg shells, however you want to describe it, but he'll figure it out and no matter how much he loves you, he'll take advantage and disrespect you. Yes, you were an absolute idiot -."

"And a prick."

"Yes," I laughed. "And a prick, but you're putting things right. You lost eight years of being his dad, but you potentially have another fifty or sixty to give him, so stop looking back and move on. Looking back is what got you into this mess in the first place."

Taking a deep breath, Sam reached for me and pulled me into his arms, wrapping me into a tight hug.

"You're so fucking amazing, you know that," he whispered against my hair. "I can't believe I got this second chance with you and this first chance with our son."

I dropped a kiss to his jaw and wrapped my arms a little tighter around him. "Because you're pretty amazing yourself, when you're not being a prick."

Sam's laughter roared in my ear. "Oh am I. You cheeky little-."

I didn't give him chance to call me anything because I kissed him again, this time my lips landing on his. It was soft and gentle and full of...well love, I supposed.

After a few seconds I pulled away, because as much as I would have like to get hot and sweaty with him on my lounge floor, he was convalescing and needed to be careful.

"Hey," he cried as I pushed away. "I was just about to start my best moves on you."

"I know, but you're ill and I have to get these boxes packed, so sorry that's all you're getting."

Sam groaned and rolled his eyes.

"And stop behaving like your eight year old son."

I slapped at his arm playfully and reached for another pile of Josh's clothes.

"Talking of," Sam said, dropping his backside to the floor and taking a box and some books. "When are we telling him about us?"

It was something I'd thought about over the few days that Sam had been staying with us and knew we would have to make a decision, but if I was being honest, I wasn't sure it was still what Sam wanted, so hadn't broached the subject. Plus, us playing happy families for the last few days, all be it in a weird way, had scared me at how much I wanted it despite all my fears.

"You didn't make any life changing decisions in the hospital then?" I asked. "You know, some come to Jesus moment while you were unconscious about wanting to sail single-handed around the world, or go back packing through Australia."

I laughed, but it was a nervous laugh, because I really was worried that something like that might have happened. The kiss a few moments earlier had been the first contact we'd had since he'd got out of hospital.

"Why would you think that?" he asked, placing a pile of paperbacks into the box he had in front of him. "I told you what I wanted, what I still want and no bang on the head is going to change that."

I looked at him carefully, noting the hardness of his jaw and the twitch in his cheek.

"Okay," I breathed out, as much in relief as needing to breath. "Maybe in a few days. Now I'll go and sort you some breakfast."

I pushed up from the floor, needing some space. Of course I

was happy that Sam still wanted both me and Frankie, but something was still holding me back from being all in with his plan.

As I moved to walk away, Sam caught hold of my hand and tugged on it, urging me to look down at him.

"You know Maisie," he said quietly. "Letting go of the past is what we both need to do, and that isn't just about you forgiving me about Frankie. It's about you forgiving me for not realising how special you were nine years ago."

I nodded and gave him a small smile before pulling away and going to make him some breakfast.

41

the present

Six whole days I'd been under the same roof as Maisie, and apart from one brief kiss, hadn't fucking touched her and it was killing me. To anyone looking in on us, you'd think we were a normal, happy family. In the day while I worked for a couple of hours from a laptop in her kitchen, Maisie cooked, read, or did housework and then when she told me I'd worked enough for one day, we'd sit and have some lunch and then watch a film or listen to some music. I'd then take a couple of hours nap while she went off to get Frankie from school and maybe take him to see her parents before bringing him home where I'd help with homework and reading, or even play a game while Maisie cooked dinner. All very fucking pleasant, but my body was burning for her.

I'd tried jacking off in the shower a couple of times, but it wasn't enough, plus it was night time when I craved her the most, knowing she was just across the landing dressed in some skimpy sleeping attire. However, as Frankie was on a camp bed in the room with me, relieving myself was an absolute no go area.

What the last six days had also done, apart from give me fucking blue balls, was to cement my feelings for her. We'd talked a lot about general things, we'd laughed a great deal too and I'd seen first-hand what an amazing mum she was. The love and attention she gave to our son was as strong and as bright as the summer sun and Frankie basked in it daily. She'd been great with me too, always attentive and caring, checking whether I needed any painkillers, looking at my stitches and making sure I was warm, fed, and happy. Truth be known, I probably could have gone home days ago, but I justified it by saying once the doctor signed me off to go back to work I'd do it, but as my doctor's appointment was the following day, I was dreading it and seriously considering telling him my headaches hadn't stopped four days ago, but were still there and I was constantly feeling dizzy. It was all in contradiction to the part of me that was desperate to get back to work and running my business. I had great staff who knew exactly what they were doing, but I still had a deep-rooted need to be there and involved, which was why Maisie had conceded to the two hours a day on the laptop answering emails and taking a daily call with Eve, my Office Manager.

I smiled as I thought of Maisie and how she'd stamped her tiny little foot where I'd suggested working from home for six hours a day. She may well have been small, but she was a force to be reckoned with and I'd soon caved and agreed to a compromise of two hours. There was so much about her that I fucking adored and I really was struggling with the idea that we might not be what she wanted any more. She wasn't particularly eager to tell Frankie and there had only been that one kiss.

Knowing she would be back from dropping Frankie at her parents' house soon, and that potentially I only had one more day to make sure we were on exactly the same page about the future, I decided to come up with a plan of action. Maisie West was going to be under no fucking illusion how I felt about her within the next couple of hours.

MAISIE

The house was quiet when I let myself in, which was unusual for the time of day. Sam was out of bed, because he'd been down to say goodbye to Frankie when I took him to my mum and dad's for the day. They'd come up with some weird little handshake between them, one that included shoulders and elbows as well as hands and Frankie had told me in no uncertain terms it was a man thing and I shouldn't worry about it. I'd left Sam making his breakfast and usually by this time music could be heard as he went on line to read the newspapers before starting on his emails. I wondered whether he'd decided to go back to bed, with it being a Sunday, or whether it was because he had a headache again and that worried me. He hadn't had any painkillers for almost three days, so maybe he'd been suffering in silence.

"Sam," I called up the stairs, but not too loudly in case he was sleeping.

When I got no response, I quietly moved down the hall into the kitchen. It was all clean and tidy, his breakfast dishes washed and put away and there was even a mug out with a spoonful of coffee in it for me; something that he'd done every morning that I'd taken Frankie to school.

I put the meat and potato pie that Mum had made for us in the fridge and flicked the kettle on, trying to decide what to do with myself while Sam was sleeping. There was no housework that needed to be done seeing as I'd had all week off and I wasn't really in the mood for watching a film, so wondered about catching up on a couple of things on *Netflix*. I would have quite liked to watch some more of *The Handmaid's Tale,* but it was something Sam and I had started to watch together, so he'd be disappointed if I did.

It struck me how we'd manage it once he left for home the following day, because I was sure that the doctor would sign him off as being fit to go back to work. The thought of him leaving made my heart clench in my chest because I really didn't want him to go. The past week of having him with us had been amazing for Frankie and for me. Just having him around to talk to and to laugh with had made me happier than I had been in years. Watching him with Frankie had been the best thing ever. I knew he was trying hard, but you would never have thought he was new to being a father. The way he talked to Frankie and gave him his attention was everything that my boy deserved. It didn't really matter if he was making an extra effort, because it didn't look that way, it all looked so natural. The way he smoothed Frankie's hair down, or nudged his plate toward him when he was too distracted to eat his dinner or how Sam instinctively reached for him when they were both sitting on the sofa watching TV – it all made butterflies swarm my stomach and my heart beat faster.

As for Sam and me, well since the one kiss when I'd been packing Josh's things, there'd been no real contact, not like that anyway. I had noticed how he always brushed my hair from my eyes when we were talking, squeezed my waist when he moved past me in the kitchen, or put toothpaste on my toothbrush if I was going into the bathroom after him. God, everything about Samuel Cooper made my legs feel like jelly and my heart full of love. I had admitted that one to myself a couple of nights before when lying in bed I found myself getting excited about seeing him again in the morning. Of course I'd have preferred to see him next to me in bed, naked, but spending my days with him would have to suffice for the time being until...I had no idea until what because I was being stupid and needed a good slap. He obviously cared about me and loved Frankie, so what the hell was I waiting for.

As I considered it again, for the billionth time that week, I decided when he woke up I was going to talk to him. I was going to tell him we should tell Frankie and start being a real couple, starting with him taking me to bed and fucking me senseless.

Feeling determined, I left the kitchen and the boiled kettle and went to the lounge, deciding I'd relax with a book for a while, in readiness for my conversation with Sam. When I opened the door, I was shocked to see him lying on the sofa. He was perfectly still and had one arm hanging down, his fingers touching the floor. In fact, he looked too still and my heart stopped for a couple of beats as I watched him, convinced I couldn't see him breathing.

"Sam," I hissed as I rushed over to him. "Sam are you okay?"

I put my hands on his shoulders and shook him, calling his name and almost screamed when he opened his eyes and gave me a huge smile.

"Hey," he said.

"Oh my god, I nearly shit myself," I gasped. "I thought you were dead."

"Nope and I'll prove it to you."

In a flash he had my back to the sofa and him on top of me, holding my hands above my head as he looked down at me with lust in his eyes.

"What are you doing?" I giggled. "You're supposed to be ill."

"Not any longer I'm not, so it's about time I told you what's what."

"What do you mean?" My chest heaved as my body recognised his, causing my blood to heat up.

"I'm sick of waiting when we both know what we have."

My mouth parted and Sam's tongue darted out to lick his lips. He looked as though he might devour me, but then he shook his head and grinned instead.

"I want you more than I've ever wanted anyone," he whispered against my ear. "Not just because you're the mother of my son, but because of who *you* are and how *you* make *me* feel. You're beautiful and sexy, you're kind and strong, things that I've told you before, but every single word is true."

"Sam-."

"Nope," he said, interrupting me with a deep, sexy growl. "I'm talking and unless you want me to slap that fucking amazing arse of yours, you'll listen to what I've got to say."

Shit, I was done over thinking things, I was going to listen and agree to anything that he said, because if the erection pushing against my stomach was anything to go by, he was going to suggest plenty of things that I'd be totally on board with.

"We are doing this," he continued. "We are being a couple and we are telling our son today when he gets home. It's too soon for me to move in here permanently, but when we get to that point, which we will, I'll sell my apartment and we'll buy somewhere for us as a family, not somewhere that you lived with that fucking prick."

He paused long enough for me to nod my head. He then kissed the end of my nose before continuing.

"I know what I did to you was fucking hideous and hurtful and I will never, ever forget that or forgive myself but I will always, and I mean always, fucking love you with all my heart. You and Frankie are such a great gift, Maisie, and I am so damn grateful for you both that I will not fuck this up. I know you think if I have to try then it's not working, but I will never stop trying to be better for you than I was the day before because you, my beautiful girl, deserve the fucking world."

I was speechless and breathless as I tried to take in Sam's words and all my head kept coming back to was that he'd said he loved me with all his heart.

"You love me?" I whispered, almost choking on the emotion

that one four lettered word could evoke. "You said you loved me with all your heart."

Sam nodded and rested his forehead against mine. "I do," he whispered. "I'm so fucking in love with you my chest aches when I get into that bed and know I'm not going to see you for six or seven hours. Everything about you makes me crave you, Maisie. I need you to be mine. I want you to be mine. I want us, I want our family."

The euphoria I felt was so intense I felt my whole body shaking and entwined my fingers with Sam's that were still holding my hands above my head.

"I get it if you don't feel the same," he continued. "But just give us a chance, please."

I was bowled over by the way the confident, cocky man on top of me had laid himself bare. He had given me everything that was in his head and in his heart, having no clue whether I felt the same way. He'd given me his vulnerability and trusted me with it, so how the hell could I not love him back.

"I love you too," I replied, ending the sentence with a soft kiss to his cheek.

His eyes stared down at me questioningly as his fingers tightened around mine.

"You do?"

I nodded. "I trust you with my heart, Sam, mine and Frankie's, so yes, of course I love you. I'm so in love with you it makes my chest ache too and I get excited when I know I'm going to see you in a few hours."

He chuckled and dropped a kiss to my neck, stirring other more primitive emotions in me.

"I was scared when you got hurt." I exhaled, as I recalled Amy's phone call and the long night of worry. "I hated to think you might be taken away from us before we'd even got started, and that wasn't just for Frankie, it was for me too. I want everything that you want and I need everything that you need and it has to be with you, because without you it would be meaningless."

Sam's lips met mine in the softest of kisses, but the way his body hardened against me and his grip on my hands tightened, I knew it wouldn't stay like that for long and soon our clothes were quickly discarded. Foreplay was hot, fast and heady – hungry kisses, grabbing hands, and bites of passion until finally Sam sank himself inside of me, filling me. With each thrust came a declaration of love and I knew we were going to fine, we were going to be the love story we should have been all along.

42

8 months later

"You sure I can't persuade you?" I asked Maisie as we walked along hand in hand.

"No way," she said with a shudder.

I bent to kiss her and earned a groan from my son who was holding her other hand. Maisie giggled and batted me away, probably because she knew if I brought my best moves out she'd agree to anything, even the tattoo I'd been teasing her about.

"Can I have one, Dad?" Frankie asked.

"A tattoo? No way, not until you're eighteen at least."

I didn't look to guidance from Maisie when answering him, I hadn't for a while, not since we'd all moved in together five months earlier. Maisie was worried it was all a little quick, but I'd been pissed I'd had to wait three months to get us all under one roof. Even when I was telling her on her sofa that day that it was too soon I was fucking ready then, but I knew she wasn't, so I bided my time and wore her down with my best moves until she was practically begging for me to find us a house.

There'd been a few teething problems, mainly me trying too hard with Frankie, but I was getting there with Maisie's help. The main thing was we had a house fucking chock full of damn love

307

and there wasn't a day that went by that I didn't show or tell them both. Elijah had even asked me if I'd become part of the unsullied, whatever the fuck that meant. Needless to say, I flipped him off and then told my girlfriend I fucking loved her – okay we were all drunk at the time, but the sentiment was there. The point was, no one was as surprised as I was at how I'd changed from a worka-holic, selfish prick who had no desire to be a father, to a home loving, family man who adored his kid, couldn't wait to have another and was desperate to make his girlfriend his wife – a proposal being something that I was in the process of planning. It involved me and Frankie, a big fuck off diamond and a picnic at our lake, oh and Maisie of course, seeing as it'd be pretty pointless without her. Before that though I had an appointment with Isaac Grainger and his tattoo gun.

When I pushed open the studio door, we were immediately greeted with a crying toddler and a slightly frazzled looking Scarlett.

"Sorry, Sam," she said as we walked to the desk. "She's ready for her afternoon nap, but won't go until she's seen her daddy and he's running over on his last appointment."

She cradled the pale blonde head against her chest and gently rocked her up and down.

"She's not normally this bad," Scarlett said apologetically to Maisie. "Sam will tell you, she's normally laughing."

"Aww it's fine," Maisie cooed rubbing a hand down little Ava's back. "Frankie was just the same when he was tired."

"I was not," Frankie objected.

Maisie raised her eyebrows at him. "Yes well I beg to differ."

For a second my chest hurt as I realised I couldn't confirm or deny the memory, but it soon soothed when Frankie started chat-tering to Scarlett, not caring about the noise coming from Ava.

"My dad is having a surprise tattoo today," he said proudly.

"I know, Ava's daddy Isaac is doing it."

"Is Isaac your boyfriend or your husband?"

Scarlett looked a little perplexed but answered anyway. "My husband, although only for a couple of months, why?"

She looked at Maisie who shrugged. I grinned knowing exactly what my little horror was up to. He was priming his mum for the big proposal, although I was hoping she didn't say yes purely because of our son's emotional blackmail.

"I was just wondering if you all had the same name, that's all." Frankie grinned at me and then ran off to look at some of the art on the walls.

"Do you think he's worried that he doesn't have your surname?" Maisie hissed, worry etched on her face.

I feigned confusion and shrugged. We'd talked about changing his name, now that I was on his birth certificate, but talking was all we'd done. I was just glad that I was now 'legally' his dad, although I only had myself to blame for that one, not being there when his birth was registered. Plus, changing Frankie's name was all part of the proposal plans.

Before Maisie could talk about it anymore, the door to the studios swung open and in sauntered Isaac, looking every inch the cool, handsome tattooist that the women seemed to love.

He looked over and smiled, offering me a wave as he said something to the client he was showing out. As the guy approached the desk, Maisie and I fell back a couple of steps as we watched Scarlett hand Ava over to Isaac while the guy paid her. As soon as she landed in Isaac's arms, Ava's crying stopped.

"Hey Sam, how are you doing?" Isaac asked, coming toward us and wiping at Ava's face. "It's been a while and no Elijah today."

I grinned because Elijah and I had always made a pact to get inked together, apart from one time and now it was my turn to do the same.

"Nope, not today. So, she's grown." I ran a hand over Ava's head that now lolled against her daddy's shoulder.

"Yeah, she'll be three soon. In fact, we have another one on the way." He beamed over at Scarlett who rolled her eyes but then gave us a mile-wide smile.

"Oh wow, congratulations."

"Yes, congratulations," Maisie added. "When's it due?"

There was a glint of something in her eye and I felt a little thrill thinking that maybe my desire for another kid wouldn't be too difficult to make happen.

"Scar's only just thirteen weeks, so a way to go yet. My mum is more excited than we are, I think."

"How are your mum and Dex?"

Dex was Isaac's step-dad and owned the studio and was one of the most sought after tattoo artists around, although Isaac seemed to be catching him up.

"They're great. My little brother and sisters keep them occupied, although Annie is still living in London after she finished Uni, she's working for some huge software company as a trainee development manager or something." He shook his head. "I have no idea what the high flying circles are that she mixes in. As for Charlie well he's got girls galore turning up on the doorstep and Savannah is getting bossier the older she gets, but it's all good. They're all happy as Larry, whoever the hell Larry is."

"I think she's asleep," Maisie said, nodding at Ava.

Isaac kissed the top of her head and sighed. "Okay, let me put her down in the back and then we'll get started."

"What exactly are you having done?" Maisie asked, dropping a kiss to my bicep.

"I've told you, you'll have to wait and see." I passed her my credit card. "Now go and spend some money because I'll be a couple of hours."

I winked, gave her a kiss and then followed Isaac to the studio.

———

"Oh my god, Sam," Maisie gasped as her finger tips gently touched underneath the tattoo that Isaac had done.

He hadn't wrapped it yet, so that Maisie and Frankie could see and although it was still a little raw and tender, there was no denying he'd done another amazing job, particularly as he'd done it free hand.

On my left ab was a man carrying a boy and above it in script were the words

"I am hers, she is mine and he is who we created"

Below the man and boy it said;

"Frankie, my son, my life"

"Is that for me, Dad?" Frankie asked, his face full of awe.

I nodded. "You and your mum."

"Because she's yours and you're hers?"

"Yep, exactly that."

I swallowed the thick lump in my throat and pulled Frankie to my side, watching Maisie carefully as she continued to study the tattoo.

"Do you like it?" I asked tentatively. "The tattoo and the sentiment behind it."

She looked up at me with tears in her eyes and nodded. "I love it and I love you." Reaching up onto her tiptoes she kissed me, taking care not to rub against me.

When she took a step back I watched her beautiful brown eyes fall onto my chest again, I knew the time was right. Fuck it and fuck any plans of a romantic picnic.

I reached into my jeans pocket and pulled out the small, velvet box and with an arm still around Frankie I cleared my throat. Maisie looked up at me and then noticed the box in the flat of my shaking palm that I was holding out to her.

"Sam," she gasped.

"Dad, now?"

When I nodded, Frankie pulled away from me and began to jump up and down on the spot, clapping his hands with excitement.

"Maisie West, you know how much I love you and I was going to do this all romantic at the lake with lanterns and wine and maybe some flower petals thrown in, which we can still do if you want to, but something like this shouldn't need to be planned. Something like this should be done when it feels right and it feels right at this exact moment, so will you marry me? Will you allow me to make us all Coopers?"

My heart pumped wildly as I opened the box to reveal a square cut diamond on a white gold band. Staring down at it, Maisie slapped a hand against her mouth.

"It's beautiful," she whispered and looked back up at me. "Seriously?"

I nodded. "Yep, and the name thing." I looked down at Frankie who was gazing at his mum. "I've looked into it and we can get Frankie's name changed easily, seeing as I'm now on his birth certificate."

"Tell us Mum," Frankie cried. "Will you marry Dad?"

Maisie grinned and nodded. "Of course I will."

As I slipped the ring onto her finger, Frankie flung his arms around us and started to jump up and down again.

"I love you so fucking much," I whispered against Maisie's mouth as euphoria I'd never felt before washed through me.

"Good," she sighed. "Because I'm never letting you go."

"I'd never want to, you're stuck with me forever."

As we kissed, hugged, and celebrated as a family, I knew I was where I was always meant to be. It had taken me a while to get my head out my arse and realise it, but there was no denying Maisie and Frankie had always been my destiny.

EPILOGUE

Two years later

As I watched Frankie struggle with his homework, I had to feel for him. I hadn't been the brightest kid at school and Frankie appeared to be following in my footsteps. Not that I cared too much, he'd work for me, if he wanted to, or he could sweep the streets – whatever made my boy happy.

"You okay there buddy?" I asked, running a hand over the top of his scruffy hair. "And have you actually brushed your hair today?"

Frankie looked up at me and grinned. His babyish looks were growing out now that he was almost twelve years old. His cheekbones were sharper and his nose a little wider; if anything he was more bloody handsome than before, but then again I was biased.

"Nope and nope," he replied. "Why do I need to learn fractions anyway? It's not as though I'm going to go into a shop and tell them I want two thirds of X as long as it equals Y, is it?"

I had to agree with his logic on that one.

"I know," I sighed, leaning over his shoulder to read what he was working on, "but you're expected to learn it to help you to get qualifications and qualifications will help you in life."

He looked at me quizzically. "How many have you got, Dad?"

My heart thumped hard when he said the word 'dad', even now after three years, it still felt amazing and strange to hear it. Yes, we'd had some difficult moments where he'd thrown it back in my face that I'd not been around when I should have been, or that I had no right to tell him what to do, but they were few and far between. Things were generally good and his anger wasn't anything I didn't deserve.

"You know exactly how many. I've told you this before," I replied, knowing full well he knew I'd only passed a couple at school and that anything else that I'd achieved had been done in my own time once I was working. "You don't have to do it the hard way, like me."

"You don't even believe in them anyway," he groaned, looking back down at the paper on the table. "Can't I just be a swimmer instead?"

We'd had this conversation many times and while Frankie was good, it would take a lot of time and effort to make him great. I was willing to coach him and put the time in, but since discovering football and girls Frankie wasn't quite so willing, so Maisie and I had persuaded him swimming for fun would be much better for him. That didn't mean he didn't smash it in the school swimming galas, because he did, even beating kids in the two years above him, but that was about as competitive as Frankie's swimming was going to get. Plus, Maisie didn't like the idea of us both being up and out of the house at four every morning and after what happened to me she would never let anyone else coach him. Also, even after three years or more, she still had the odd panic about when Josh took Frankie. Thankfully though he wasn't a problem for us any longer. After getting a six month prison sentence, of which he only served three, he moved back to his home town to live with his Dad. We'd heard he was working in a call centre selling solar panels, but it didn't matter because he was of no significance to us, Maisie was just glad there was no chance of me bumping into him and getting myself into trouble.

"Hey, babe."

And there she was, my beautiful wife, looking incredible despite only having three hours sleep the night before.

She came over to me and wrapped an arm around my waist, dropping a kiss to my bicep, her favourite spot for kisses.

"She gone down okay?" I asked, lifting my arm to pull her closer.

"Hmm, she fought it, but mummy won. Yay go me." Maisie grinned and fist pumped.

Our nine month old, Dotty, was not a good sleeper and kept both of us on our toes. We tried to share the night feeds, but as I worked long days, Maisie insisted that I slept, but without her in bed next to me I couldn't always settle anyway. It was weird, for a man who was adamant he wasn't settling down and didn't want a wife or a family, I was fucking lost if they weren't close by. I was totally gone for all three of them to the point of being a pussy about it. I'd even added an amazing 3D pretty pink Princess crown with Dotty's name in it, to the collection of tattoos on my chest. Yeah it looked girly, but I didn't give a shit, I adored my baby girl.

"What are you doing, sweetheart?" Maisie asked Frankie.

He pointed at the sheet of paper. "Maths and Dad is no help."

"Well don't look at me," Maisie sighed. "Maybe we should call Auntie Amy."

I shook my head. "You try getting her out of the house without my brother putting a stop to all non-essential movement. He's a real daddy bear at the moment."

"Poor Amy." Maisie giggled. "She's got three weeks to go until she has the baby, he can't keep her inside until then."

Amy had almost lost the baby at three months, but after bed

rest for a few weeks everything had been okay, and we'd soon have another strong and healthy Cooper boy to add to the mix. To say Elijah was excited *and* worried was an understatement and he was counting the hours until the safe arrival of Jacob Elijah Cooper.

"He can and he will," I replied, remembering how protective I'd been when Maisie was pregnant with Dotty. I would never forget how I'd missed out on Frankie, through my own stupidity, so when we found out Maisie was pregnant, just two months after we got married, I was determined I wasn't going to miss one minute and I was going to make sure Maisie knew how lucky *I* knew I was.

"Can we go there, to ask Auntie Amy?" Frankie asked. "Because you two really are rubbish." He looked up at us and grimaced. "And please stop cuddling all the time."

Maisie and I laughed and I reached out for my boy, pulling him into the hug with us, almost dragging him from his chair.

"Dad," he groaned, but with a huge smile and a giggle.

"We're having a Cooper hug," I replied.

"Well we don't have Dotty with us, so it's not a proper one," Frankie said, getting off his chair and wrapping his arms around both our waists.

"This is a special one for our first baby," Maisie sighed, kissing the top of Frankie's head.

I swallowed the lump in my throat and kissed her softly as she raised her gaze to me.

"Do you know how much I love you?" I asked.

"Ugh no," Frankie howled, but not letting go of us. "It's gross."

"Yeah, I think I do." Maisie snuggled closer. "I love you too."

And then as if on cue, a loud, demanding cry rang out through the baby monitor as Dotty let us know she wanted in on the action.

"I'll go," I said, kissing Maisie again before doing the same to the top of Frankie's head.

As I left the room to go and get my Princess, I turned to watch them for a few moments. They were my life and I loved them more than I could ever show and I was just glad I'd been given a second chance, because without them I was nothing.

The End

PLAYLIST

Mercy – Lewis Capaldi
Out on The Floor – Dobie Gray
Do I Love You (Indeed I Do) – Frank Wilson
Like I Did – JC Stewart
Beneath The Streelights and The Moon – JP Cooper
Silhouette – Tom Grennan
Heaven Must Have Sent You – The Elgins
Soul Time – Shirley Ellis
I've Been a Fool (Toy Guns) – Lotus
To The End (2012 Remaster) – Blur
Release Me – Agnes
What Hurts The Most (Radio Mix U.S.) – Cascada
Shadows (Inpetto edit) – Those Usual Suspects
I Found U (Radio Edit) – Axwell, Max C

Find It Here

ACKNOWLEDGEMENTS

I've said it before and I'll say it again, this part gets harder and harder, because the list of people I need to thank gets longer and longer. This time I'm going to do something different, this time I'm going to acknowledge two people who probably won't ever see this, or even know that I write books.

I would like to thank Mr Jennison and Mr Pace, two teachers who encouraged me to write and express myself and who taught me that there's nothing wrong with having an imagination.

NIKKI'S LINKS

If you'd like to know more about me or my books then all my links
are listed below.

Website
www.nikkiashtonbooks.co.uk

Instagram
www.instagram.com/nikkiashtonauthor

Facebook
www.facebook.com/nikki.ashton.982

Ashton's Amorous Angels Facebook Group
www.facebook.com/groups/103948092950o429

Amazon
viewAuthor.at/NAPage

BOOK LINKS

Guess Who I Pulled Last Night
No Bra Required
Get Your Kit Off
Rock Stars Don't Like Big Knickers
Rock Stars Don't Like Ugly Bras
Rock Stars Do Like Christmas
Cheese Tarts and Fluffy Socks
Romans Having Sex
I wanna get laid by Kade
Box of Hearts (Connor Ranch #1)
Angels Kisses (Connor Ranch #2)
Secret Wishes (Connor Ranch #3)
Do You Do Extras?
Pelvic Flaws
Elijah (Cooper Brothers #1)

Audio Books

Find Them Here

Printed in Great Britain
by Amazon

35794282R00193